4/17

P9-DGL-430

WITHDRAWN

lucky GIRL

AMANDA MACIEL

lucky GIRL

BALZER + BRAY
An Imprint of HarperCollins*Publishers*

Balzer + Bray is an imprint of HarperCollins Publishers.

Lucky Girl
Copyright © 2017 by Amanda Maciel
www.epicreads.com

ISBN 978-0-06-230533-6

Typography by Erin Fitzsimmons
17 18 19 20 21   PC/LSCH   10 9 8 7 6 5 4 3 2 1
❖
First Edition

For my mom and my sister: I'm so lucky to have you.

1

"YOU BROUGHT BALLOONS." Ryan's face doesn't move as he stares at the mess of color floating over my head. "To the airport."

"Is that not a thing?" I ask. My arm hurts a little as a gust of late-summer wind yanks on the bouquet.

"No, they're . . ." He laughs. "They're great. And she'll be able to see us from a mile away! It's perfect."

I stick out my tongue at him. Maddie won't have a problem finding us in the Omaha airport, which is basically just one big room. But I thought the balloons would be nice. And it's the kind of thing my best friend would do for me, if I was the one who'd spent half the summer at a cool science/soccer program in Spain.

Plus, I think Maddie could use some cheering up. Early in the summer she was telling me all about this guy she'd met, asking for flirting advice like she always does. Maddie's the sporty, STEM-y one and I'm the one who knows about boys, so I think my tips were pretty solid. But then she stopped talking about him and I never saw any pictures, so . . . I guess we're back to square one.

Ryan strides toward the airport doors. "I know she was a walking disaster before she left, but you didn't have to get her a hospital present."

I pull the balloons down fast, so that some of the low ones bonk Ryan in the head. He yelps and we both laugh, and the automatic doors *swoosh* us into the freezing baggage area. "*Hospital present* isn't a thing," I tell him. "But if it was, it'd be flowers."

Okay, maybe I feel like I owe her a present because of last year. Like how her date, Ben Perez, left in the middle of Spring Formal without telling her or even sending a text until two days later. And how I wasn't even there, because I was busy driving to the lake with my boyfriend at the time, Paul.

And then the week before she left for Europe, Maddie's parents announced they were getting a divorce. She came to see me at my job, crying, and all I could do was take a fifteen-minute break and hug her while she cried. I really wanted to say the right thing, but I don't know—Maddie's parents are weird. At least with the Ben Perez thing I knew what to do—unfollow him on all the socials and cough "loser" when I saw him at school. What do you say about someone's parents?

Luckily my job at Dairy Queen has left me a lot of time to think this summer, particularly about being a better friend. Or at least getting back to being the fun friend with good advice about guys. Even if the jerk in Spain didn't work out, we'll find Maddie someone awesome this year. She deserves that.

"Seven o'clock," Ryan mutters, turning toward me and jerking his head a little, back and to the left. "You've got another admirer."

I look past his shoulder and see a boy about our age, sixteen or seventeen, not much taller than either of us. But solid. Not cute, exactly—sort of rust-colored hair and dark eyes and almost a mean look on his face. Or not mean, maybe. *Intense.* As soon as the guy sees me looking back, his glance flits away. He's waiting at the same baggage carousel Maddie should be headed for, from her connecting flight from Chicago. An older guy, probably his dad, stands next to him. They don't talk.

"Oh, and him, too. *He's* hot." Now Ryan's looking past my shoulders at someone else.

"You don't think they're just checking out the balloons?"

He snorts. "Get it? The *balloons?*"

"Oh my God, you're ridiculous." I shake my head, but actually I'm going to miss this, having Ryan to myself. The way guys stare at me sort of makes Maddie crazy, even more than it bothers my mom. Sometimes she seems jealous, sometimes worried—it's always something. Another reason that life would be better this year if Maddie had a good boyfriend. Win-win-win, or however the saying goes.

"Where is that girl?" Ryan asks, and then he jumps. "Madelyn Costello, report to carousel three!"

I hear Maddie's squeal before I see her, and her arms are around me before I can even get a breath. She smells like flowers, and she hugs me tight, like always. We hop around, holding each other, and then she's hugging Ryan. We're all laughing and it's old times again—until she steps back and I get a good look.

And gasp.

"I know!" she cries, smiling so big it looks like it must be hurting her face. "My hair got super blond!"

It's true, but also—Maddie is *gorgeous*. She's always been pretty, but now she looks like a girl from TV. She looks like she should be trying out for a modeling reality show.

"Good on you, girl," Ryan says, reaching out and touching Maddie's long hair. *Very* long hair. Long and beachy and definitely *super blond*. "Love."

Her face is bright and freckled and she really can't stop grinning. "We were outside all the time, you know. With the soccer and everything. Seriously, you guys wouldn't believe how into it they are. It's not even a sport, it's a *religion*."

I nod vaguely. How did I not know she'd changed so much? We talked all the time. But her Instagram was all blue skies and old cathedrals and stuff. Maddie's not a selfie girl, at least not without me around. My brain struggles to put together the Maddie who left two months ago—the sweet and pretty but very sporty, kind of plain girl—with the girl here. This girl has amazing hair and beautifully tanned skin and legs that are totally longer than they used to be and clothes . . . I mean, even her clothes look exotic. . . . Foreign.

"You could be a model," I finally manage to say. She laughs like I'm joking, and I'm glad because that means she can't hear how jealous I sound. Am I jealous? God.

"You've got competition," Ryan says, elbowing me.

"Now you're just being ridiculous." Maddie rolls her eyes.

"Okay, now let's talk about how pretty *I* am," Ryan says.

Maddie laughs and turns to grab her suitcase. I'm still smiling but it's starting to pinch a little.

It's not that she's so pretty. Or not just that. She's *different*. I watch as she strolls alongside the conveyor belt, casually tossing her hair over one shoulder. Last spring Maddie was still wearing Keds and shorts that came down to her knees. Now she has on a skirt and chic, strappy sandals and she's laughing with some random airport guy who's helping her with her bags.

Without meaning to, I glance over to where Intense Boy was standing earlier. But he's gone.

I've never been jealous of Maddie. She's good at sports and her parents can afford stuff like summer programs in Spain, but I have my own things. And unlike most girls at our school, Maddie never turned our friendship into a big competition over guys or prettiness or whatever.

I blink, trying to shake off the weird feeling. She looks happy. That's what's important. And if she also seems a million times more confident than when she left, then . . . great. That's great.

Ryan picks up Maddie's carry-on as she wheels two big duffels back toward us and the doors.

"You guys are so nice to pick me up! I missed my R 'n' R!" Maddie grins at us over her shoulder, and then *finally* she seems to notice that I'm basically that old man from *Up*. "And you brought balloons! Oh, Rosie, you remembered!"

I feel a sudden rush of warm reassurance, because of course Maddie remembers that one time in eighth grade when she brought me a balloon. I'd gone to Arizona with my mom for her dad's funeral, and when we got back from the airport Maddie was sitting on our porch with a big balloon shaped like Elmo. For some reason it just made us both laugh really hard, how silly it was. That was when I decided that even though Maddie didn't care about makeup or stalking boys online or hanging out at the right mall on Saturdays, she was going to be my best friend.

Ryan and Maddie drop the duffels near the back of my mom's old SUV. I click it open and let them put the luggage in before I stuff the balloons in the way-back space.

"Okay, *what* happens if you have to see out the back window?" Ryan asks me.

Maddie hugs him again. "Don't pick on her—she brought them for *me*." And then she hugs me again, too, and this time I have both hands free to hug her back.

"Okay, okay." Ryan rolls his eyes at us, but in a nice way. "I told Father Matt I'd come help with the relief boxes we're sending the church in Beatrice, so I gotta run."

Maddie makes a pouting face. "You're not coming with us? But Village Inn! *Pie!* A million photos of Spain on my phone!"

He just kisses her forehead in response. Maddie's almost as tall as Ryan now. And they're about the same level of tan—that golden shade that I'd kill for but just cannot achieve. My mom tells me to be thankful for my pale complexion, and I do get a lot of Angelina Jolie comparisons, but still. Sometimes I wish I could just be *cute*. And wear an SPF below 2 million.

"Tell *David* I said hello," I say to Ryan as I walk toward the driver's side.

"Who?" he replies, but his cheeks are red. Neither of us knows for sure if David, who goes to St. John's and volunteers almost as much as Ryan, is actually gay. But he's got this dimple that we've spent half the summer admiring.

"Oh, man, I want to hear about *David*," Maddie says.

"Next time. Maybe." Ryan waves and hurries across the parking lot.

I climb behind the wheel, start the car, and roll down the windows. As soon as hers is lowered all the way, Maddie sticks her head out and yells, "Hello, Nebraska! I'm home!"

I steer us toward the exit and laugh again. Maybe she hasn't changed so much, after all.

After I pay the short-term parking fee, Maddie turns sideways in her seat and says, "Tell me everything. *Everything.* What's going on with—um. Are you still hanging out with Cory Callahan?"

I shrug. "Sort of. But who cares, *you're* supposed to have the stories! You've been hooking up with *Spaniards.*"

"Well, I told you about Miguel, and how he was all tongue." She shudders, and so do I. "But there was actually an American guy who was really nice. And smart. We were study partners for a while."

I feel a little jolt. She didn't tell me about an American guy. Why not? "Oooh, *study partners*," I say, ignoring my stupid worries.

"No, not like you're thinking. I mean, I took your advice, I 'got out there.'" She makes air quotes and shrugs. "But this guy was just really fun to hang out with. Great footballer, too. Not as hot as Cory Callahan, though. God, remember when I was in love with him for all of freshman year?"

I turn onto the freeway, enjoying the little surge of adrenaline as I press down on the gas pedal. Above us, the sunny sky is starting to turn gray, as flat and dull as the road. It must look so boring after Europe.

"Oh—yeah," I say. I'd actually forgotten about her Cory crush. She didn't talk about it that much; had she really been in love with him for an entire year?

"Anyway, I met Aaron at the pickup games we used to play at night, you know, when all the dorm kids would hang out."

I nod. I'm not jealous, definitely not. I don't even like soccer.

"But he lives in North Carolina, so I guess I'll just have to move on with my life." Maddie laughs, sounding genuinely chill about it. Which is also weird, because Maddie is fun but she's rarely *chill*.

"Well, if you want to start moving on *tonight*, there's a thing out in that new neighborhood where Gabe Richmond lives," I tell her. "A bunch of the houses are, like, half finished, so we've been taking beer and picnic blankets and stuff. Gabe has all that weird hunting gear. Did you see his awful dead-deer photos on Instagram?"

"Ew, yes," she says. "Wait, are there dead animals at these parties?"

"No! It's just, that's why Gabe has, like, the entire Cabela's fall collection. *Lanterns* and shit. It's actually kind of cozy."

Maddie takes a lip gloss out of her bag, checking her face in a pocket mirror I've never seen before. I ease the car onto the exit ramp, angling the steering wheel with one hand onto the side road that leads to Village Inn. I don't remember Maddie ever touching up her makeup in the car. Or anywhere else, really.

"Isn't that illegal, though?" she asks.

"Probably. But it's fun, and it's not like we graffiti the place or anything."

"Ha, okay. Let me just see how the parents are."

We're in the parking lot now, so I get my own lip gloss and take a second to smooth my hair in the rearview mirror, waiting for her to text her mom and then her dad. I think about asking what's going on with them, but the words feel awkward in my throat. We haven't talked about them all summer, and I figure Maddie will tell me what she wants to whenever she's ready.

But probably a better friend would ask. Would know how to ask.

Maddie turns and looks toward the back of the car. "Will those be okay while we're in there? We could give them to the hostess or some kids or something."

"No, you have to take those home! And treasure them always!"

"Okay, for always," Maddie says as she climbs out of the car. "Hey, does that waiter still work here? The one who loves you so much and gives us free stuff?"

I stick out my lower lip and shake my head. "He hath forsaken me. But there's a waitress who maybe digs me a little bit . . ."

"Dishy!" she cries. "See, this is the *tell me everything* I was talking about! Are you joining Ryan over the rainbow, or what?"

"Not unless they have football players there."

"They do, but probably not lesbian ones," she says. "At least, not at our school."

"Yeah, no. You'll have to go away for a lot longer than one summer if you want things to change *that* much around here."

Maddie throws her arm around my shoulder and walks me to

the restaurant door. "Tell you what, if Rosie Fuller is my best friend and still snagging free food because she's crazy gorgeous, then I'm happy to be home."

"Me too, lady," I say. "Me too."

Turns out our waitress is older, maybe forties, and doesn't care about flirting with anyone, especially not us. So Maddie tells me more about Spain, shows me pictures of the North Carolina study partner, laughs at my stories about DQ.

I watch her tucking her hair behind her ears, eating her slice of chocolate cream pie. Try to convince myself she hasn't changed that much.

When Maddie told me about her parents getting divorced, I genuinely didn't know how to feel upset. My mom was never actually married to my dad, and I only half remember her getting together with my stepdad. And Maddie's parents have never liked me very much; it's always been pretty clear they think I'm not smart enough for her.

But she needs me. I make sure she has fun, I force her to wear cuter outfits than she'd dare to otherwise, I have no problems talking to boys and she freaks out when anyone sends the most harmless of texts.

This weird feeling will go away. So what if she didn't tell me everything about Spain? She's back now.

Plus, now I know I haven't been a good enough friend. Maybe I don't know how to change, exactly, but I'm going to at least try. I can be happy for her that she had such a good trip. I can be happy that she's so blond and gorgeous. I really can.

"You sure you don't want a bite?" she asks, pointing her fork at her plate.

I make a face and she laughs.

"See, this is why we work, Rosie. If you liked chocolate cream pie, I'd actually have to share with you."

"But I *actually* think it's disgusting."

"Exactly. So more for me."

I put a protective arm around my cherry pie and she laughs again. "*Forever.* All that gross chocolate cream pie for you forever, Maddie."

2

"THERE'S A ROOM upstairs," Cory says, his long quarterback fingers digging into my hip and pulling me closer.

"But it doesn't have *walls*," I say, giggling. "You are such a perv. And we have to wait for Maddie, remember? I thought she'd be here by now. . . ."

Cory just makes an *mmm* sound and buries his nose in my hair, tickling my neck.

"Oh, there's Ryan," I say, waving. Before I can catch his eye across the crowd, Cory's grabbed my other hip and started grinding with me. In addition to Gabe's Coleman lanterns lighting up the half-constructed house, someone brought iPod speakers that are filling the place with pounding hip-hop.

I laugh again, letting Cory dance with me. Adorable freckles scatter across his cheeks and late-night stubble defines the shadows on his strong jaw. He looks like someone's Hollywood version of a corn-fed Midwestern boy. Last year I dated a couple of basketball players and even made out with a random college guy at a party.

Now I guess I'm into big, blond football clichés. Or for a couple of weeks I have been, anyway.

Someone bumps into us and Cory jerks around, hands up, like he's going to throw a punch. "Hey!" he yells, but it's so crowded I can't even tell who he's trying to start with. I reflexively grab one of his elbows, pulling him over to the keg. It's late, I've lost sight of Ryan, I still want to find Maddie, and as much as I like having my whole body pressed into Cory's, I'm starting to feel sweaty and thirsty.

Cory grunts and lets me lead him away. "Beer, yeah. Good call." He grabs us a couple of Solo cups from the plywood floor. Another football player comes over and shoves him in the shoulder on purpose, and this time Cory shouts, "Bro! Sick practice today!" and they fist-bump.

I take my beer and sip, even though it's still half foam. Maybe it's better that I couldn't catch Ryan's eye. He's not that into the jock thing. Last year when I broke things off with Paul Maziarz, one of the basketball players, Ryan went, "Oh, thank *God*," and when I got offended he just said, "I'm sorry, but *dude-bro* is my least favorite breed."

I watch Cory talking to his teammate, gesturing wildly about some drill they ran. He's fun and he never takes things too seriously—I mean, I've never seen him *actually* punch someone—and I happen to like jocks just fine. They're easier than guys who think they're into music. And obviously they're *so* much easier to hang out with than girls.

The Midcity jocks have the best parties, too. We seem to be

disproportionately blessed with tall boys who have access to alcohol and reliably absentee parents.

My eyes wander around the room, but Ryan must've gone back outside, and Maddie definitely isn't here yet. I see another familiar face, though. It takes me a few seconds to place it, and then I nearly choke on my beer.

The guy from the airport is here. The intense one, the redhead. He's standing against the doorframe that will someday lead out to the porch and yard, but for right now is nothing but a big rectangle with the black night behind it. His hands are shoved in his jeans pockets, and he seems about as comfortable as Maddie will probably be, if she ever shows up.

"Hey, isn't that Costello over there?" Cory shouts in my ear.

I turn toward where he's pointing, and at the same time I hear Maddie's laugh ringing out over the blaring music. It is her, though she looks even more different here than she did at the airport. Her hair is glowing in the lamplight, and her eyes are dark with eye shadow and mascara. And her shorts are *short*. She has all these bohemian necklaces on, plus a bunch of bracelets, and she is completely pulling it off. If she weren't my best friend I'd be hating her right now, hating even more how pathetically boring my black tank top and white jeans skirt look in comparison.

"I didn't know she was *hot*," Cory says.

"Let's go say hi," I yell, ignoring his comment. I grab his hand and drag him through the crowd again.

Back in ninth grade, when we started high school, I was suddenly surrounded by boys all the time. Maddie was still more interested in soccer and riding our bikes to the creek, and it started feeling weird, like I was leaving her behind. That's when I started trying to help her get better at flirting. I taught her all this stupid shit, like how to flip her hair and bite her lip and stuff—things I probably looked like a moron doing myself, but figured must be working, because for the first three weeks of high school I hooked up with a senior. Instead of an older boyfriend, though, Maddie started getting into student government and Spanish club, and by the time she went on a few dates sophomore year, I had way better advice.

But now, as Cory and I elbow our way over to where Maddie and Ryan are talking to Olivia Thorpe and Annabelle Wilhelmi, I watch in total amazement as my best friend flips her hair. And bites her lip. And smiles at us in this way . . . it's almost . . .

"Hey, sexy, welcome home." Cory leans over and gives Maddie a one-armed hug, and *now* I'm jealous. Because what the hell, dude-bro. But also—she *is* sexy. And again, what the hell?

"Hey, guys!" Maddie breaks away from Cory and kisses both my cheeks. I've only seen people do that in movies, and I'm so surprised I almost drop my drink. When she leans back again she winks at me, though, and I realize she's just doing that other thing I taught her, back in the day: get all handsy with your girlfriends because guys think that girls kissing or touching other girls is super hot. I don't know whether to laugh or cry that all my worst advice is working so well for her.

"Maddie, you remember Cory *Callahan*, right?" I shout over the music. My lungs feel hot as I realize I'm showing off—I'm literally showing her what I did this summer. She might've had all sorts of amazing experiences across the ocean, but I hooked up with one of the hottest seniors at Midcity.

Who she was apparently in love with two years ago.

The burn moves to my cheeks, but I can't help it—I want to still be the prettier one.

"Duh!" Maddie cries, putting her hands on Cory's shoulders for a second. All her bangles slide down her golden arms, and it's nauseating how cool she looks. "From school! From middle school, Sunday school . . ." She throws back her head and laughs, and he is . . . dazzled.

Whaa . . . at.

And now they're talking—Maddie and Cory just start chatting like old friends. I mean, they *are* old friends, we've been in school a year behind Cory since junior high, and we're all at the same church.

"I thought Gabe was here?" Ryan shouts, pulling me closer. Annabelle and Olivia have scooted away, probably still pissed at me for that game of spin the bottle last year when I kissed Annabelle's crush, Finn Kramper, right in front of her. I know *I'm* still pissed about it—the kiss was gross, and then Finn wouldn't stop texting me for weeks afterward. It was just *spin the freaking bottle*. I wasn't supposed to get a stalker *and* a sworn enemy out of the deal.

"Yeah, most of this stuff is his," I tell Ryan, angling my face so I can talk into his ear and keep an eye on Maddie and Cory. Is she still into him? Does she think I'm *not* that into him?

I mean, I'm kind of not. And she seems *very*.

"I thought there'd be more people here I know," Ryan says.

"You know me!" I bump my shoulder into his. "And have you met Sam Adams? He's a super-chill kind of dude." I tip my cup, pointing to the beer inside, but Ryan shakes his head.

"Getting up early tomorrow," he says. "No rest for the theah-tah."

I nod. Ryan's always telling us how damaging cultural stereotypes can be, but he swears that gay people *are* better in the arts. "We know what it's like to respect the fourth wall," he declares to anyone who will listen. Which is usually just Maddie and me, because he's honest with us about being gay, and also because we understand what the "fourth wall" is. Because he told us.

"Whatever, it's still technically summer. You can be a little late."

"I sort of can't, though. You know, since I'm in charge. As student director."

I stare at him for a long second, then I'm screaming and throwing my arms up, and it's just lucky that there isn't any beer left in my cup to spill on us.

"WHAT!"

Annabelle and Olivia wrinkle their noses at me but who cares? Ryan is legit *blushing*.

"It was supposed to be Charlotte Lewis, but she—"

"Yeah, no, I know, she took all the damn jobs!" I say. Ryan and I comanaged Maddie's student council campaign, which by default made us semiprofessional Charlotte Lewis haters. Ryan did most of the actual work, and I was in charge of hating Charlotte, who ended up winning president while Maddie took VP. And then I hated Charlotte even more when she also took the best theater gig.

I lower my arms, wondering why that all feels like such a long time ago.

"So I guess she just told Klonsky it would be too much work," Ryan's saying, "and I'm not such a bad fallback option, so . . ."

"Fallback?" I squawk. "You were *robbed*, and now you have what should have been yours to begin with! This is so amazing!" I give him a big hug.

Ryan hugs me back, then pushes me away again. "Stop or people will think you're in love with me."

I stick my tongue out. "Am I not a—what—pretty good fallback option?"

"From Jonathan Groff? No, sorry."

"Well, let's have a toast anyway." Ryan starts to protest again but I'm already pushing him toward the keg, back across the room, where I was standing with Cory a minute ago. Where I was being humped by Cory, basically, and now I'm most definitely not.

"Maddie seems to be having a good time," Ryan observes as I pour him a cup of foam.

"Yeah."

"And you seem . . ."

"What? I'm fine," I say, but too quickly. "I am. Maybe she likes that guy, whatever."

Ryan rolls his eyes and mutters, "that guy," under his breath, but he takes the beer from me without further comment.

"Hos before bros," I say with as much conviction as I can muster. Then I tap my plastic cup against his and we both drink.

"She looks freaking amazing," Ryan says, and we both watch

Maddie laughing at something Cory said.

"Yeah," I say. Maddie deserved to have an awesome summer, to have something go right. And if the only thing in her way now is me . . .

Ryan nods toward another corner of the room. "I heard Marcus Weaver still pines for you."

I spot Marcus's big Afro floating above the crowd. "Come on, *pines?*" I snort.

"Yes, *pines* is a perfectly acceptable way to phrase that! I also hear that he's been *jonesing* for your *groovy kind of love.*"

I drop my head, giggling too hard to look him in the eye anymore.

"Seriously, though, do you really like Cory? Isn't he kind of . . ."

I look back up. "What, hot? Yes, he's *kind of* hot. And he's funny."

Ryan's eyes get huge and serious. "He is *not* funny."

We stare at each other silently for a few long seconds, until I crack up again, shaking my head. "No, he's not!"

Ryan smiles but mostly just looks relieved. "I mean, you've probably laughed *at* him."

"Don't be mean! What if Maddie really does like him? You'll have to find a way to enjoy his company."

Ryan shrugs and I feel sort of buzzy with a new idea. Maybe a balloon bouquet was immature, but ditching Cory so Maddie can have him . . . that's something a really good friend would do.

Out of the corner of my eye I see someone standing very still, a dark column of silence in the room. I turn and don't even feel surprised to see that it's Airport Guy again. He's looking at Gabe Richmond, barely nodding while Gabe talks, though his face is alert and almost friendly. I stare at them for a minute, wondering why Airport Guy is so totally different from everyone else in this room. It's not just because he seems sober, and focused, and quiet. It's also . . . I don't know. Interesting. Sophisticated.

Maybe he went to Europe this summer, too. Snort.

"You were looking for Gabe, right? He's over there," I tell Ryan. "Who's he talking to?"

"Where? Oh. Oh!" Ryan puts a hand on my shoulder like he's steadying himself. "Isn't that Alex Goode?"

"Alex Goode? Like, *the* Alex Goode?"

"Yeah. Remember we heard he might move here or something? I guess he did."

I only half remember, honestly, because I'm terrible at keeping up with the news. But now that Ryan says it, I realize I've seen Airport Guy on TV. He's Alex Goode, and he stopped a school shooting last year, over in Iowa. He caught the gunman, another student named Brian Hinckley, and somehow talked the guy out of a massacre. Brian killed himself, but everyone else was okay. And Alex became a national hero.

"Jesus," I say under my breath. "No wonder he seems so intense." Then I look at Ryan, suddenly suspicious. "Why didn't you recognize him at the airport today?"

"He was at the airport?"

"Yeah! You were all, *seven o'clock*."

Ryan's face is blank for a minute. "Nope. That guy was black. I for sure did not see Alex freaking Goode at the airport."

"Huh." I turn back to watch Alex nod at something else Gabe is shouting over the music. "This is the smallest, weirdest town."

"Let's go say hi," Ryan says.

Gabe smiles as we walk up, but Alex just looks at us blankly as Ryan shouts, "Hey! I'm Ryan. You're Alex, right?" and sticks out his hand. Alex nods and shakes hands but still doesn't say a word. I'm about to pretend to faint or something, anything to avoid the awkwardness, when Ryan points at me. "This is Rosie."

"Hi," I say. I reach out and Alex takes my hand. It's very serious.

I bite my lip to keep a silly giggle from escaping. Something tells me Ryan will not approve of me giggling at National Hero Alex Goode.

Alex's hand is strong and warm and dry, smooth in a way that shows this guy doesn't sweat. At least, not over stuff like girls. The giggle evaporates in my throat, and I manage to meet his eyes and smile. They're dark and at the same level as mine, and I'm wearing heels, so that means he's only a few inches taller, and in a flash I remember every single shred of gossip I've ever heard about him. And then I go full maniac and blurt, "You're on the team! Football! I mean—you play football. Right?"

Fabulous. It's because he's famous, I think. I've never met a famous person before. Or a hero. Unless you count all my friends' parents who are in the military, they're heroes, obviously, but besides them. I've had too much beer, and I don't know how to be normal around a celebrity, that's all.

Alex nods at me and that's it. Thank Jesus, Gabe starts telling us about something football-related and Ryan laughs—which is weird, because even though Gabe is very entertaining Ryan doesn't usually care about football, but whatever. But Alex and I just stand there, stuck in the awkwardness vortex I created.

"I gotta go," Alex says suddenly, and without another word he disappears into the crowd, heading toward one of the not-yet-a-door holes in the wall.

The three of us watch him leave and Gabe goes, "He didn't even want to come to this. The dude is totally shy, it's so random."

"I don't know," Ryan says. "Kind of makes sense to me."

I pour the rest of my beer down my throat. I don't know what I expected Alex Goode to be like, but *shy* wasn't it.

Gabe and Ryan keep talking, but I tune out, scanning the room. Cory is touching Maddie's hair, and she's gazing up at him. Olivia and Annabelle are dancing with each other. My head is doing that floaty thing.

Ugh, I'm drunk. I check my phone, and it's later than I'd thought. It's almost curfew, and I'm tired of watching Maddie flirt with Cory. I'll deal with all that tomorrow.

"Can I get a ride?" I ask Ryan. "I don't think the guy who brought me here wants to drive me home."

He raises his eyebrows. "You don't sound too broken up about it."

"Yeah, well. Maybe I'm growing as a person."

Ryan glances back at Gabe and then shrugs. "Let's go tell Maddie we're leaving."

"Nah. She's good. I'll text her."

Ryan doesn't argue and we turn on our phones, lighting our way across the muddy expanse of not–front lawn to his car.

"This is going to be an interesting year," he says.

I grunt.

"In a good way," he adds.

"Ha, yeah. Definitely. Though I'd settle for just some better parties."

Ryan laughs, a sharp bark that gets swallowed in the humid night air. "Good luck with that, kid."

3

"YOU WERE OUT late last night." Mom leans against the counter, a giant mug of coffee cradled in both hands just below her chin.

"Not really," I automatically mutter, shuffling to the fridge and pulling out the frozen waffles.

"The dog next door started barking around two—"

"Mom, I was home *way* before that." I push the toaster button down so hard it doesn't stick, then jab it again a few more times out of frustration. She never believes me.

"Hey, okay, calm down."

I watch the metal coils turn red around my waffle, and neither of us speaks for a long time. Finally I look over, taking in my Disney-princess mom in her pale lavender scrubs. Even when she's tired, even when she's annoyed at me, she is beautiful.

"I was home by one, I swear," I say softly.

She nods, but then her eyes travel down to the hem of my shorts, and anger flares up behind my eyes again.

Before she can say anything else, though, Ayla comes in and yanks open the fridge.

"Where's all the yogurt?" my sister practically shouts.

"Oh my God, are we all on our periods, or what?" I snap.

"Rosie, that's vile," Mom says, while at the same time Ayla nearly takes my head off yanking open the freezer.

"Watch it!" I jump out of the way as the door swings shut again, and there's a completely different twelve-year-old standing there now. A serene, smiling one, holding a cup of yogurt and a bag of frozen blueberries.

"Ayla, honey, the moods *are* getting a little . . ." Mom stops herself as Ayla's smile fades.

This has been the story of the summer, basically. My sister turned from the sweet angel my mom had always wanted *me* to be into a hormonal beast, and now no one is safe. Not even Ayla's dad, my stepdad, Dave. Who is probably upstairs right now, pretending to be asleep so he can avoid the morning drama of the three Fuller women.

My waffle pops up, and I back away, finding a spot on the counter that's not too close to either of them, and sneak a look at Mom again. She meets my eye and smirks a little, and just for a second, we're on the same team. The same *What the hell happened to Ayla?* team. I give her a tiny smile.

Then I remember that I need something. "Can I have the car?" I ask, and she sighs. Moment over.

"I still need stuff for school." Ayla has her back to both of us, but her voice is loud and clear.

"I know," Mom tells her. "I just have a short shift today, so I can take you later. Or your dad should be around, right?" She turns back to me. "Maybe you should ask him for a ride, too,

Rosie. I have to leave pretty soon here."

I'm careful to not look pissed when I shrug. Dave's always nice about taking me to work, or anywhere else, but it's starting to get seriously embarrassing being the only person I know who doesn't have her own car. Obviously not everyone has a cool new Fiat like Maddie got for her birthday, but some old used junker would be fine.

The last time I brought it up, though, Dave just cheerfully pointed out that I'm making my own money now, so we could discuss a payment plan. I guess he's right, but if that's the option, I'd rather walk to DQ and have some money of my own.

"Is Maddie back?" Ayla asks.

"Yeah," I say. "Yesterday."

"Wow, good story."

"Ayla . . ." Mom's tone is a warning, but Ayla just makes a face and pours blueberries into a bowl. There's an awkward silence until Mom asks me, "Did she have fun at her program?"

"Yeah," I say again.

Maddie already texted to say sorry for not hanging out more last night, and I said it was no problem, and neither of us said anything about Cory. So right now I don't really want to talk about Maddie, because I don't really know how I feel about any of it.

"I'm gonna walk," I say. "I should go." I make a point of rinsing my plate and putting it in the dishwasher, hoping this will show Mom that I'm not the awful teenager she seems to think I am *and* make Ayla look a little bad, since she never does dishes. But they're already looking at Ayla's eighth-grade supply list and talking about

26

Target, so it's pretty much a wasted effort.

Upstairs, I stuff my uniform shirt and hat in my backpack, swipe on some mascara, and grab my iPod. I can hear Dave singing an old Foo Fighters song in the shower, and all second thoughts I might've had about not asking him for a ride vanish. Dave is pretty much the best guy for your mom to marry, especially if your own dad left after getting her pregnant in college. But he's also way more into music than I am, and he thinks it's a tragedy that I don't want to listen to his old CDs all the time. He once tried to explain to me how Coldplay apparently used to be cool or edgy or something, and it was the longest conversation of my life.

But then I walk out the door and the humidity smacks me in the face, reminding me that a car would be a pretty awesome thing to have.

A mile and a half later and my hair is stuck to my neck, but at least I don't mind changing into my dry Dairy Queen polo shirt. Pulling my ponytail through the back of the white baseball cap they make us wear, I check my reflection one last time in the tiny office bathroom. Not bad. Not an outfit Selena Gomez would ever wear, obviously, but with my cutoffs I almost look like a perky girl-next-door type.

Steph Barnes is already behind the counter, cleaning the toppings case. She's a literary magazine/Tumblr kind of girl, and at Midcity we run in completely different crowds.

But at work, she cleans. So at work, she is my hero.

"Hey, Rosie," she says now, not looking up. "Can you get the front?" She nods toward the wall of windows with the door, where a high counter runs the length of the small store. There are a few stools in here, but most people sit outside at the picnic tables.

I stifle a groan and grab the washcloth she holds out to me.

"How's your last weekend going?" I ask. The Formica I'm wiping down will never really be clean, but it's satisfying to send the crumbs of old sugar cones raining to the floor.

"Okay, I guess. At least everyone's back from their exciting travels."

There's a hint of bitterness in her voice that makes me turn. She shrugs.

"Didn't your friend Maddie go to Spain?"

"Yeah," I say. "You know a lot of people who went away, too?"

She shrugs again, and I wonder why she brought it up if it's such a sore subject.

The door opens and our first customers of the day come in— about fifteen little girls in soccer uniforms, basically tiny Maddie clones. Their coach does a double take when he sees me. I pretend I don't notice. He's old and it's gross, but I get that kind of look often enough that I can just block it out.

For almost an hour it seems like everyone has decided to have soft-serve instead of lunch, and Steph and I don't say anything to each other except, "She ordered the Blizzard," and "Hand me those wrappers?" It's mindless but it keeps you from getting cold, and every time I look up to smile at a new customer, I feel a little jolt of connection. It's weirdly fun, serving people. Especially serving ice cream, which tends to put people in a good mood.

When there's finally a lull, I take out my phone and scroll

through my feeds, but no one's doing anything interesting. I already studied all the party photos when I woke up. The only ones with Cory showed him yelling or drinking. Maddie's in the background in one of them, looking the other way. My genius plan of gifting this boy to my BFF doesn't feel so awesome anymore, but I'm probably just cranky because I'm at work.

"So, you were saying about the summer?" I ask Steph, glancing up from Instagram for a second.

She sighs. "There was this camp I couldn't go to," she admits, picking out a red M&M and popping it in her mouth. "This guy I know, not from Midcity, he went. He's one of those, you know, lives-in-the-neighborhood, our-parents-are-friends people."

I nod. Steph lives in a much nicer neighborhood than I do—it's not within walking distance of this DQ, so she drives here in a pretty new VW—and she talks about her junior high and neighborhood friends a lot.

"Anyway. I was fine, you know? Until he came back and wouldn't shut up about it. I don't think he even liked it as much as he likes knowing I couldn't be there."

"Sounds like a hell of a guy," I say drily.

"Oh, yeah. I'm *definitely* gonna marry him."

I laugh, surprised, even though by now I've figured out that she can be really funny.

Then the afternoon crush kicks in, the worst time of day. It's late enough that the pool kids are coming by, dripping chlorine all over the floor and shouting at us because they have water in their ears. By the time I've made my fiftieth chocolate dip cone I feel like

I have water in my ears, too, and I'm dying to hide in the bathroom with my phone for a few minutes, when suddenly there are two tall, dark shapes in the doorway, and my stomach goes all fluttery.

"Rosie Fuller," Cory booms. He makes my name sound kind of dirty, but in a way that—and yes, I'm embarrassed to admit this—kind of turns me on.

I hate that I'm blushing, though, because I'm kind of mad—or something?—at Cory. And I really hate that I'm blushing in front of the guy who's with him: Alex Goode.

They stride up to the counter like a two-man starting line, practically blocking out the sun with their shoulders. Alex is wearing a Midcity Lions jersey already, and for a second I'm afraid they're here for some kind of team hazing ritual, making him eat his weight in Butterfinger crumbles or something. But then Cory leans his elbows on the counter and grins at me, and I take another guess—Cory's showing off for the new local celebrity.

"What can I get you guys?" I ask. My voice comes out all breathy and flirty, which isn't really how I feel. But Cory's eyes flash, so: worth it.

"You know Alex?" Cory asks. "Alex Goode? He's on the team this year."

I smile at Alex, whose gaze is fixed on the menu over my head like it's showing porn.

"We met at the party last night," I say charmingly.

But Cory's already turning to Alex to ask, "I'm starving, bro, you want something?" The new star player just shakes his head.

"Parfait?" I say to Cory, knowing from the two other times he's visited me at work what he's probably going to order. His grin goes from wolfish to triumphant, since obviously I've just made him look like a ridiculous stud. Not that there's anything studly about the word *parfait*, which I wish I could point out to him right now. But if he wanted to make Alex think he runs this town, having the ice-cream girl remember his "usual" isn't the worst way to do it.

I'm grateful to have an excuse to turn my back to them, pouring vanilla and chocolate syrup and peanuts into one of the plastic parfait cups, making the layers come out even. I'm kind of proud of how much better I am at this than I was a few months ago. Which is maybe kind of pathetic.

When I hand the cup to Cory and collect his five dollars, he smiles again, and Alex blinks in that intense way of his, and then they leave, and a weird empty feeling opens up between my lungs. The pointlessness of everything I've done since school let out hits me: hooking up with a guy who's more interested in my best friend—and vice versa—and learning how to make his favorite ice cream treat exactly right and . . . that's it.

"So weird," Steph says as soon as we're alone again.

"What?"

"Oh, God. Never mind. It's—no, it's nothing."

I poke her arm. "Now you *have* to tell me."

She flinches away, shrugging at the same time. "It's just, you know. That guy. I know he's a big deal and whatever . . ."

"Alex?" I guess. Though Cory's a big deal, too, even if he hasn't been on the news for anything but football.

"Yeah." She laughs nervously. "I've just never seen a guy, like, not look at you. I'm sorry, that's totally weird! I mean, it's weird that I'm saying anything. But it was *unusual* to see a guy just . . . not drool on you."

I laugh, wishing she would stop looking so anxious. And I wish she wasn't so right. Cory clearly wanted Alex to be impressed that he can come in here and flirt with me—but Alex didn't seem impressed at all. Even when I caught him looking at me in the airport . . . I don't know. I guess he really was looking at the balloons.

"He's kind of odd looking, right?" I say.

Steph frowns. "I don't know, I just thought he seemed serious. He's not as classically handsome as Cory, obviously."

I'm checking my phone again, but I pause to roll my eyes. "I don't know. Cory's a little basic."

She scoffs. "Yeah, basically perfect."

I don't reply because I've found a new photo on Maddie's feed— someone else took it, but she reposted. Of her standing with Cory at the party, laughing. It's . . . cute.

Suddenly there are noises from the back office, and in a flash Steph and I are both tidying up the counter, the spoons. I grab another washcloth and clean the soft-serve machine.

"My favorite girls!" Joel comes through the office door with his hands raised, and we laugh in relief.

"Oh, it's just *you*," I say, tossing my rag in the sink.

He gives me a mock-offended look, and then we smile at each other in that way that we probably shouldn't, given that he's twenty-two and one of the night managers and I'm still in high school. But it makes the empty feeling in my chest disappear completely.

"You girls hustlin' that paper?" Joel asks, rubbing his fingers together like a cartoon villain.

I roll my eyes at his pathetic slang. "We were, but then Steph ate all the M&M's, so I think we're back where we started." I grin at Joel and then at Steph, but she narrows her eyes at me. She *did* eat some M&M's, but whatever, so did I, and obviously Joel doesn't care. Or I guess she's probably glaring at me because she thinks I shouldn't flirt with our manager.

"I'm gonna clock out," she says, and before I can tell her it was just a joke, she's disappeared into the office.

Joel doesn't seem to notice anything is wrong. He's got his nose in the cash register, and when he looks up and finds me still standing there, he just smiles again.

"Go on," he says lightly. "Go enjoy your soda jerks and your sock hops."

I swing my ponytail as I turn away, smiling when I hear Joel laugh. But by the time I've clocked out, Steph is halfway across the parking lot already. I wait by the Dumpsters near the back door, watching with envy as she slides into her Volkswagen and literally drives off into the sunset.

My phone vibrates.

Movie night? Maddie asks.

My thumb hovers over the screen. Girls are so *hard* sometimes. Is Steph actually mad about the stupid M&M's thing? And maybe *I'm* supposed to be mad at Maddie for all that flirting with Cory? At least with Cory—with boys—it's obvious: they want the shiny thing, the pretty thing. And usually the *new* shiny, pretty thing is

33

even better. But with girls, I really don't know sometimes.

Then again, it's Maddie. Of course I want to see her. And screw it. She can have pretty, shiny Cory. She needs him more than I do. And I need her more than I need him.

Pick me up in an hour?

She sends back a screen full of smiley faces and hearts. Which, let's face it, is the kind of perfect thing that a boy would *never* do.

I send back one fist bump and start walking home, smiling again.

4

"I CAN'T BELIEVE—it's—" I look up at Maddie. "You didn't have to get me anything!"

"Seriously? I'm basically the worst person ever for not giving it to you as soon as I got back! I just wanted to unpack and wrap it and . . . Are you sure you like it?" She twists her fingers together, looking genuinely worried.

I smooth the scarf against my legs. It's a thinly woven silk in a dusky blue. When I move it in the light from Maddie's bedroom lamps, it almost looks like a very dark aqua color.

"I thought it would match your eyes," she says. "And maybe help you forgive me for not only going away for our whole summer, but then coming back and hanging out with your boyfriend."

I roll my eyes at her, but my hand clenches a little around the cool fabric. We're sitting on the floor with a package of Oreos and a bowl of microwave popcorn in front of us, getting ready to have a *Pitch Perfect* marathon. This is the right time to do the good-friend thing.

But I just want it to kind of *happen*. Maybe I could stop texting him and let high school nature take its course. . . .

Maddie's still twisting her fingers together, looking nervous. Something loosens in my chest, settles back to where it's supposed to be. This is us, like always. I'm her Boy Coach.

I take a deep breath. "Listen, Mads. He's not my boyfriend. We hooked up a bunch of times, but if you *like* him, you should go for it."

Her eyes light up and I can tell she's biting the inside of her cheeks to keep from smiling.

"Oh my God!" I cry. "This is pathetic, for real. If you don't mind that I've already, like, *done stuff* with him . . ." I'm just teasing her, but for a second the light in her eyes definitely dims.

"That is awkward, isn't it?" she says softly. "This whole thing is so stupid. I'm sorry. I don't know why . . . He doesn't even play soccer! I'm being a total asshole."

Maddie doesn't swear, ever. Or pre-Spain Maddie didn't, anyway.

"Maybe Europe *changed* you," I say in a dramatic voice, trying to turn it into a joke.

"Ugh, I know!" She covers her face with her hands and groans. "I really don't want to be that girl who goes away and then can't shut up about it!" Her hands drop and she grabs an Oreo and holds it up, showing me. "You know the truth? I ate these every day. *Every day*, Rosie! Because they reminded me of home. I had a stash in my room."

I smile. "That doesn't sound so bad. Oreos are delicious."

"I know!" she cries, her mouth full of cookie. "But it just made me feel like such a kid, that I *needed* them. Everyone else there was so sophisticated and smart and just, I don't know. Grown-up."

"You're sophisticated," I say. "And the smartest person I know."

She uncrosses one leg so she can poke my knee with her toes. "You're too nice to me. I can't be a total loser *and* ask for your blessing with Cory. That's too much."

"Um, okay, well you definitely don't have my *blessing* because no one is getting *married*, right?" We both laugh. "But I do think I should text him and say I've moved on. Because I have."

She leans forward. "You *have*?"

I open my mouth to say, *Of course not! It's been like twelve hours!* then snap it shut again. What's a little lie between friends? She's never going to stop beating herself up over this if I don't give her a solid out. Or at least as solid an out as I can commit to.

Plus, if I'm being honest, there have totally been guys I lost interest in overnight. Most of them, actually.

So I shrug and say, "I have a crush on someone. It's totally distracting, and I was feeling like the thing with Cory was unfair. For a while now."

Maddie looks entranced, like I've just told her some wonderful fairy tale. Though I guess it does make for a pretty conveniently happy ending—which, hey, maybe I've figured this whole good-friend thing out after all.

"Who is it?" she breathes. "Do I know him?"

And then for some reason I couldn't explain in a million years, Alex Goode's face pops into my head. His not-handsome, not-smiling, not-flirting-with-me face, with those deep, serious eyes and that permanent scowl. That face that's attached to the only mysterious high school boy I've ever met, the only real-life hero-celebrity. The only guy I can't seem to get to look at *my* face.

I wave my hand in the air between Maddie and me, brushing away thoughts of Alex and her question all at once.

"It's new," I say. "It's really too new to talk about—I don't even know if it's real yet, I don't want to jinx it."

She frowns. "I thought you said it'd been going on for a while?"

"No, no, I mean I wasn't that into Cory for a while." As soon as the words are out of my mouth, I sort of wonder if they're true. I like who Cory is on paper—his looks, his popularity. I even like his big, grabby hands, how they always made me feel so wanted and sort of, like, tiny and feminine. But Cory himself . . . "He's not really my type."

She's still frowning, and I know this might be a lie too far. No one knows my type better than Maddie. And besides, Cory is *every-one's* type. I may as well have just said that Channing Tatum has an okay body.

"Seriously, look," I say quickly, getting out my phone. "I'm going to tell him I found somebody else." *Not Alex*, I add to myself. "See? And then you should write him and ask for a ride to school on Monday, or something."

Maddie's face finally clears and she lets out a small laugh. "I can't ask him for a ride to *school*."

"Why not?" I ask, but I'm only half listening. I'm mostly focused on my phone, on trying to write something friendly but final. *That was an awesome summer, but I think we should see other people this year.* I stare at the words, wanting them to be less lame but not knowing how to fix them. I try adding a thumbs-up emoji and then delete it.

Maddie leans over again, trying to see what I'm typing, and I panic. I hit Send, feeling virtuous and idiotic and relieved and confused, all at the same time.

I cling to the feeling-virtuous part. This is going to make Maddie happy, we'll have a fun junior year, and I'll be the friend she can turn to for boy advice again.

She needs me. I'm helping her.

My thumb is still hovering over the screen when she grabs for my phone and cries, "Let me see!"

I just hold it up high and shout, "It's done! Your turn!"

"No!" she shrieks. "I can't! *You* can't!"

She's still trying to pull my hand down and I squirm, sliding the phone across the carpet and then full-on tackling her.

"Give me *your* phone!" I yell.

"Ack! No!" She's screaming and laughing and I manage to pin her long enough to grab the cell behind her.

I hold it at arm's length, out of her reach, and then stop. "Crap, you need his number, right?" But as I'm saying it I'm also unlocking her screen and opening her texts, and that's when I see that she *doesn't* need his number.

They've already texted.

I drop the phone like it's a snake and Maddie's laugh dies in the air between us.

A text exchange shines up at us, resting in the pool of the fancy Spanish scarf on the floor.

All I can see are the words *cool party* from Cory.

"Rosie, I'm the *worst*," she says.

I can tell she's too afraid of me to move, to grab or turn off the phone, but that's fine because I'm not reading anymore. My eyes feel dull and blurry.

"It's okay," I say. I know the words are true, somewhere in the future, but I can't make them sound right. "It's obviously fine."

Then she finally takes her phone and tosses it across the room, letting it land near mine over by her closets.

"Let's just watch the movies," she says. "I missed you so much, I don't care about stupid boys. I couldn't even talk to a stupid boy before I met you! You're way more important than all that crap."

"I know," I say. I can't stop staring at the scarf. I'm doing a *horrible* job being cool about all this. How can I feel so uninterested in Cory and at the same time, so hurt that Maddie already has his number?

"Seriously, it was just a stupid text. Please don't be mad. Please?"

I sigh, looking up at her worried face. "I'm not mad," I say, and at least for a minute I'm sure I really mean it. "You're *way* more important to me than Cory could ever be. He was just a summer thing, and it's over. Okay?"

She studies my face for a minute, then nods. I reach over and pull her into one of those awkward we're-both-sitting-cross-legged hugs, and it's not enough, but I think it makes things feel a little more normal.

"Do you need another Coke?" she asks, pointing at the food we've barely touched.

"Nah, I'm good. Let's just watch the movies, like you said. It's been way too long since I got to see you on a Saturday night."

She grabs my hand and squeezes it, another one of those things that only Maddie can do, and with her other hand she lifts the remote and turns on the screen.

We laugh at all the usual parts and shout our favorite lines along with the characters. When the first song comes up, we sing like we always have, and I look over at my best friend and feel really, really good. I missed her so much. And now I'm really doing it, I'm really being the better friend I thought I could be. Maybe it's still just boy stuff, but I don't know—it feels good.

Then this thought flashes through my mind, that I'm lucky. Lucky that Maddie's still so insecure. Because seriously, there's no way she needs my help with boys anymore—if she just looked in a mirror, she'd know that. Didn't she see the way Cory made a bee-line for her? The way he gave her his number? Hasn't she noticed that life is different now? I've had some time to get used to the stares, the attention, so I guess maybe it's all still new to her. Still, though.

She doesn't know what it means, yet, to look the way she looks. She still thinks she needs my help, even though she obviously got Cory all by herself.

No matter what I think I'm bringing to this friendship, Maddie would be completely fine without me. I should be happy that she just doesn't know it yet.

"Ayla, go see if your sister is coming with us."

"Do I *have* to?" she whines. "She never comes; can't we just *go*?"

"Ay—"

"It's okay, Beth, I'll go."

I flop over on my bed and groan, wishing my family would have their conversations about me somewhere else, or at least realize that I can *hear* them. I can hear Dave coming down the hall right now. He taps lightly on my door, probably hoping I've gone back to sleep since getting home from Maddie's. Since leaving *another* conversation about whether I want to go to Mass today. I don't want to discuss it with him any more than I did with Mrs. Costello, but I take a deep breath and yell, "Come in," in as not-shitty a tone as I can manage.

"Oh, hey, you're up."

Dave's head is poked through a small opening of the door, his black hipster glasses slightly askew where they're leaning against the wood.

I wave an arm over my fully clothed body, though whether I'm agreeing with him or pointing out that actually, I'm *not* up, I'm lying down, I'm not sure.

He's easier than Mom, though, and doesn't take offense at stuff like that.

"We're heading to Mass in a few minutes. You can catch a ride, if you want?"

"I have to work later," I say. *And I would so much rather lie around the house until then*, I don't add.

Dave nods. "I don't think we can leave a car—your mom has a shift, and you know how mine—"

"I know." Dave's car is really nice and he doesn't like me driving it. Sometimes I wonder if he'll let Ayla drive it when she's old enough—if he doesn't trust me because I'm not really his kid. But probably it's just that I'm not a great driver under the best of circumstances, and Dave's car is a stick shift. He did try to teach me a few times. I could drive, mostly, but not in a way that didn't scare the crap out of both of us.

"Okay, well. We'll see you at dinner? Or maybe we'll stop by to watch you work."

This makes me smile, and he does, too. Mom doesn't go for ice cream in the middle of the day. And lately, Ayla has gotten all health-conscious in this way that's making even normal meals kind of a nightmare. I won't be surprised if I have the frozen waffles all to myself pretty soon.

"Light a candle for me," I say.

He laughs. "Will do."

A few minutes later I hear the garage door opening, and I pull out my phone. Oh, look, Cory and a bunch of the football guys went to the lake. I think I spot Alex's shoulder in one of the photos, but it's hard to tell. Cory's everywhere, though—cannonballing into the water, posing for a shot with his arms flung around Marcus on one side and Brianna Kelly on the other. Brianna's been dating Brian Greenburg for years. The only thing grosser than their matching names is their waiting-for-marriage rings. Which they got in ninth grade, when, hello, no one should be doing it yet.

Still, I wonder if the photo will make Maddie worry. Or if she wishes she'd gone to the lake, like I'm sort of wishing, even though I'm not really into getting my hair wet with a bunch of senior jocks.

I hope what I saw at that party on Friday was the Cory that

he's capable of being. I hope he acts like a horny dude-bro with me because he thinks I like it. Or—okay, maybe I don't *hope* that. But it would make me feel better about handing him over to my best girlfriend if I thought he'd be a gentleman with her. Not send late-night texts that are clearly just code for *NOW will you have sex with me? Or do some more of that other stuff we've been doing?*

I go to texts and erase all of Cory's old messages, then send a quick *What up* to Ryan. Then I get in the shower and spend a long time there, letting the steam lift off all my conflicting feelings about everyone. I take an extra-long time drying my hair and putting on makeup, too, telling myself it's practice for before school tomorrow. The truth is, it just makes me feel better. To be as pretty as possible. To know I look really good, maybe better than the other girls I'll see today. Pretty enough to hook up with whoever I want, whenever I want. Prettier than all the other girls.

And it totally works, just like always. Every guy who comes into DQ that afternoon practically loses his eyeballs trying to check me out. My shorts are tight and I'm extra friendly, and I'm getting away with not wearing the baseball cap because Joel is working this shift, too. He's staring at me the most.

It's not as fun to see the dads' reactions, obviously, but I don't really care. Cost of doing business, as Dave would say. Though I've never seen Dave look at anyone but my mom. I think he might be the only guy in this sad suburb who actually likes his wife better than whatever teenage girl just walked by in cutoffs.

"You're gonna melt the ice cream," Joel says when we hit a lull in the traffic. "I mean, you always look cute, but today . . ."

I smile at him, and he clears his throat. It's harmless enough, flirting with Joel. I kind of like how there's this invisible wall between us, both because of his age and the fact that he's my boss.

"Should I put on a parka or something?" I tease. I even jut out one hip and do a little pose, which I know makes him look at my legs again. It's funny, how powerless people can be. How predictable. How I never get tired of it.

He shakes his head and laughs. "I have payroll stuff to do in the back." With another look at my hips, he shakes his head again. "Try not to hurt anyone out here, okay?"

I do a pouty face, and he bites his lip. I could probably ask for a raise and a promotion right now and get both.

Instead I just wave as he swings through the door to the back, and when I hear the office door click shut, I pull out a cup and fill it with M&M's.

Maybe I didn't learn anything new and exciting this summer, but hey. I haven't forgotten any of my old tricks, either.

5

"I can't believe you're wearing a fedora."

Ryan checks his reflection in the rearview mirror of his car and looks a little smug. "Maddie says everyone in Spain wears them. And you know I look good in hats."

"Yeah, but your *best* quality is your modesty," I say, poking him in the arm.

"Did she get you that scarf?"

I touch it self-consciously. I don't usually wear things like scarves, at least not in the summer. And definitely not to school. But when I tried it with the flowery, flowy dress I put on this morning, it looked perfect.

"Do I look like I'm trying too hard?" I ask.

"Harder than the guy rocking this Spanish fedora, you mean?"

I laugh. "You can't wear it into school, you know."

"Pshh. How unfair is that? I don't understand how we're supposed to remind everyone that *their* best friend didn't go to *España*."

"You can share my scarf," I offer. "We could wind it around both our necks."

"Which won't look weird or choke us to death at all."

I grin. "At least I'd always know where you were."

His eyebrows shoot up. "I don't know if that's something you really want to know, babe."

I poke him again. "Thanks for driving my sad, car-deprived ass, by the way."

Ryan flips on his turn signal and leans over the wheel, looking both ways. We're just a block from school now. Our house is so close to Midcity that Mom thinks I should walk, but she doesn't understand how pathetic that would be. Plus, thanks to Ryan, I'm not sweaty, my hair is intact, and this conversation is distracting me from the first-day-of-school nerves that always hit me way harder than they should.

"Young lady," Ryan says in a haughty voice, "there are kids your age who don't even have a *smartphone*. Think of how privileged you really are."

"Yeah, yeah, yeah."

"Besides," he adds, his voice back to normal, "look at this so-called senior parking lot. One more car in here and then what? I'm parking across the street? Or on the other side, with the *teachers* and *lowerclassmen*?"

"Uh, Ry, we're not seniors."

"Please," he says, and with a last, swift jerk of the steering wheel, we have a prime spot right next to the side doors. "What are they going to do, ticket me?"

We grab our bags and Ryan bares his teeth at me. I shake my

head—no food—and he does the same for my teeth. Then I point at his hat, which he takes off and chucks into the backseat.

And now we're officially juniors.

Maddie's been here for an hour already, doing student council stuff and missing our annual tradition of arriving together. It doesn't take long to find her, though, since it turns out that "student council stuff" means "handing out IDs and locker assignments in the front hall."

"R 'n' R!" Maddie yells, loudly enough that we actually hear her over the apocalyptic level of noise. "Come and get it!"

We fight our way through the crush of upperclassmen and she gives us each a kiss on the cheek, which I guess is her usual thing now. At least it's only one kiss each this time.

"Nice scarf," she says with a smile.

I fluff it a little, smiling back. She still looks different, with her natural blond highlights and another boho top under a feathery necklace. But something about the box of IDs and the clipboard on the table in front of her makes the whole thing much more Maddie. Much more normal.

She leans forward and drops her voice, asking us, "Have you seen *Alex* yet?"

I shake my head, confused.

"Everyone is *freaking out*," she explains.

"No shit," Ryan says. "Nothing even remotely exciting has ever happened at this school."

Maddie rolls her eyes. "People are ridiculous. Charlotte Lewis gave this big speech to us this morning about how we're even safer now, having him here, but we should still petition the school board for more security. Because we can't rely on other students to protect us."

"What the hell does *that* mean?" Ryan says.

"Right? I have no idea! Mrs. Walsh was like, 'Uhh, okay, let's maybe just go over the dance schedule for now.'"

All three of us crack up. Then someone shoves me from behind, and Maddie waves as we move out of the way.

"Charlotte Lewis is an idiot," Ryan mutters. "You remember when she said she couldn't watch *Ellen*? Because she was *Christian*?"

"That was sixth grade, dude," I point out. "You have to stop worrying about it."

"Whatever, you're still mad at her, too."

I laugh. "Yeah, but only because she basically bought that stupid election with all those damn *cronuts*."

"Those were good," Ryan says under his breath.

"Hmph. She did have the best party of the summer, I guess. You totally missed it."

Ryan narrows his eyes at me like he thinks I'm joking but can't tell. I'm serious, though, it *was* a good party. Charlotte has a huge pool, and there was catering and everything. Some of the football guys snuck in a bottle of vodka, and I ended up in the pool house with Cory, which was . . . oh, well. It was a long time ago. Like a month. Ancient history.

We reach the part of school where the hall splits, and before Ryan leaves to go to his locker he gives me an exaggerated kiss on the cheek. "To Spain," he says.

49

"I don't care what Jesus says, I'll watch *Ellen* with you anytime," I reply, kissing him back.

"Jesus is cool with it," he assures me, and walks away.

I turn to find my locker and see Mrs. Walsh coming toward me, her eyes locked on my face. Anxiety pricks the back of my neck. I can't be in trouble already, can I? She's always really nice to me, even that time I snuck out with Paul Maziarz (well, that time we got *caught*). But she also has her extraserious student counselor face on.

Then I see that Alex is walking with her, and the prickles turn into actual chills.

"Rosemary Fuller!" Mrs. Walsh calls, suddenly all smiles. She's stopped now, standing right next to my locker, and I have no choice but to join her there.

"Hey," I say uncertainly.

"How was your summer?" she asks with a big smile. I don't know why I get nervous around her, except that teachers make me nervous. Because they always want something from you, and in my case it's never something good.

"Fine," I say. My eyes dart over to Alex, who's just standing there, all calm. Everyone who passes us is turning their heads, getting a look at him, lifting their phones to snap photos as they walk past. It almost makes me giggle.

"This is Alex Goode, our new addition to the junior class. Alex, this is Rosemary Fuller."

We nod at each other, neither of us bothering to point out that introductions have already been made. I sort of like that Alex doesn't say anything. He does smile, though, just the tiniest bit, and heat starts to spread through my chest like ink soaking into paper. I wonder what would happen if I met someone who was famous for real. Would I faint?

"You guys have lockers right next to each other, Rosie, so I thought you could show Alex around today?" Mrs. Walsh goes on. "And it looks like your schedules are pretty similar, too. He's already been here, working out with the team, but he doesn't know how to find all the classrooms, do you, Alex?"

He shakes his head politely, giving her a perfect adult-appropriate smile, and she beams at him.

"Okay! Have a great first day, you two! Alex, you know where to find me." We both nod again, and she pauses like she wants to say something more. In the end she just raises a fist halfway and yelps, "Go Lions!"

We watch her walk away, stopping to chat with other students every few feet. Alex turns to me, and for a second we stare at our lockers in a completely awkward silence.

"Go Lions!" I say softly, and out of nowhere he lets out this huge laugh. It makes me laugh, too, just once, and I sneak a glance at him.

"Do they really call the pep rallies 'Pride Parades'?" he asks, a smile still on his lips.

I pinch my mouth closed and nod.

"What a world."

"I'm sorry she assigned you a babysitter," I say. "I'm sure you could find your classes just fine, I mean."

Alex shifts his eyes from me to just over my shoulder, then back again. "Yeah, and everyone seems super friendly."

I angle slowly around and notice that there are people *staring* at us. Standing there, totally still, staring. Even one of the teachers, Ms. Fiedler. And Ms. Fiedler doesn't get distracted from calculus for *anything*.

"I think we're gonna need a bigger boat," I say softly. It's an old family joke from *Jaws*, which Dave insisted on watching with me when I was way, *way* too young to handle it. I'm mostly talking to myself, but Alex raises an eyebrow at me.

"You like movies?"

"Sure," I say. "I'm also quite fond of air and food and the blood that keeps my internal organs from collapsing."

He just stares at me for a long beat, long enough for me to wonder what the hell I've said, and then another one of those huge laughs comes booming out.

It breaks all the spells at once—the kids behind us scatter, the last warning bell for homeroom rings, and I burst into a big smile.

I made the hero laugh. *Twice*.

"Come on," I say. "Who's your homeroom teacher?"

He takes a piece of paper from his pocket, folded into the size of a quarter, and starts smoothing it out. By the time he hands over his schedule I've already tested my locker combo and slammed the door shut again. I take the creased paper and see that Mrs. Walsh was right—we have a ton of classes in common. Starting with homeroom.

"Okay, you can basically follow me around all day," I tell him. It sounds decidedly flirty without me even meaning it to, but he just shrugs. Hiking his backpack onto his shoulder, he waits expectantly until I start walking.

I'm reminded how easy it is to get down the hall when everyone makes way for the guy you're next to. With *this* guy, though, it's also awkward as hell, trying to pretend we're not being gaped at like some kind of zoo exhibit.

"So," I say, hoping I can distract him from how pathetic my fellow Lions are acting, "did I see you at the airport the other day?" As soon as the words are out, I realize I'm being almost as creepy as all the gawkers around us, so I hurry to add, "I mean, I was picking up my friend Maddie, and, you know, it's not a big place, and I thought I maybe recognized you. After I saw you. Probably."

Oh, wow, I'm making it *even awkwarder.*

But Alex just says, "If it was Friday, then yeah. I was there."

"Why were you flying in from Chicago? Didn't you move from Iowa?"

If it surprises him that I know way too many personal details, he still doesn't show it. "We were visiting family," he explains. "All my stuff was already at my dad's house, so we just flew back."

I nod, biting my tongue before it can babble something else that makes me sound like a stalker. But I still have a million questions, a million rumors I wish I could verify directly. Everything I heard last year, like that his dad has lived out here for a long time, and that Alex moved here to get away from his old school three hours away in Iowa. Because of the traumatic memories. Which all makes sense, but might not even be true.

I don't want to be a nosy jerk. But then I hear myself saying, "It must be weird, that everyone already knows everything about you."

"Probably not *everything*," he jokes.

"Well, I mean. I know where your homeroom is." I stop outside Mr. Richnow's door and smile. Before I can think better of it, I also flip my hair and tilt my head a little. Like an accidental flirting move.

But he just furrows his eyebrows and looks past me through the door. "Yeah, I guess you do," he says.

And then he gives me a brief little smile and walks ahead.

Okay.

I let Alex get ahead of me and scan the room. I guess I should sit with Alex, but it's kind of exhausting, feeling so nervous around him all the time. Even if I did make him laugh, now he seems like he can't get away from me fast enough.

Unfortunately the second bell rings and Mr. Richnow yells, "Everyone find a seat and sit in it!" and I get stuck next to Olivia Thorpe. She doesn't scowl at me, though, so maybe it's not that bad.

"Hey, sexy."

I turn to the right, and there's Finn Kramper, grinning at me.

Perfect.

"Okay, people!" Mr. Richnow booms. The room gets marginally quieter but he doesn't wait for silence, just keeps yelling. "Remember where you are now, because that will be your seat for the rest of the year!"

Per. Fect.

I turn around, careful to rotate away from Finn, and catch

Olivia sneering at me. I sneer right back, then keep turning until I find Alex. Of course *he* snagged a seat in the back row, right next to this guy Emilio, who's totally cool.

"When I call your name, tell me if you're here or not!" Richnow says, voice still booming.

"How can we tell you if we're not here?" Finn calls out. I accidentally look over at him again and he grins at me, so very proud of his clever joke.

Mr. Richnow ignores it all. "Marisa Ang!" he shouts.

Well. I made it a whole half hour before I remembered how much I hate school.

I keep up with Alex for the rest of the morning, but he gets quieter and quieter. Maybe because people keep gawking. And the way people stare at him isn't the way they stare at me. It's way more . . . serious. Like they *need* something from him.

So that's how roughly two million years go by, and then it's time for lunch.

We've just rounded the corner to the cafeteria when I feel a slap on my ass. Not hard, but not soft—and it's followed by a loud, "Keepin' it high and tight, girl!"

Ah, Marcus Weaver, he of the famously fluffy Afro, now bigger than ever. He laughs and winks at me, and I laugh back, relieved to see a friendly face.

"Just keepin' it *high*, Marcus?" I joke.

He's surrounded by a bunch of the other football players, including, I notice, Cory and Gabe. They all go, "Oooh," or make pot-smoking faces, laughing along with me. But it only lasts a second before they spot Alex and get distracted fist-bumping him and talking about practice. Cory throws an arm around me, keeping me included with the group, but I'm no longer part of the conversation. And when we reach the cafeteria, they all scatter, Marcus dragging Alex away to the french fries and the other guys hurrying to the burger station.

I scoot to the side and check my phone. There's nothing from Ryan or Maddie, even though I texted them both this morning to ask when they have lunch.

I've just ducked out the door to try them again when I finally see Maddie heading toward me. She's in the middle of a group of student council–type girls, all of them listening to something she's saying, laughing at whatever it is. Even Charlotte Lewis is giggling, and, I have to admit, looking slightly less stuck-up than usual.

I wait for them to get closer so I can walk in with them, but then someone to Maddie's left starts talking and her head turns away from me. So they all keep strolling, not even noticing I'm there.

Which. Okay. Not a big deal.

But for some reason, I feel like I'm about to start crying. Like it's my first day of kindergarten instead of junior year.

My phone buzzes in my pocket, making me jump. I let out a strangled yelping sound that, thank God, is too quiet for anyone to have heard, and grab it.

Ryan: *Stuck in theater bring chips!!!*

It's to Maddie, too, part of the group text I sent earlier. But I'm so relieved to have a plan that I don't pause—just haul ass to the vending machines. Because there's never been a day so weird it couldn't be improved by junk food.

6

"Have we discussed how his last name is literally *Goode*?"

"Right? Super on the nose."

"And now you know everything about him."

"Oh my God, not even close."

Ryan spritzes glass cleaner in my direction and I squeal, even though I'm sitting all the way across the dressing room. "We're counting on you, Fuller. Get that gossip!"

"Sorry." I lean closer to the mirror, adjusting the straps of my bra under my top, snapping a few photos. It's boring in here, but the lighting is great. "So is cleaning the green room really what being student director is all about? Because it kinda blows. No offense."

Ryan pulls a chair over to the mirrors and stands on it, gently spraying and wiping down each vanity bulb. "I'm not doing this because I'm director," he says. "I'm doing it because this place is full-on *disgust*."

"That's true." I poke at the paper-towel roll on the counter and look around. Every inch of the room seems to be gray with dust or grime.

Ryan stops spritzing. "Are you gonna help, or what?"

"Probably *or what*." I shrug. "Plus, I already helped—your Doritos are right over there, remember?"

"Hmph," he grunts. "You got Cool Ranch."

"They were out of the super-cheesy ones, I told you!"

He climbs down, moves the chair, and starts washing the next mirror. "You really don't want to convo about Alex Goode? You were with him all morning! Did he do anything gallant?"

I snort, shaking my head. "I feel kinda bad. Everyone just stares at him."

"Well, duh. He's famous. Plus, he's walking around with *you*."

"Ha, okay. Thanks?"

"He's way more interesting than some quarterback, anyway."

Our eyes meet in the mirror and I roll mine.

He laughs. "Maddie told me you guys were doing a little Cory-swapping, yeah? I'm just happy to hear you've already got someone else to be all paparazzi-patrol with."

"You are seriously a lunatic."

Ryan goes back to cleaning. "So, what's happening now? You into Alex *Goode*?"

"Dude. It's not like I need a boy every second!" I'm still fiddling with my phone, adding filters to the new photos. Maybe that's why my voice sounds so whiny.

Ryan steps down from the chair and gives my head a cursory little pat. "It's a small town. Sometimes you're gonna have to share the cute boys with your friends. Especially when you're already moving on to the hot new mystery guy."

I laugh. "That is not what's happening, okay? Whatever." I

finish the pic I like best and post it. Then I turn off my phone, like I always do right after a post. A watched selfie never gets liked, as they say. "Anyway. You saw them on Friday. She's totally into him."

"I know, right? And seriously, I'm so relieved she told you how obsessed she's always been with that boy. Even if I don't understand it."

"Wait—you knew about that? I swear she never told me!"

Ryan gives me a weird look and goes back to cleaning.

I throw my head back, shaking a fist. "Maddie! Curse you and your saintly, silent suffering!" It makes us both laugh, but I'm still not sure if I knew about Maddie's old crush or not. Honestly, I might've known and just not taken it seriously, because . . . well, Cory Callahan was kind of out of her league. At least, before this summer.

"Thank God you never get attached to these guys," Ryan says, turning away again, setting down the Windex and picking up a broom. "She really would've kept suffering in silence, you know. If you'd actually liked him."

"I did like him." The words come out before I think, and Ryan gives me a look in the mirror. "For like a minute," I add quickly. "Not now."

"Well, yeah. The timer went off."

I narrow my eyes at him. "There's no *timer*."

"Oh, for sure there is. The famous Rosie Fuller Stopwatch? Everyone knows you have a short attention span."

"Jesus, you're making me sound . . . skanky."

"No! No. You're *fun*. You love life. You love boys. We all love boys! No shame, no shade."

I keep watching him in the mirror. He's sweeping, glancing up now and then, just casual chitchat. I unwrap and bite down on another Starburst but the back of my throat tastes kind of sour.

"So you think I should have a longer 'attention span'?" I put air quotes around his phrase, which makes him look up again.

"God, no. What for? You're hot, you're young. Trust me, if I lived somewhere a little less provincial, somewhere I got hit on as much as you do? I'd be swiping right all over the place. Or is it left?"

"Dunno." I look down at my phone again. Enough time has passed, and there it is: fifteen hearts. Pull down, refresh. Twenty.

"Typical," he grouses. "Life is so easy for you normative bitches."

"Yeah, I guess." I scroll down, zoning out.

Football starts this weekend. There will be parties and boys everywhere, and Maddie will finally come along to all of them with me, and I'll always be able to crash at her house, where there's no psychotic little sister and they always have good cereal. It's all working out for the best.

At the end of lunch I find Alex still in his huddle of jocks, all of them yelling about some video game. Well, all of them except Alex, who's doing that silent almost-nodding thing I'm starting to think of as his signature move. When Marcus spots me, his face lights up, and the next thing I know I'm being carried down the hall, flailing and giggling and hoping to God he doesn't move his arms and shove my skirt out of place.

"Put me down!" I squeal, because that's what you're supposed to say, and he grunts like a caveman, the way he's supposed to.

The other guys are laughing, but I'm careful not to look at Alex. We probably seem so stupid to him, after everything he's seen. Then again, maybe this is just what he needs—some normal high school crap. That's sort of why he's here, isn't it?

"Ms. Fuller, that's enough!" Ms. Fiedler's voice shouts, and without warning my feet hit the floor again.

"Sorry Ms. F.," Marcus says, giving her a little salute. She's glaring at me, though, obviously not pleased that I can't stop giggling.

"Try to set a better example for our new student," she snaps, then turns and storms back into her classroom.

Some of the guys go, "Oooh," as soon as she's gone, and Marcus reaches out to tickle me. I yelp and jump back and he goes, "Yeah, Fuller, why don't you stop messing around?"

"You're such a dork!" I yell at him, swiping at his hands. Cory's there laughing, too, and when I meet his eye, he winks at me. It makes my skin go hot and cold at the same time, and suddenly I don't feel like laughing anymore. I smirk back at Marcus and say, "Thanks for the ride."

"Hoo, baby, anytime." He high-fives Gabe Richmond, and then they all swagger off, totally full of themselves.

Finally I turn to Alex, and sure enough, he's barely smiling. There's a little glint in his eyes, though, I swear. "Did you have a good lunch?" I ask. I'm trying to sound friendly, but it comes out total mom.

"Yeah. Thanks for coming to get me."

I feel my cheeks go from pinkish to magenta. "Sure. Sorry those guys are so . . . dumb." I wave down the hall, in the general direction of Marcus. "Anyway, we're right here."

We walk into history class and end up sitting together. A few people look over, more subtly than this morning. I notice some raised eyebrows in my direction, almost like they're impressed to see me with Alex. But not the way people look at me when I'm with Paul or Cory or whoever. *Surprised* impressed.

I open my mouth to say something to Alex, prove to everyone that I am impressive, but I've got nothing. He gets out his books and I check my phone, and the day continues—confusing and weird, but, I remind myself over and over, *interesting*. Ryan has drama, and Maddie has her whole group of smart girls, but I am the only person at Midcity who got assigned to Alex Goode for the day.

Lucky me.

I don't even get my laptop turned on after dinner before Ayla wanders into my room.

"Ever heard of knocking?"

She ignores me and walks over to my desk. Her fingers rest on the box of charcoal pencils I had to get for the art elective I'm being forced to take.

"What's this?" she asks.

"Arts credits," I say. "Intro to Art."

"I didn't know you drew."

"*Intro* to Art," I say again. I'm already sitting comfortably on my bed, and it would be a waste of energy to get up and shove her out of my room, but I keep a careful eye on her.

"I heard Alex Goode is at your school now."

"You guys get gossip at the junior high, huh?" I can't believe I'm actually curious to know what she's heard, but I am.

"He goes to St. John's," she says. "Which you'd know if you ever came to church anymore."

"Ayla, come on. What do you care, really?"

She glances at me, her face tight, then looks away again. "I don't. It's just—Mom won't let me sit with my friends, and if you were there I know she would."

I sigh. I don't know how to explain that when I got on birth control, I started feeling uncomfortable at church. It was like I had to choose one or the other, and church was the boring, way more optional one. So.

Ayla turns away again, starts picking through my open closet, and now I'm feeling too bad about my heathenish ways to yell at her to stop.

"Can I borrow this?" She pulls out a miniskirt that's probably too mini on me now, but I still want to say no. She stands in front of my full-length mirror and holds it up to her hips. It's awfully mini on her, too.

"I don't know," I say. "You're taller than I was in eighth grade."

"You wore this like a month ago."

"But now I'm *older*."

She narrows her eyes at me and looks so much like our mom that it's sort of scary. "Are you body shaming me?"

"No! Oh my God, Ayla, take the stupid skirt, but *get out*!"

She smirks triumphantly, and then she's gone.

I sigh, staring down at my homework feed. It's mostly blank now, a bunch of white space where the rest of the year will start filling in, getting complicated. I start to open one of my social pages, but then my phone buzzes and I figure, screw it, and push the laptop closed.

Send pics grl.

Ah, great, Marcus has decided to follow up. I feel flattered until I remember he's probably sent this to a dozen girls at the same time, to better his odds. Then, for some reason I think about Alex, how he looked at us when we were goofing around in the hall today.

On a whim I lift my middle finger, snap a photo, and send it back to Marcus. It makes me laugh, so I send some smiley emojis, too.

Marcus doesn't respond. Guess he'll pick up some other girl in the hallway tomorrow.

Not that I care. Much.

7

"This place is beyond insanity." I lean forward in Maddie's passenger seat and stare at the school parking lot. "It looks like they're giving away free ice cream or something."

"It looks like they're giving away free *drugs*," Ryan says from the back.

"Yeah, and wasn't it smart of us to carpool?" Maddie chirps. I know she's trying to joke, but her hands, choking the steering wheel, tell me she's stressed.

"Ryan, doesn't Maddie look amazing tonight?"

"Baby, you're a firework."

"Ah, shut up, you two." Maddie smiles with clenched teeth. All her post-summer chill seems to have evaporated since she started sort-of dating Cory. They've hung out four times this week, mostly at school, and I know the exact number of times (and duration of hangouts) because I've been debriefed and quizzed after each one. I also happen to know that Maddie really, really wants to kiss him, and despite the fact that it's only been a week since I kissed him, I really want her to, too. For one thing, she can't worry about kissing him when she's *actually kissing him*. Probably.

Though I have to admit, it's nice to be needed again.

"I picked her outfit," I brag to Ryan. "She has those crazy summer-soccer legs and she was trying to wear *jeans*."

"Whaaaa?" Ryan gets extra flamboyant when we're trying to cheer Maddie up.

"Stop talking about me like I'm not here." She still has that fake half smile plastered on her face—the face that also looks great, thanks to me painstakingly dabbing on exactly the right amount of makeup.

"Oh, for Chrissake, the *media* is here," Ryan says suddenly. I follow his eyes, and sure enough, a couple of local news vans are set up close to the field entrance. "Your boy Alex is blowing up the joint."

I roll my eyes. "He's not *my* anything." After a whole week sitting next to each other in history, across from each other in art, and *near* each other in almost every other class, I still don't really know anything about Alex Goode. Except that he's very serious, extra polite to all the teachers, and ridiculously not good at flirting with me. Or, possibly, totally uninterested. Though I did make him laugh again. Three more times.

Not that I'm counting.

But it's started to drive me nuts, to be honest. Everyone keeps looking at us like there's something going on, to the point where I wonder why there's *not* something going on, and whatever, if someone's going to hook up with the famous new guy, shouldn't it be me?

Except that's not really it, either. It's . . . I don't know, he has this *magnetism*. I feel like I'm being physically pulled closer to him whenever we're in the same room. And we're *always* in the same damn room. It's just that he doesn't seem to particularly care.

Meanwhile, I'm obviously not the only one who thinks he's compelling—from the looks of the license plates, most of Nebraska and a lot of Iowa is here to get a glimpse of the Goode goods.

"We're missing half the game," Maddie says, squeezing the car into a tiny space at the far end of the lot. We can't open the doors all the way, but we edge our way out and start hurrying toward the lights and the noise. "But I guess, no matter how good Alex is, they're probably only going to put the seniors out there tonight." Her voice goes up a little, and I know she's thinking about watching Cory.

"Actually," I say, trying my best to keep my voice light and nonargumentative, "I think last year's first game was sort of a free-for-all. They scored a ton of points in the first quarter, so everyone got some field time. It was really cool."

That game was the first real date I went on with Seth Thiesen, and he spent most of the time explaining what was going on. At first it was kind of cute that he wanted to take care of me. Then it was kind of frustrating that he didn't want to sneak away—even at halftime!—to make out. And finally, it just got super annoying, since I actually knew more about the game than he did. Like he thought that just because I'm a girl, I'd need a whole tutorial. Maybe I'm not as smart as Maddie or Ryan, but I can follow a ball around a field. And I'm not gonna play dumb if the guy I'm being dumb for isn't going to at least *reward* me for it.

"That is a shockingly accurate recollection," Ryan says to me. He doesn't sound like he believes my story, and all my annoyance from that night with Seth flares up again.

"I pay attention, okay? And I know the whole team, practically! It's not that hard to follow along!"

Maddie and Ryan exchange a look, but before I explode again, Maddie grabs my hand.

"I think we're all a little stressed out," she says. "But we're about to be on camera, so maybe we should just be glad that we clean up real nice, yeah?"

"Work! Work!" Ryan sings, throwing his arm up. I let myself laugh. The air is crisp and it's Friday and Maddie already has the boy she wants.

All that's left is to start having fun.

"Wow, he keeps throwing the ball to Alex, huh?"

I nod without looking at Maddie, and she doesn't look at me. We stare at the field, transfixed.

All of Alex's quiet intensity has exploded into action tonight. He's obviously Cory's favorite receiver, catching every pass and sprinting past the Bellevue players like they're made of smoke.

We move closer and closer to the field, cheering when Alex takes possession again, running the ball to the ten-yard line, tripping just before he can take it all the way in. The crowd is losing its collective mind—and I swear I can see people in the away-team stands clapping a little, too.

"Okay, so I maybe get why people like this game," Maddie breathes.

There are three minutes left in the first quarter and we're already up 10–0.

"Do you think Coach Veylupek sold his soul to get Alex out here, or what?" Ryan looks at me like he's expecting a real answer.

"I think he's here to live with his dad," I say, trying to sound casual. I think I might be getting a little addicted to talking about Alex, even if I really only talk about school stuff *with* him. Today I tried to ask if he likes movies, too, but the bell rang and after class he hurried off with Cory. Then I sort of low-key stalked his profile pages and found some highly suspicious photos with a girl. But he hasn't posted anything for almost a year, so who knows if the girl is even still a thing.

Not that I care either way. Probably.

"I guess if he doesn't want attention he should stop being so awesome," Maddie says. She waggles her eyebrows at me and I laugh.

There's something about home games at the beginning of the year, the way everyone is tense and happy, the air full of energy. It makes me want to walk around and smile at everyone. I don't know why people make fun of cheerleaders—if I had time to go to all those practices, or the patience to hang out with Olivia and Annabelle on a regular basis, I would totally squad up. Jumping is literally their whole job. If I want to jump around, I have to pretend it's because I'm cold, or I have to wait until something important is happening on the field. But right now the team is just taking the break between quarters, and I'm dying to do a cartwheel. Obviously I resist.

"Oh, hey! They're waving!"

Maddie throws both hands over her head, wiggling like a puppy. I bet she'd do a cartwheel with me if I asked.

I turn and there's Cory, holding his helmet up high and smiling at her. Not leering or smirking, but really *grinning*. And she's grinning back. They are so perfect together. Even I'm grinning at this point, so much that when Alex catches my eye, I forget to stop. I realize I'm also waving when Alex lifts a tentative hand in response. It's like I've tricked him into saying hello—but I don't care. I lift my hand higher and yell, "Go Lions!" as loud as I can.

Alex's whole face shifts as he laughs. He's sweaty and his shoulders are all bunched-up looking, thanks to the pads under his uniform, but the stadium lights make everything shine. His eyes, his smile. With his head all sweaty his ears stick out a little, but maybe that's kind of cute?

I've never seen him look so . . . not sad. Huh.

I keep my eyes on Alex even after he turns back to the coach and his team, even after he takes a seat on the bench next to Cory's big blond head.

He looks less sad because he *is* less sad, I realize with a jolt. He's in his element. He's good at this. He feels the same energy as I do—probably a million times more than I do, since it's all directed at him. He's happy.

I turn to Ryan, bumping my shoulder into his. "Isn't football *magical*?" I shout over the noise of the crowd.

"You're such a nerd!" he shouts back.

But it is magical. And I'm happy. I'm in my element, too.

Ryan wanders off just before the end of the half, and then Charlotte comes over to talk to Maddie, so I figure it's time for a bathroom break. "Save my spot, okay?"

Maddie nods and I start squeezing my way through the crowd.

The concession stands are a zoo, blocking the shortest route, so I cut behind the bleachers. It's all shadows and muffled crowd noise back here, the empty track over to my right and the school off in the distance. I'm almost feeling creeped out when I notice a flash of light up near the back door of the school.

There are two people, though they're so close to each other it almost looks like one. The prestorm clouds make everything a little brighter, but at first I can only see the faint glow of light clothing.

Then they shift, and the person closer to the wall is—huh. It's a guy from the team. I can't tell which one, and he's not wearing his jersey or pads, but the short, shiny white pants are a clear giveaway. He must've snuck out of the locker room to—kissing! They're definitely kissing. That's sweet.

The other person is tall and their shirt is a pale color, but I can't really see anything else from this far away. And I don't even know why I'm spying, except that it's all so *secret* looking. The football player should definitely be inside, getting a lecture or a pep talk from Coach Veylupek.

As if he could read my thoughts, the player turns back toward the school doors, slipping inside. The girl starts walking down the hill toward me.

And it's not a girl. It's a yellow shirt and straight-fit jeans, short hair. Squared shoulders.

Aha. Ryan obviously thinks football is magical, too.

I start to move forward, start to wave and shout and get all *Who's the GUY??*—but then I stop.

Ryan's never had a boyfriend before, at least not as far as Maddie or I know. What we do know, because he's spent a lot of time explaining to us, is that coming out isn't anyone else's business or gossipy story or whatever. And that he's met other gay people at this youth program he goes to—one that Father Matt told him about, but that's run through a way more liberal church than ours—who have a much harder time with their friends and families and communities than he does. So it's not like every gay person feels the same way about everything. And just because he's out to us doesn't mean he wants to talk about his gayness all the time, or be constantly public with it, or spend hours explaining the intricacies of his lifestyle choice.

And when he says "lifestyle choice" he's being sarcastic.

So I stop myself while I'm still hidden in the shadows, and I try to figure out what I should do. More than anything I want to ask Maddie, but maybe that would be gossiping?

But *kissing*! I'm so happy for him! I really want him to know that I'm happy for him—except, okay. This isn't about me.

So finally, just as Ryan has walked close enough that he'd clearly see me if he looked up, I step into the sliver of light between the concession stands and say, "There you are!" I throw my hands up, and he jumps about a foot in the air. "Sorry! We were just wondering what happened."

Ryan puts a hand on his chest, breathing hard. "You scared the *shit* out of me!"

"Sorry," I say again, laughing. "I was trying to get to the bathrooms, and then I saw you . . ." I let the words hang between us, but he doesn't fill in the space.

Instead he puts an arm around my shoulders and starts walking again, steering us back to the bright lights of the field.

I really want to say something. Just not the *wrong* thing. If he would say something first, we'd be fine. But the longer he doesn't, and the longer I don't, the more I feel like I'm keeping a secret from him. Which is not something I ever do.

And then we're back in the light of the field, the noise, and all I can do is blurt, "Hey, I forgot to ask if you're coming to the party tonight?"

He looks at me, his eyebrows raised. His lips are red, his hair a little messed up. He doesn't seem upset *or* particularly happy, just steady.

"Oh, yeah. Maddie said I could catch a ride with you guys."

"Awesome. We can do *shots*."

Ryan thinks doing shots is the worst, most unoriginal activity ever, and he's given me more than one lecture about how I should not be one of those "basic bitches" who lets the group rope her into a Jäger party.

He doesn't laugh at my joke, though. He nods absently, scanning the crowd until we both see Maddie, craning her neck to watch the far end of the field, where the team is swarming back into position. Cory pumps his helmet in the air, and I hear Maddie cheer.

I glance at Ryan. Which player is he looking for? I mean, it's none of my business. But why isn't he talking to me about it?

Then again, Maddie didn't tell me she had a crush on Cory, either.

Maybe I'm the only one who isn't keeping secrets around here.

8

"BRO, YOU DON'T want a shot? Do a shot!" Cory holds up the bottle, his whole face goofy with confusion.

"I'm good," Ryan says for the third time. He starts to back away, but Gabe and Marcus are right behind him, blocking the kitchen door.

"C'mon—" Cory starts, but I step closer to him and shove my boobs into his arm.

"I want one," I say.

I'm just trying to distract him a little, but when Cory looks down at me with that crazy midparty smile of his, I feel a laser of heat zip down my spine. And then I wish that Alex hadn't gone straight home after the game. Maybe I could make him laugh again if he was here. Maybe I could get him to notice me.

Ugh, maybe I'm being one of those annoying girls at school who talk to him just because he's famous.

"Yeah, man, we should be getting the *ladies* drunk, am I right?" Marcus holds up a hand, and without either of them turning their heads, he and Gabe high-five.

Ryan finally slips away, probably going outside to find Maddie. Or his mystery guy. I take the tequila from Cory and bat my eyelashes a little. In a harmless way. Or an old-habit way, I don't know. I don't care! It's a party.

"This is what I'm talking about," Marcus says.

It's just too easy.

"Callahan, you know we have practice tomorrow," Gabe says, his voice slurring.

Marcus groans. Gabe takes a sip from his beer can, realizes it's empty, and tosses it toward the sink, where it clatters just a little more loudly than the music being pumped through the house speakers.

Must be nice to have a giant house with a cleaning service and parents away at some corporate retreat. At least Gabe's good at sharing.

"Coach doesn't understand that partying makes us *better players*," Cory says passionately. "We work hard. We play hard. We party hard!" His arm circles my waist and he lifts me up, doubling down on the *party hard* with a big "Whoo!"

Some of the other team guys are sitting around the kitchen table playing cards and drinking a little more slowly, but they all echo Cory's "Whoo!" with a big one of their own.

After a long second Cory puts me back down. I'm laughing and I know my cheeks are red, but it all feels a little distant. I drank a beer and did that shot, and I can feel the room separating itself ever so gently from my brain. My knees are tingly. I can feel the best part of the night, the just-beginning-of-drunk part, starting to happen.

Cory sets another shot in front of me, and I drink it fast. He rubs my shoulders like a prizefighter's coach, and we jump around a little.

"That was so awesome that you got to play tonight," I tell him. "You were awesome!"

"Oh, man, it was *so* awesome," he says, and I start laughing again at how many times we're both saying *awesome*.

"Where's Maddie?" I ask, but right then something happens over at the card table and Jack Gawecki is standing up, shouting.

"Whoa, man, calm down," Gabe says without moving from where he's leaning on the kitchen island.

"We all need to get in the *pool*," Cory announces.

The card guys stop yelling at Jack and everyone shrugs. Half of them are seniors and probably don't care about this party anyway, but more important, no one ever argues with Cory. Plus, Gabe's pool is awesome.

Ha! *Awesome.*

It took *forever* to convince Maddie that she had to wear a bikini under her clothes tonight, just in case. I tried to get her to bring a whole new outfit, like I did—swapping my jeans for a maxi skirt in her car on the way over here was super easy—but that part she refused. Anyway, I totally need to find her and get in the pool now. That would be fun. This party is so fun! I am having the *best time.*

I follow Cory through the screened-in porch that leads down from Gabe's kitchen, stripping my tank top off along the way. I toss it onto one of the porch couches and giggle when Cory turns around to gape at me in my bikini top.

"What?" I say. "This view isn't yours anymore, you perv!"

He makes a disappointed face and shoves the screen door open, letting me through first. "Damn," I hear him mutter, and I just shake my head. Boys are so obvious.

As soon as I step out the door, a hot blast of wind throws my hair in my face and makes my skirt flap around my legs. "Uch, why!" I yell, shaking my head until I can see again.

There are at least five people in the pool, but none of them seem to be Maddie or Ryan. Cory pushes past me and takes a flying leap into the water, yelling something I can't hear, and as soon as he splashes down there's a crack overhead.

The sky lights up with the brightest blast of lightning I've ever seen. It lasts for several impossibly long seconds, long enough for us all to stop moving and turn our heads up.

Everything just turns white. No bolts, no streaks of electricity. Just the dome of clouds, illuminated from within. And a faint sizzling sound that makes the hairs on the back of my neck jump up.

Then, everything is dark again, and wet. Water hits us so hard, so thoroughly, that for a second I think maybe I fell in the pool.

"Get inside!" Gabe is yelling from the porch door, but he doesn't need to tell anyone. I'm scrambling up the stairs, and behind me I hear everyone screaming and splashing and laughing.

"Oh my God!" Olivia's voice screeches. "Oh my God!"

At first I think she's overreacting—because that's what she always does—but when I turn back to look out the sunporch windows, I see that the rain has turned into hail, giant balls of ice slamming into the brick pool deck, transforming the pool water into some kind of terrible, frothy nightmare.

Everyone from outside is huddled and dripping at the windows with me now, all of us silent, as the world outside becomes unrecognizable.

"Damn," Olivia says softly. "This is messed up."

And that's when I *know* it's the end of the world, because Olivia Thorpe just said something I completely agree with.

Almost immediately a bunch of people bail. The hail turns back into rain, and for some reason most of the seniors rush out to their cars and drive off, like it's not still stupidly dangerous out there. Gabe tries to stop a few of them but I hear Tamir Windham say something about how much he loves driving in storms.

I'm shivering a little in my bikini top, but I'm too distracted trying to find Maddie to bother going back for my shirt. Finally I see her in the front living room, standing with Cory at the windows, watching the storm. He's got both arms around her, holding her close, gently. Their conversation is low and private. Nothing for me to hear. Nothing I've ever had with Cory. Or anyone.

Something new twists in my stomach. A fresh feeling of jealousy, I guess, that Maddie has everything now. I *want* her to have everything. She's my best friend. I just maybe want her to not have everything right now, right in front of me. Without me. A chill reaches all the way to the bottom of my stomach and settles there.

There's something sticky and warm, too, wrapping itself around my lungs. Guilt. Because Maddie doesn't have *everything*. Not everything perfect, anyway—some of the things she has are problems, like anyone else. Like her parents' divorce. All her crappy luck with boys up to now.

And I shouldn't have flirted with Cory tonight. Those words my mom used to say to Ayla and me all the time pop into my head: "Just because you *can* doesn't mean you *should*."

Before the happy couple can see me, I turn away and edge silently back into the hall.

In the kitchen I see Gabe talking to Ryan, pointing in my direction. For a second I'm confused until I see that the basement door is open—I guess the party is moving downstairs now.

I wait for Ryan. He comes toward me with a *What can you do?* look on his face, and I shake my head.

"This is insane," I say.

"Just a storm," he replies, but he puts a hand on my shoulder to guide me down the basement stairs, and it makes me feel a little better.

"Here," Gabe says, crowding into the stairwell behind us. He's handing me something—a sweatshirt. "If you're cold," he adds, then disappears again.

The Richmonds' basement is gorgeous. Fully carpeted, TV and video game station, bar area, bathroom and guest room—it's basically like the nicest main floor of a really beautiful house, except it's just one of four floors in this place. I haven't been here since last year, when Gabe threw an Oscar party and we all dressed up. I'm not sure why we did that, but it was really fun, especially since my mom let me wear the elbow-length gloves she still had from the 1920s-themed gala at her hospital.

Now the basement is filled with people huddled in towels, I guess waiting for Gabe to grab their clothes or more sweatshirts from upstairs, I'm not sure. I pull on the hoodie he handed me, but I don't zip it up. It's at least three sizes too big and says *Creighton* across the front, so I guess it's his older brother's. Either way it's not very flattering—but it is warm.

Olivia seems to have recovered from her panic earlier. She's laughing at something Marcus is saying, and Annabelle hovers nearby, her eyes darting from Marcus to the TV and back. Someone turned on the news, but no one seems to really be watching it. There's a local reporter being slammed with rain and wind, all on mute.

In the pocket of my skirt, my phone buzzes and beeps angrily, and around the room I hear everyone else's doing the same— Weather Service alert.

"Shut up, phone! We know it's fucking raining!" Marcus's laugh sounds like a bark.

"Come on," Ryan says to me. "Let's call our parents or whatever in case we lose service."

The two of us perch on stools at the bar area and start typing. I text Mom *OK at party in basement* and her *Good! Stay there!* reply comes so fast that I feel kind of guilty for needing Ryan to remind me to even be in touch.

"Are you staying?" I ask. Across the basement I see Maddie and Cory coming down the stairs with Gabe right behind them. It looks like the whole party is here now, and the TV area gets a lot louder as the football guys start a video game.

"I don't know," Ryan says.

I catch Maddie looking around the room in a lost kind of way. The tequila is still giving me a nice swimmy feeling, and this is kind of fun, hunkering down in the basement with just the key people. *Except Alex*, my brain says, which, great, now I am totally fangirl-ing.

Maddie spots us and hurries over. She's dry and fully dressed, not an artfully messy curl out of place. But her lip gloss looks a little . . . absent. She's waving her arms and talking before she's all the way across the room.

"I was stuck with Charlotte for like half the party, and right when she left, all this started happening!" She swings her hands back, indicating not just the basement, but the storm outside, which we can still hear, faintly.

"I didn't even know Charlotte came," Ryan says. "What was she talking about, student *council*?"

"Ugh, yes. She lives like two blocks from here, and to tell you the truth"—Maddie lowers her voice to a whisper—"I think she's kind of in love with Gabe."

Ryan snorts, and Maddie gives him a look.

"You're so mean! Charlotte and Gabe would be cute together," she says.

"I'm just surprised," Ryan clarifies. "I thought Charlotte was a lesbian, is all."

Maddie elbows me with a smirk. "I thought only people Ryan *likes* are gay?"

"Yeah, I thought that was the rule."

"Whatever," he says now. "I was right about that guy at the coffee shop downtown, wasn't I?"

"*Any*way," Maddie says, glancing back at Cory, who's deep into Madden with Marcus and Gabe, "isn't this crazy?"

"You don't want to go home?" I ask.

"Do we need to?"

"A bunch of people did," Ryan says. "But we're good if you are."

She shrugs. "Yeah, whatever. It's just weather. Plus, I've missed the whole party so far!"

"Are you sure about that?" I say. I'm trying to sound teasing and funny, but it comes out a little shrill, and my hand veers drunkenly as I try to point to where her lip gloss has clearly been kissed off. "I think I see party evidence on your face."

"It's nothing," she says with a grin that definitely means *It's everything!*

"You and Cory smooched, that's so surprising," Ryan says, pretending to yawn.

"Hey!" Maddie smacks his arm. "It was really romantic!" Then she covers her mouth with both hands, realizing how loud she's talking.

"*I'm* happy for you," I say.

"Phew!"

She smiles again, right at me, but the jealousy in my gut just gets more pointy and uncomfortable. *Your new boyfriend checked out my boobs tonight*, I think of saying. I don't even know why I think it—it's so awful. But she looks so *satisfied*. So proud of herself. So *I've been to Europe and you haven't*.

We're both kind of being jerks, but it'll pass. I think.

Ryan checks his phone and says, "Yikes. My dad says there's a whole clusterfuck of tornadoes headed this way. Even if we wanted to leave, it might be too late."

"Your dad said 'clusterfuck of tornadoes'?" I ask.

He shrugs, ignoring my giggles. "For once I guess the weather alert meant something. Sounds like everything's about to get a lot worse."

Right then I hear the faint but unmistakable whine of a siren, one of the faraway horns that go off every Saturday morning in the summer for testing. I've never heard one in an actual storm.

When Ayla and I were younger, Mom and Dave would wake us up and take us down to the basement at least twice every spring and a few times in the summer, but now they don't bother. The warnings are common, but we never get anything but bad thunderstorms. Like we're getting right now.

Tornadoes only seem to like hitting tiny towns in the middle of the prairie. Places that already have almost nothing get reduced to rubble every year, while our huge, sprawling city only has to deal with some fallen trees or jacked-up electrical wires.

But for some reason my stomach goes sideways as we listen to the siren wailing in the distance. I should probably either have another shot or try to throw up the ones I already took.

Maddie's looking back at the gaming boys, laughing at the victory dance Cory's doing. For her, the stupid weather is working out perfectly.

"Let's get *drunk*," Ryan suddenly declares. He smacks his phone down on the counter next to us and jumps off his stool.

And that's when I decide it really is the apocalypse, because Maddie goes, "Yes! Let's *shall*," gives me a high five, and sits down next to me at the bar.

"Party round *twoooo*!" Cory howls, and my best friend smiles at me, and something in my chest loosens up.

"Okay, okay, twist my arm," I say.

Maddie puts her head close to mine, holds out her phone, and we take a selfie. "We're so hot," she says conspiratorially. "Isn't it *fun*?"

I nod. It totally is.

9

As soon as Ryan starts pouring drinks, most of the guys leave the TV and join us at the fully stocked basement bar. All the bottles are in a low cabinet along the wall or a sleek wood-front minifridge. My mom would go on a total rant about how crazy the Richmonds are for leaving alcohol out in the open with teenagers in the house, but of course that's exactly what makes Gabe's the ideal party spot. In any weather.

"Just leave the nice stuff," Gabe calls. He seems more sober now. Maybe corralling everyone into a storm shelter—even one this swank—is a buzzkill. But after a second he leaves the TV, too, and walks over to join us. "Here," he says. "I'll do it."

In minutes I'm holding a plastic cup full of what I'm pretty sure is a splash of every different liquor he and Ryan could find.

"Long Island iced tea!" Gabe says, holding up his cup.

I try a sip and am surprised that it's not that bad. It doesn't taste a thing like iced tea, but it's actually pretty good.

Maddie picks up two cups and carries them over to Cory. Now

that the game has broken up, Olivia and Annabelle have switched the news back on. The same reporter from before holds an umbrella and squints into the wind. He looks like he's going to fly away if they don't let him back inside soon.

"Remember those pointless tornado drills we used to do in elementary school?" Ryan asks. He already sounds a little drunk, but his face is glowing in a really wonderful way.

"Yes!" Gabe shouts, slapping Ryan on the arm and then laughing when he stumbles a little to the side. Ryan laughs, too, and Gabe yells, "What the hell *was* that?"

"Here, kids, just curl into a ball, cover your head, and wait for the End Times," Ryan says in a teacherly voice.

"Don't worry about that whole section we just did about Joplin," Gabe says in the same official tone. "You guys are *probably* not gonna die in this soulless hallway outside the principal's office!"

I laugh and watch as Marcus and this guy Eric wander back to the PlayStation, arguing with Olivia over the remote. I notice that Maddie and Cory have disappeared, but it doesn't bother me. The strange cocktail in my hand is making it easy to not care about things.

"You know what they made my little sister do?" I ask. My voice comes out too loud, but Ryan and Gabe just look at me expectantly.

"*This* sounds like a messed-up story." Ryan makes a show of resting his chin on his hands, waiting for more.

I wave my hand at him like it'll help me explain. "They made her whole school have these, like, emergency drills. For shootings." I snap my fingers as a new thought occurs to me. "Like what happened to Alex! Except all these little kids would have to make barricades out of their desks to practice for, like, a crazy gunman coming in and trying to *kill* them all."

Gabe nods like he's heard about this, but Ryan looks kind of sick.

"Seriously," I add for emphasis.

"High schools do that, too," Gabe says. "I bet you anything Midcity will start this year."

For some reason this makes me laugh, and both boys give me weird looks. I want to explain that it's not *funny*-funny, it's just . . . I don't know. I guess Ayla's okay, even though she hid in a closet with all the other second graders . . . but I can't say anything because my brain is starting to disconnect again. *Balloon brain*, I think. *Hashtag.*

Snort.

"Messed up," I hear Ryan say, and it makes me giggle again. I toss my head to the side to see if my brain wobbles—I think it does!

"I'll have another, bartender." Ryan's voice is very far away. Or right next to me.

"Sure," says Gabe. "But, um. We're out of vodka. I think there's some back in the pantry, can you help me find it?"

"You're the boss, bartender." Ryan's laugh sounds weird, but I'm having a hard time focusing on his face. He and Gabe wander off, and I spin around on my stool, just once before I decide that's not such a good idea.

Oh! I could go upstairs! There's totally a bottle of vodka in the kitchen. And my shirt! I should put on my shirt. Good, this is good.

I'll just run upstairs while no one is watching. Good good good.

The other side of the basement door is both a lot quieter and a lot louder than the basement. No people, no PlayStation, but still there's a definite roaring in my ears—or wait, that's outside. It's *roaring* outside! Like a bunch of lions!

I giggle to myself and tiptoe down the hallway toward the kitchen. *Don't wake up the lions!* I think, then giggle some more, because *duh*, they're obviously *super awake* already. Just listen to them!

Stopping at the kitchen island, I look around the room. Why did I come up here again? I should have brought someone with me. It's kind of creepy. The clock over the stove says 2:07, and I wonder what kind of conniption fit my mom's going to have when I get home so far after curfew. No, wait, I'm not going home, I'm going to Maddie's. No, not Maddie's, I'm—my shirt!

Another roar shakes the house and there's a snapping sound that's louder than any noise I've ever heard in my life. My hands hold on to the cold tile of the kitchen island in front of me and the rest of my body goes perfectly still, suddenly sure that something much scarier than lions is about to rip into the house.

And then all the lights go out.

An hour passes. A minute. A second.

I'm too scared to move or breathe or scream. My brain floats around in my head.

But from downstairs I hear lots of screaming—and laughing, and something crashing to the floor. It all feels as far away as the moon, though, compared to the wind still rushing around the house.

I wonder if we're in the air. Maybe the Wicked Witch is riding by on her bike outside, laughing at me.

Don't think about witches, I tell myself, squeezing my eyes shut.

I just need my shirt. If I can just get my shirt, everything will be okay.

Still holding on to the island, I edge my way around one sharp corner toward the back door. My eyes are starting to adjust, finally, and now I can see that it's still surprisingly light outside—there's a glow coming through the back porch windows. I don't know how, but by the time I reach the doorway, I can sort of see.

"There you are," someone says behind me, and I leap straight into the air, choking on a scream.

I turn around so fast that my skirt tangles between my legs. There's a huge hulk of a person right behind me, getting closer.

"Hey, hey," he says, chuckling. "It's just me."

It's Cory, I realize. It's Cory, I'm not about to be murdered, we're—

He wraps his arms around my waist and presses his mouth down onto mine, hard and hot.

Oh.

We stumble backward through the porch door—he's pushing us, I realize, to the sunroom couch. *That's where my shirt is*, I think stupidly.

Cory's pushing too fast and the back of my right leg knocks into the corner of something hard—a table, a metal table, *fuck*, that hurts—but he's also kissing me too insistently to talk, so hard I can barely gasp. Then I'm under him, lying down, and his hands are in seven places at once. On my breast, pushing my bikini top out of the way. On my hip, pulling the waistband of my skirt.

His hips dig into mine and there's this shock of feeling there, this flash of heat, a second when my body just responds to his because we used to do this. A couple of seconds ago, this was a thing I did that felt good.

But then the feeling is gone because everything hurts—he's going too fast and his fingernails scrape the soft skin of my belly.

And *Maddie*.

Jesus Christ!

My brain slams back into my skull with a sickening *thud* and I'm all the way conscious, all the way here.

Cory's still got his tongue in my mouth. And I have my hands around his back! What am I doing! *Nononono*, I think. *MaddieMaddieMaddie.*

His shoulders are so wide that I can't really get my elbows back around the way I need to, but then he shifts a little—oh, shit, he's pulling on my bikini *bottom* now—and I'm able to tuck my arms in and brace my hands on the front of his pecs. I start pushing, gently at first, and then harder, and then as hard as I can. I don't think he can even feel the pressure. Or he does and doesn't understand—his mouth tastes like beer and lemons and I know he's drunk, too.

I know he thinks I'm into this.

I try pushing again because now my skirt is stuck and the kissing has gone on *forever*, oh my *God*, just come up for air already!—and then he does. His face moves.

I take a big, gasping breath that's almost a laugh. This is so not okay! What is he even—*shit*. I feel my skirt being pulled down clumsily, painfully. The stinging in the back of my leg flares up, and suddenly I'm sitting upright so fast that I accidentally headbutt Cory, another sickening *crack* that echoes in my skull.

"What the *fuck*!" he sputters. He reaches up to touch his forehead, and right then there's another burst of lightning outside and I can see his face.

He looks *furious*.

The laugh dies on my lips, and everything seems to slow way, way down. Everything inside my head gets super quiet.

"Come on, let's just do this," Cory says, and I'm back down, he's pressing me back down.

Just before he crushes his lips against mine again I gasp, "Maddie!"

But he just goes, "Nope, Cory," and I can't see anything because his face is too close, and the stench of alcohol fills my mouth, and he's clawing at my clothes again. And at his clothes.

This isn't happening like this, though. Cory's so sweet—I've seen him be sweet, I know he's a good guy.

Well, he's sweet with Maddie, a voice in my head says. Unhelpfully.

One of Cory's knees jams its way between my legs, and that same little voice adds, *I guess we're just doing this.*

But no, I can't—I didn't mean to flirt with him, I want Maddie to have him, I want her to be happy—

My hands scramble in the tiny space between my chest and his, trying to push or scratch or *something,* but it's no use. I wrench my head to the side to breathe, but I just hit a wall of shoulder and arm muscle and *Spring Break Cancun* T-shirt.

This is so stupid!

Why am I so stupid?

I bite his arm.

There's a rough grunt. And then a release.

I can see his face again, almost—and then I'm blinded, I can't see anything.

The lights are back on.

Another shaky laugh rushes from my lungs, though it might just be the beginning of a sob. I didn't know there were so many lights on this stupid porch, but look at them all! And the kitchen—the kitchen is brighter than the *sun* right now!

Cory's face is still twisted in something like rage, but he's blinking furiously, too, and so disoriented that he's sitting all the way up. Still on top of me, still with one leg twisted in my skirt and the other braced against the floor, but the weight is off my rib cage.

I take a ragged inhale, and when it comes back out I'm laughing again. I'm so relieved I can *breathe* now! Look at me, breathing! Stupid Cory, you almost suffocated me!

There's not enough air to talk yet, but it's fine. He stopped.

I'm still half laughing, half panting when I notice there's a shadow in the kitchen doorway. I turn my head almost lazily—I'm suddenly so tired, and it's so late, and that was so hard, trying to get him to stop crushing me—I think I'm still smiling moronically, and maybe my eyes haven't adjusted after all.

Because it's Maddie, there, in the doorway.

"You're here!" I say. I practically sing it. Like it's a good thing. Like she came to save me.

"Typical," she spits.

And things click back into place. My smile disappears and so does my not-boyfriend—Cory stands straight up from the couch, easy as pie. No pushing necessary.

"You just do whatever the *hell* you want," Maddie's saying, her voice as coarse and painful as the burn I can feel on my cheek from Cory's stubble. "What, was this all a joke? Were you guys just laughing at me this whole time? Or can you seriously not keep it in your pants for *five seconds*?"

I can sit up now, but it feels like it takes an hour. My arms are like jelly, and it's hard to pull my bikini back into place. But I can't sit here half naked while Maddie screams at me. I can't even understand what she's saying—I was laughing at her?

"No," I say, but it's too quiet. Why can't I get my voice to work? "No, Mads, it was just a mis—"

"Just *don't*," she snaps.

Cory's standing there, totally still, staring at something off to the side. Waiting for us to figure it out, I guess.

My skirt is bunched under me and I can't get it pulled up, but I feel too weak to stand. I wish I could stop thinking about my clothes and just say something to Maddie—I have to *say something*— but my head is like Cory's hands were just now, trying to do three things at once and fumbling with all of them.

The thought of Cory's hands makes my insides lurch, and for

a second I think I might throw up. I almost want to throw up, to get all this stuff *out* of me, to show Maddie how sorry I am—but then I don't.

She's just staring at me with tears in her eyes, and all I can do is sit, my fingers scrambling uselessly around the stupid hoodie Gabe gave me, pulling it closed as best I can. Hiding my skin.

Maddie isn't even looking at Cory, just at me. I'm the one who did this, who betrayed her. I'm the one who said it was okay, the one who was happy for her and him. She thinks I didn't mean it.

But I did. Right? Of course I did.

I force myself to lift my eyes to his face, and there's a fresh wave of pain because there it is—he's sorry. He's grimacing with regret.

At least, I think that's what it is. He's not looking at Maddie, either, and for a second I grasp some awful energy between them. A fight? But they barely know each other, they aren't even—

"You're not even going to *say anything*?" Maddie is screaming now, her whole body is turning red.

I jump back a little on the couch. It feels like I've been slapped.

"You're just going to fucking sit there," she adds at a much lower volume. "Well, that's just terrific, Rosie. What a way to be a *friend*."

My mouth drops open but still, nothing will come out. *Nothing nothing nothing* chants that awful voice in my head. Where did that voice even *come* from, anyway?

"And *you*," she says. She still isn't looking at Cory, but we both know who she means. "I guess you knew where to go to get what you wanted."

It's not until she spins on her heel and starts walking away that my body finally remembers how to move, how to *do* something. I stand up so fast my head spins, but I ignore it. I pull up my skirt and lurch forward, hitting the *front* of my leg against the goddamn metal table this time, and trip after her.

"Wait!" I say, my vocal cords still miserably failing to work properly. "Maddie, please, you don't—"

Everyone's coming upstairs now. The basement door is vomiting a bunch of laughing, stumbling idiots into the hallway, Gabe and Olivia and Ryan and Marcus, just a blur of noise blocking me, letting Maddie get away.

"Ryan!" I say as loudly as I can.

He stops, a huge grin still on his face, and gets a good look at me.

I can see what he sees. I can *feel* what he sees. I'm clutching the unzipped front of my sweatshirt and my skirt is still twisted around. My hair is everywhere and I know my makeup is gross and smudged. I can feel the hot, sweaty wall of Cory standing behind me. I can *feel* how his clothes must look, just as screwed up as mine.

A couple of screw-ups. I can see it.

And then Ryan's head swivels to the right, to the other end of the hall. I lose track of everyone else as they scatter, and it's just Ryan's eyes watching Maddie as she throws open the front door.

We both start moving at the same time, both start calling out for her and rushing to get to her, but Ryan has a head start. Ryan can get his feet under him, can move in a way that doesn't feel like torture. He gets to the door so easily I want to cry, and then I see that Maddie *is* crying.

They're both out on the front steps so fast. Then they're hurrying down the lawn. I don't even get to the door before the screen is slamming in my face, and Maddie's car is lighting up as she climbs into it. And Ryan climbs in on the passenger side.

For an eternity I stand there behind the screen, watching it all happen. The rain is lighter now, hitting the earth the way rain is supposed to, insistently but not violently. Not cruelly. The yard and the street tell the story, though—leaves and branches cover the grass and the cars and the sidewalk and the road. They flutter in the wind, but from the way the rain falls on them, you can tell they're dead. You can tell they got ripped away from their trees and flung to the ground without mercy.

Maddie's taillights are an angry red, disappearing into the darkness.

10

I DON'T KNOW how they're going to make it home. I don't know why she'd try to drive right now—it's so late, and she was drinking, and the roads are a mess, *beyond* a mess.

My legs give out under me, and I find myself kneeling on the hard ridges of the welcome mat just inside the front door. The storm window feels cool under my forehead as I rest there, breathing. Catching my breath.

I screwed everything up. I secretly resented Maddie, and look what happened. I'm a tiny, small person. I wanted Cory's attention. I *needed* it.

I didn't care about Maddie until it was too late.

The voice in my head won't shut up. It runs around in circles, reminding me how I felt when I saw Maddie at the airport. How I felt scared that she was so pretty all of a sudden. What kind of friend doesn't want her friend to be pretty, to be happy, to have everything she wants?

The kind of friend who didn't know what to say before Maddie even left, didn't know how to be there for her when her life was bad. And now tries to ruin it again, just when it's getting good.

At least Alex wasn't here.

Ugh. What a stupid thought.

Everyone will know some version of the story by morning, obviously—Olivia will take care of that, no problem—and most of them will probably roll their eyes and make some stupid comment about me being a skank or whatever. But perfect Alex Goode seeing me be such a loser would've been a million times more humiliating.

The house behind me feels huge and quiet, and I remember everyone who *is* still here. Cory. Gabe and Marcus. Freaking Olivia.

With a strangely calm feeling, I stand up, grabbing the door handle to help myself off the floor. Then I click the heavy wooden door closed and lock it.

I know it's not safe to stay upstairs, especially in the front rooms with their huge windows. But I pad to the sitting room anyway, my feet sinking into the soft carpet. My leg burns where it hit the table, so I carefully sit on the tufted leather couch and lie down on my other side.

But it doesn't feel right. I don't want to lie down on a couch.

So gingerly I get up again and lower myself onto the stiff armchair. It's too straight and the seat is barely big enough for me to tuck my legs under me, but I don't care. It would be impossible to have sex on this chair. If a girl was going to sleep with her best friend's brand-new boyfriend, she couldn't do it like this.

I keep shifting until my cheek is resting on the cold, leather arm of the chair and my legs are pinned awkwardly by the other arm.

The chair creaks painfully, and I know I might be damaging it, but I don't care.

I'm not safe, but I'm secure. And I'm not comfortable because I don't deserve to be.

I close my eyes. The voice in my head is taking a break, so I slow down my breathing and try to sleep.

It's a long night.

There's only the faintest hint of daybreak when I open my eyes again. My legs feel rubbery as I slowly unfold them from the chair, and my neck is definitely not going to be okay for a while. There's an enormous clock on the mantel behind me. I've been listening to it tick loudly for what feels like a lifetime, but when I turn around—carefully, trying to save my neck—I see that it's only been a few hours.

5:30.

I sit perfectly still and let the clock *chunk* its way to 5:31 or 5:32, it's hard to tell exactly, and then I stand up, inch by inch. I'm either hungover or still drunk—or stuck in some terrible purgatory between the two. Whatever I am, I am *not thinking*. I am walking down the hall to the kitchen, quietly. I am stepping out onto the sunporch. I am finding my tank top and sandals and carrying them back to the front door and opening the front door and closing it behind me and not wondering if it will lock and putting on my shirt and my shoes and walking down the steps and not falling on the leaves that are everywhere, everywhere, everywhere.

I am not falling on leaves for a long time. The whole front walk is covered, and the sidewalk is even worse—there are branches to pick my way over, and I'm not sure if I'm stepping onto sidewalk or grass underneath all the debris. My shoes really aren't great for this, but they're flat, at least. I wish I still had my jeans from last night, but I left them in Maddie's car, along with everything else but my phone.

At the corner of Gabe's street, I stop and roll up the waistband of my skirt a few times, making it a little shorter and easier to manage. I realize I'm still wearing his sweatshirt, and it's too warm out—even at this hour, even after such a huge storm, the air is thick with humidity and the sky is low, gray, too close. I'm already sweating.

I take off the sweatshirt and throw it on the nearest car—then hold my breath. After a few seconds I exhale, relieved that I haven't set off an alarm, and then, still *not thinking*, keep walking toward the main road.

My phone is closer to my hip now, and I can feel it pressing against me with each step. I could call someone. I could—I *should*—call Maddie or Ryan and see if they're okay. I should call and apologize.

But it's so early. And if I called anyone else, like my mom, I'd have to explain, wouldn't I? I'd have to have some pretty good reasons why I'm hungover-slash-drunk and walking home at 5:30—5:45 now—in the morning.

When I reach the main road, I think of another reason I can't call anyone: the whole city is a *mess*. The power company is down the street about a quarter mile, fixing wires attached to telephone poles, and trucks that look sort of like snowplows are sweeping the street itself. But otherwise, I might as well be the last person alive. I feel like that robot in *WALL-E*, wandering around what's left of Earth.

Across from the Omaha Public Power truck, I find my sidewalk blocked by an actual tree, a *huge* tree that stretches from its no-longer-rooted roots to the middle lane of the street on my left. It's some kind of pine tree, and for a while I just stand there, staring at the branches sticking up in the air, the highest needles reaching well above my head. My options are pretty much nonexistent, and despite my best efforts to keep my brain turned off, it's forced to struggle awake.

I can't get over this thing. If I go right, toward the grass and the roots, I'll have to deal with an extraordinary amount of mud and yet more fallen branches and leaves. Plus, it's a steep decline into a little ravine. An image of sliding in the mud and falling down that short hill flashes through my mind, and it doesn't look like fun.

But going left will put me right in the middle of the street for as long as it takes to get around the top of the tree, and that doesn't look fun, either. I also don't want to attract the attention of the power company guys. There's something about the postapocalyptic-wasteland atmosphere that makes me wonder if I'm not actually allowed to be walking down this road, or be outside at all.

Plus, I want to be alone. A sick, sloshy feeling starts rising in my stomach, and I have to swallow once, twice, to settle it back down.

I don't want those men to see me. I just want to be invisible for a little while longer.

I try not to think about what a strange new feeling that is, wanting to be invisible.

Finally I turn, looking back the way I came, deciding to cut around and into the neighborhood to take the side streets. It's at least two miles from Gabe's to my house, but hopefully at this hour everyone's still asleep, waiting as long as possible to deal with the aftermath of the storm. I wish I was still asleep, too. Or I wish I could wake up from this nauseous, foreboding feeling inside my stomach and my heart and my muscles.

Never mind. Walking.

I find a street that wasn't too hard hit, and I walk down the very middle of it, almost enjoying my personal Mad Max moment. I hear a machine whir to life—a chainsaw, I guess—but it's far away.

I don't hear the car. It's driving so slowly that when I see it, I wonder if it's just rolling by itself down the street that intersects the one I'm on. It's a pale silver sedan of some kind, ghostly in the flat morning light. The shadow of a person fills the driver's-side window and I stop, waiting for them to keep moving. For an instant I'm tempted to lie down in the street, cover myself with leaves, and hide. I remind myself not to be dumb—this isn't *really* a dystopian wasteland, and that driver isn't a zombie—but the urge doesn't go away.

The car stops. I've been spotted.

And I just stand there, paralyzed, wondering if this is what happens to deer when they get caught in the headlights, not that I've ever seen a deer, the most I've run into is a really big raccoon that scared the shit out of me and Maddie when we were driving one night, it looked like it was going to grab the car and bite it but instead there was just a gut-churning *thump* and I realized I'd killed something and it would never make it back home and oh, God, that's how I feel now, I'm so far from home, I'll never make it, why am I even trying—

"Rosie? Is that you?"

I haven't covered myself in leaves, but I've done the next most embarrassing thing: I'm standing there with my hands over my eyes. The old *I can't see you so you can't see me* trick. Which only three-year-olds think actually works.

It's pure insanity, but for a few seconds I stay there in the dark, steadying my breath. The voice is close—whoever was in the car has gotten out. I hear them stepping carefully on the leaves.

"Hey, Rosie, are you okay?"

Oh, for the love of *shit*.

"Alex, hi." My hands fall to my sides like dead weights. The tendons on the insides of my elbows ache, reminding me that my arms have been trying to protect me all night, to push back, and they're just too weak. They can't do anything.

"I thought that was you. I mean, I was just . . ." He points back at the silver car. "Do you need a ride somewhere? It's probably faster to walk, honestly, but there's air-conditioning. And a ton of bagels. I was just taking them over to the church."

His face turns a litttle pink at the word *church* and I'm suddenly afraid that the next breath I take will make me start laughing or crying. What a combination—Mr. Way Too Goode and Walk-of-Shame Girl, out on the town.

"I'd kill your whole family for a bagel, actually," I say. It's definitely the wrong joke to make to this guy, but I just let it hang in the thick air between us. Who even cares anymore.

"It probably won't have to come to that," he says easily. "I have more than enough to share."

I follow him to the back of the car, and sure enough, the trunk has five big, open boxes of supplies: several bags of bagels in one, a few gallons of orange juice in another, and various paper products and cleaning supplies fill the rest.

"Wow. What are you, saving the whole city this time?"

Alex opens one of the bagel bags. He's good at ignoring my awful jokes. "Plain and cinnamon raisin in here," he says. His voice is flatter than the gray clouds over our heads now, and I'm sure I've gone too far this time. I should just stop trying to be funny, ever.

Ryan once told me that no one could ever hear me being funny, anyway, because I was too pretty. They were always distracted by my looks. "Nobody can hear what you're saying, dollface," he said, smiling affectionately, like he meant it as a compliment. Maddie had argued, said that was ridiculous. But I didn't need him to tell me that, and I didn't need Maddie defending me. I already knew it was true.

"Plain," I say to Alex. The hunger that had flared in my stomach at the mention of bagels has disappeared, and now I just want something soft to hold. Maybe bite down on a little.

Alex hands it over and slams the trunk closed. I'm not sure whether the offer of a ride is still on the table, but before he climbs into the driver's seat he turns back to look at me.

"I don't know how far you're going, but you should let me take you," he says. "Those shoes aren't going to get you two blocks."

I get in the car. For a while we drive in silence. The only sounds are the murmuring of the radio news and the sharp breaths we both take every time a particularly huge branch blocks the road. It's like we're watching the same scary movie.

After a few minutes I start pointing the way to my house, but we still don't speak. My mind flits back to last night, to Maddie's face, and I squeeze the uneaten bagel in my hand until the image goes away.

"I'm sorry," I say to Alex. It's the wrong person, but I do owe him an apology. And maybe this can be practice.

"It's fine, I was going out here anyway."

"No, I mean—about the stupid jokes. I wasn't making fun of you. But I was being, you know. Insensitive. I didn't mean it."

"Oh," he says. There's so much surprise in that tiny syllable, I can't even understand it. "That's okay. I wasn't offended."

"It's really amazing, what you did. I mean, I wasn't there, obviously, but I know about it from the news. Like everyone else. And it's amazing."

I thought it would be a relief to talk about Alex's famous, heroic act—I thought that once I got to know him well enough, we could openly discuss what a great person everyone thinks he is. What a great person *I* think he is. But it feels wrong, somehow. It feels like it should be a compliment but is actually the opposite, and I have no idea why.

"Sorry," I say again, before he's had a chance to reply. "I'm gonna shut up now."

He leans over the steering wheel, creeping around a garbage

can that's landed in the middle of the road. "Well, don't shut up quite yet," he says, still concentrating on the street. "I still don't know where you live."

"Ha, right. Okay."

He's silent for a minute, and at the next intersection he looks at me so I can wordlessly point the way.

"Honestly," he says softly, once we've made it another block, "it wasn't that amazing. In real life. Somehow it got pretty amazing when other people told the story, you know? So you don't have to . . ." His hands lift for a split second, releasing the wheel, palms up. Then he clamps down again, his knuckles white.

We stare out the window and go back to not talking. The streets have suddenly gotten so much cleaner, and I'm sure it's because we're driving past the nicest neighborhood around here, Emery Woods. My house is on the other side of school from here, in an older group of streets, and pretty much the only thing we have over Emery is that our trees are taller. And I'm sure their trees will catch up in a few years. Probably get gigantic, make ours look sad.

For a whole block, it's like there isn't a blade of grass out of place, and then we pull up to another stop sign, and for some reason we both look to the left at the same time.

"Oh my *God*," I say.

Alex's hands slide off the wheel, into his lap.

The street—an entire block, just on one side—is leveled. Pipes stick out of the ground here and there, but otherwise what should be houses has been reduced to piles of rubble. Smoke hovers over one of the piles and I see a fire crew nearby. They're all standing so still they look like statues. The truck behind them blinks soundlessly.

A third of the way down the block, closer to us than the firemen, a car has been flipped onto its roof. It looks almost peaceful, almost normal. There's an American Girl doll sitting on it, probably right where the engine is. She's staring straight at us. For a second, I think someone must've put her there on purpose, but the longer I look, the more I realize her hair is supposed to be blond. Not gray. And her face is gray, too. She's covered in ashes. Her eyes stare into me, through me. I feel empty.

"I heard there was a touchdown, but I didn't know . . ." Alex shakes his head. "This is awful."

He waits another few seconds before pulling away from the stop sign. We drive slowly past Midcity, and it looks fine from the outside. The fences around the fields are standing as straight and strong as the light posts; the big school sign out front still says *Welcome Back Lions!*; the windows passively reflect the clouds, uncracked, unfazed.

And then we're on my side of town, and everything's fine. The roads are messy, but the houses look good. The cars are upright. There aren't any toys sitting where they shouldn't be.

When Alex turns onto my block I reach out and grab his arm, hoping he'll stop before he gets to my door. I can see Dave and Ayla outside, raking.

"Here?" he asks, braking hard in the middle of the street.

If I get out here, Alex will keep driving right past my house. Maybe I could pretend to walk up to the Brezinskis' door, but that would be super weird.

And yet. Look at my family. They're so normal. Whatever Alex must think of me right now, walking home alone, obviously up half the night— God, I don't even know what I look like! Why didn't I check a mirror before I left Gabe's house?

Just the thought of Gabe's house brings on a wave of nausea so intense that I'm pretty sure I'll vomit in Alex's car. Which, I mean. Is not going to make me feel less like an asshole right now.

Who says you shouldn't *feel like an asshole?* the voice chimes in.

"Sorry," I say for the millionth time. "It's that one up there. With the happy family." It's supposed to be a joke, but yet again, it's completely unfunny.

"Okay." Alex eases the car forward, stopping more gently at the foot of my front yard. Dave and Ayla look up, squinting at the car.

"Okay," I whisper to myself. "Here we go."

"I should walk you up, but I'm already late . . ." Alex trails off, gesturing vaguely toward the trunk of the car.

"Right," I say. "Do you guys need more help? Should I"—what am I even saying right now?—"come over there later or something?"

"That would be great," he says, his voice full of surprise again. "I'll give you my number if you want to text me." He pauses, as if exchanging numbers suddenly seems like a terrible idea, but then he keeps talking. "I'm just not sure where we'll be, exactly. But you can just come to St. John's, obviously. That'd be great, if you want."

I blink. This is a lot of words all at once, especially from Alex. Especially this early in the morning.

"Okay, yeah, just put your number in." I hand him my phone.

When he gives it back our fingers touch, and the little flare of heat it sends up my arm is familiar, expected. But I'm not expecting the way the nausea hits me again, almost as bad as before. My urge to crawl under something and hide is so strong that for a second I can't even move.

"Thanks for the ride," I say quickly, yanking the car door open.

"I'm glad I saw you," he says.

He saw me.

A million things I'd normally say to a boy skitter through my brain, like coins falling out of a bag onto a hard floor. But this isn't "normally" and Alex doesn't look at me the way boys usually do, not even now, post–number exchange. And I'm so tired.

I give him a small smile and climb out of the car, my leg shouting with pain. On the lawn my stepdad and little sister are looking at me like the trainwreck that I am, and I just have to hurry, slipping and shuffling in my stupid, worthless sandals, to the safety of my own house, the soft, quiet darkness of my own room, where I can finally, finally hide away. Preferably forever.

11

"ROSEMARY? THOUGHT YOU might want to come out now— we're getting pizza and Ayla's picking a movie, so I could use your help . . ."

Dave has my door cracked open, but I know without even looking that he's keeping his eyes averted—fixed on the ceiling or the wall, sometimes his phone—to give me a little privacy. It's one of those things we do, like how he calls me Rosemary, and I call him Dave. We're family, but we respect each other's space.

When I squint out from under my quilt, though, I see something I wasn't expecting: it's almost dark outside. I slept all day.

And no one woke me up. Not even to go to my shift at Dairy Queen, which—crap.

"Did work call?" I ask, sitting up so fast my vision blurs, threatening to go black.

"Yeah. Actually, I called them," Dave says, sounding embarrassed for some reason I can't figure out yet. "We tried to wake you earlier and it just—I told them you were sick. Sounded like it wasn't a problem."

"Oh." I haven't missed work before, even one time when I think I really *was* sick, which was kind of messed up, probably. I used to skip school last year, basically whenever Paul wanted to, but skipping work seems stupid. They give me money to go there. And it's just ice cream—I mean, it's not something hard, like calculus.

An uncomfortable mix of relief and guilt worms around my insides. I do feel sick, but not the kind that medicine would help. Not the kind that gets you a day off.

"Anyway, I figured you'd probably be hungry by now. Are you feeling okay?"

I can't look directly at Dave, for some reason. He's tall, and though he's not as wide as the football players I was with last night, he still blocks the door in this way that feels . . . I don't know.

"I'm okay." The lie falls out, like when you accidentally laugh with gum in your mouth. It's out and it sticks. And I can't take it back, so I add, truthfully, "I could eat."

"Great! We were arguing about the pineapple situation, and I couldn't remember where you fall on the issue."

"I like it if there's no ham," I say.

"Right! Gotcha. Ayla's acting like she wants mushrooms?"

Now I look at his face, and the confusion I find there is kind of hilarious. "I think she's trying to be more mature? Or maybe she read that they help you lose weight." I seem to remember reading something like that myself, or that the mushroom flavor made you less hungry, maybe.

"It better not be the weight thing," Dave says, his face instantly going serious. "Ayla!" He starts walking away, calling to her as he goes. "You better not be on a diet, young lady!"

I shake my head, even though there's no one here to see me. Dave is always giving us these male feminist lectures about stuff like body image, which, I don't know. I guess it's good that he tries with Ayla, but it usually ends up sounding ridiculous to me. Besides, I don't really have any body issues, aside from usually wishing I could lose like five pounds. And have smaller ears.

But then I swing my legs over the side of my bed and feel the sharp stab of pain behind my knee. So there's *that* body issue.

I'm still wearing my skirt and bikini top and tank from last night, and within seconds I've jumped up, ripped off all my clothes, and run across the hall to the bathroom. I'm so desperate to take the hottest shower possible that it doesn't even occur to me that someone—like Dave—might see me *naked*, which is definitely worse than wearing my stupid skirt for five more seconds. But he and Ayla are laughing about something downstairs, and Mom's at work again, and I'm alone.

I spend twenty minutes in a scalding stream of water, thinking about nothing but how much it hurts. I never realized how helpfully distracting pain could be. Even the scratch on my leg— it's just a really bad scratch, already scabbed over, at least until the water hits it—is keeping my brain focused in this way that I'm grateful for.

By the time I'm ready to get out and open the door, letting steam billow into the hallway, the smell of pizza has reached the second floor. I dig through the back of my bottom dresser drawer until I find my oldest yoga pants, but none of my shirts feel right. Finally, keeping my towel pressed to my chest, I tiptoe down to Mom and

Dave's room. Mom has a whole collection of huge sweatshirts, plus all her body-disguising scrubs sets. I choose a bright red UNL pullover. It's like wearing a blanket.

Finally I grab my phone. I'm afraid to look at it. Maddie and Ryan must think I don't care what happened to them last night. They must think I really did want to hook up with Cory, that it was all my idea.

You were flirting with him, that voice in my head pipes up. *And you drank enough for a shipload of sailors.*

I can't argue with that. How can I explain what was happening when Maddie walked in if I can't even explain the rest of the night? Or the whole week—everything since we picked her up from the airport. Since school started. Since Alex. Everything is *off*. I didn't mean to flirt with Cory. It was just habit. Right?

"Pizza's here!" Dave calls from downstairs, but I don't answer. I stand in the middle of the dark hallway and click my phone on.

The light from the screen reflects off the family photos on the wall next to me, our smiling faces hidden behind the glare. Most of the missed calls and unanswered texts are from Ryan—saying they got home okay, hoping I did, too. Wondering what happened. I'm sure Maddie told him everything and for a second I fall in love with him a little bit, just for wanting to hear my side of the story. Then I remember that this is how Ryan survives being our third wheel: he doesn't pick sides. He doesn't carry messages back and forth, he doesn't let one of us vent to him about the other. It's smart. It's annoying as hell sometimes, but it's smart.

There's nothing from Maddie, though. Mom called once, and

so did DQ, and there's even a text from Alex about volunteering. Shit, of course, *of course* I said I might come help out and then slept through the whole thing. I don't even know what *our* yard looks like right now.

I open a new message to Maddie and stare at the empty white box. I can't think of a single thing to say. I even scroll through the emojis, wondering if there's a tornado one. There is. It's too small, though. It doesn't say anything I'm trying to say. Even if I knew what that was.

Experimentally, I click on the funnel cloud, a football, and a crying face.

Delete, delete, delete.

"The *movie's* starting!" Ayla shouts.

"O-*kay*," I yell back. I send Ryan a *So glad yr ok I got home fine slept all day such a fk-up*, then toss the phone into my room. It lands safely on my bed, and I leave it there, hurrying downstairs to watch whatever horrible British rom-com my sister picked out this time.

LOLOLL go home tree yr drunk!

Donating just $1 to the Red Cross saves so many lives and homes, you guys. Follow this link, seriously.

Look at this FCKIN CAR HAHAHAHA

I can't stop crying today. Some people lost EVERYTHING.

No lights on at school yasssss

We're going to Emery after church tomorrow if anyone wants to join. So much work to do!!

I blink and yawn, but I can't sleep. This is what I get for staying in bed all day—a night full of everyone's Saturday updates. There are photos from the party, though I'm not in any after the storm got going. I mean, you can see my elbow in one, probably lifting a shot. But I'm not tagged. I'd be offended if I weren't so zonked out.

Cory Callahan smiles at me from his pictures, his eyes extra blue in the camera flash. He's in Gabe's kitchen, in the basement. His profile photo is a soft-focus shot of him looking out over the football field, his face serious. Majestic, sort of. Or *HAWTTT*, as some girl I don't know posted a month ago.

At the party there's a photo of Cory and Maddie—she took it. She's laughing so hard her nose is wrinkled, which I know she won't like, even though I always tell her it's cute. It is cute. She looks beautiful.

And there's one of me and Cory. I'm making a face at him, my mouth dropped open. It's extremely flirty.

I stare at it, at my stupid face, the way you pick at a zit. Like I can make it better by making it worse first.

Then I open up chat and send him a note: *Have u talked to Maddie? Did u explain?*

I don't know what I expect him to say to that, but I send it anyway. Then, quickly, I add, *We shld talk 2??*

My fingers twitch, wanting to write something to Maddie, but I still don't know what to say. Her page is full of charity links and the volunteering stuff she's doing tomorrow. She and Charlotte already have a whole action plan for any Midcity juniors who want to help out. I could do that—I could show her that I'm not just a useless party girl. But on one of the posts about it I see Cory say, *See you tmrw!* and I know I should stay away. I should let them be alone, or at least let them see each other without seeing me.

That moment last night when I saw him holding her, watching the storm from Gabe's front windows, keeps coming back to me. It's easier to see than anything that happened after that. I wasn't as drunk then. I wasn't in the dark shadow of his body as it loomed over me.

Nope. Thinking about something else.

I click on Alex's page. Other people from St. John's tagged him in photos from today, and I stare at them. He never smiles—not that it was such a smiley day, I guess. But that face he had on at the football game, that joy that radiated off him, it's like that was a different person.

Finally I scooch down and let my eyes flutter closed. I can feel the white, blank light of the laptop staring back at me, but I leave it on my stomach. The heat from the battery burns through my sweatshirt, and I wonder if I'll get cancer or something. Electronics are bad for you, right? Maybe I'll get some really painful bone cancer in my hips and everyone will stop being mad at me because it'll be so sad. I'll lose my hair and get a bright blue wig because I'm so edgy, and I'll get really good at art class and make some devastating tribute to everyone who ever loved me, and everyone will sob and sob at my funeral. . . .

My breathing slows and the light from the computer darkens into screen-saver mode, but I'm still awake when I hear Mom get home from her shift. There are the usual sounds in the kitchen of keys dropping into the bowl on the counter, the fridge opening and closing. I hear the beep of the coffeemaker being set for tomorrow morning. The click of lamps being turned off.

I keep my eyes closed and my breath steady, just like when I was a little kid pretending to sleep. Mom's footsteps climb the stairs slowly and I realize I'm expecting her to stop at my room, check on me. But of course she's not, I'm not a kid anymore. Maybe she'll check on Ayla, but she won't—

My door opens. I can feel the cooler air from the hallway and smell Mom's perfume. She sneaks across the floor so quietly that it almost surprises me to feel the laptop move away, the sudden chill on my stomach, the even-darker dark behind my eyelids when she closes the screen.

I wonder what she thinks happened to me last night. Usually she wouldn't let me sleep all day, but maybe she felt sorry for me, getting caught in the storm. Maybe she's just glad I got home safe.

I can tell she's looking down at me, and for a second I think I'll reach out, ask her to stay. Ask her for one of those stories where I'm a princess and I convince a dragon to stop being mean, give me his jewels, and be my pet. Those were good stories.

I don't move. She tiptoes out as quietly as she came in.

"I'm sorry, I said I'd bring this stuff. She's just—whatever. You should talk to her."

Ryan holds out a bag and looks like he'd rather die than be here. It's one of those reusable bags they sell at Whole Foods. The kind the Costellos have twelve thousand of.

I take it and look inside. My jeans, my purse. My stuff from Friday.

"What is she, breaking up with me?" I try to smile.

Ryan just shrugs. Which seems like a bad sign.

"Do you want to come in?"

We're standing on my front porch, the noise of a thousand leaf blowers and chainsaws making it hard to talk. Dave's working on the gutters, and I'm pretty sure if we stay out here any longer he'll ask us to help him.

But Ryan hesitates, looking over his shoulder. I follow his gaze, suddenly worried I'll see Maddie waiting in his car, but there's no one.

"I'm going to that clean-up thing," he says. "Do you want to come? You look like you could maybe get out of the house a little bit. No offense." He's looking at me again, clearly concerned by my shapeless sweatshirt and unbrushed hair. He's still in his church clothes, a crisp plaid button-down tucked into dark-wash jeans, and I do feel pretty grubby standing next to him.

"Won't everyone . . . be there?" I say slowly.

He shrugs again. "Rosie, you know they'll all be at school, too." His voice has this heavy weariness to it. Like we've had this conversation too many times. Like I've always been some kind of shut-in that he's had to reason with.

I open my mouth, but stop when I realize I'm about to say, *Will Alex be there?* because Ryan won't understand why I want to know. I don't even understand until the thought pops into my head:

Alex won't make me talk.

Suddenly the thing that was driving me crazy about that guy sounds like the best thing ever. All morning I've been avoiding Mom, Dave—even Ayla wants to chatter on and on about the storm, the damage, the various clean-up efforts she should be driven to around town.

"I don't know," I finally say to Ryan. It hurts that he's not trying to talk me into it. Or I'm glad he's not? I seriously can't even tell.

"Okay. Listen, I've been meaning to ask you. I need tech people, and Mrs. Walsh said you still have open elective credits. So you should do it."

I blink at him. "You mean theater stuff? Stage . . . things?"

Finally, finally, Ryan smiles. He almost laughs, in fact. "Yes, *stage things*. You'll report to me. Hang on my every word, fulfill my every whim. You know, like always."

I smile, too, and it feels weird. Maybe I've been frowning. "Do I have to?"

Ryan sighs. "No, you don't *have* to. I just figured we could hang out. You're always saying how Maddie and me—how we're more involved at school than you are."

That's true, I guess. "Sorry, you're right. That sounds good. Thanks for asking me."

We stand there in silence for a minute. I stare down at his fancy wing-tip sneakers, and he shoves his hands in his pockets. Isn't this what I wanted? To feel closer to Ryan again, to not be the last to hear about what's going on in his life? To know who that football player was he hooked up with at halftime on Friday?

I slump against the doorframe. That game feels like a different life. I have way bigger problems now.

"It's okay," Ryan says finally. "I'm just worried about you."

"I could come by at lunch. Is that okay?"

"Only if you bring the good Doritos this time."

I try to shrug, but I end up just tipping forward until my head is resting against his shoulder.

"Oh, you poor, confused girl."

He wraps his arms around me. No one's touched me since Friday and my body does this involuntary shuddering thing. The way you convulse before you start crying, except I'm not crying. It's super weird but Ryan squeezes me closer for a second, then steps back and says, "For *srsly*, though, maybe some real clothes? Your pjs are cute and all, but no one's hangover lasts this long."

I choke out a small laugh. "Thanks for coming over."

"Shower. Then *call her.*"

I stare at my feet and nod. And for some reason I wait until I hear Ryan's car door slam before I look up again, watching him drive away. The bag is heavy in my hands, and I wish I could just throw it all in the trash at the side of the house.

I don't, of course. I haul it inside and dump it on my bed. Then, because my stuff is taking up all the room, I lie down on the floor and open my laptop. It'll just make me feel worse, but I need to see what everyone else's post-storm life looks like today.

12

"ARE YOU OKAY?" Steph keeps her eyes on the floor she's mopping. "You seem a little . . . off."

I'm standing behind the counter, mindlessly staring at the rainbow sprinkles, the dull silver spoon handle sticking out, perfectly still. I blink a few times and force myself to shift my gaze to Steph. It's sort of amazing how much you notice without having to actually pay attention—the way her head was angled down, the fact that her hair is in a ponytail that seems particularly bouncy today. I knew all that, and I haven't actually looked at her since we started our shift half an hour ago.

"I don't feel great."

"Still?"

"What?"

"You were sick yesterday, right?"

I open my mouth and move my hands to—I don't know. I don't really know what to do with them right now. Letting them fall back to my sides, I nod at Steph. "Yeah. It's probably still whatever that was."

"I could handle this, tonight," she tells me. Behind her, the night sky has turned the windows into mirrors. Steph's mom-like khaki shorts are reflected back at every angle, but I'm just a shadow behind the cash register. I forgot my hat, and I'm wearing the red polo shirt today, so only the faint glow of my pale face floats in the glass.

"Nah," I say. "I'm fine."

It's not so bad, being here. I needed to get out. Ryan was right. After he left and I showered, I felt better. Was feeling better for a little while, anyway.

"Is your house okay? You're over on this side of school, aren't you?" Steph hoists the mop into its old, yellow bucket and starts wheeling it behind the counter.

"Yeah, we were good. Trees got beat up, but my sister said no one on our block lost power or anything."

Steph shoves everything into the storage room and comes back out to wash her hands. It's so quiet tonight that the radio feels louder than necessary. I turn the volume down until we can just barely hear Shania Twain singing about being a woman.

"You weren't with your sister?" Steph asks. "There was a huge outage at like two in the morning, pretty sure most of the city went dark."

"Oh, right. No, I was—out."

Steph nods and something passes over her face. Like she feels dumb for not knowing that already, for not assuming I'd be some-where, doing something in the wee hours between Friday and Saturday.

I think about all the places where my smiling face is posted, photo after photo at party after party. All summer, all last year. Maybe Steph thinks I'm the dumb one.

"Ryan and Maddie and a bunch of us were hanging out after the game," I say. I don't know why it makes me feel better, to try to convince her that my night wasn't *that kind* of party, but it does. For a second, it does.

But Steph just nods, and my stomach goes hollow. She's already heard where I was on Friday. God knows who told her or what they said, but she heard something.

I'm tempted to ask her, but it would be mean to put her on the spot like that. And whatever, I'll find out soon enough, anyway.

"What about you guys?" I ask instead. "Is your house okay?"

Steph takes a big inhale. "The one here is. But my grandma is over in Council Bluffs, and her power still isn't back on. And my parents have a lake house they're worried about. None of the neighbors checked in with them about it yet, so I think my mom's driving out there tomorrow."

She sounds so grown-up and responsible, and all I can do is nod. I mean, we don't have a lake house. But I didn't even help Dave rake the yard.

My Friday night was messed up because I messed it up. I might have bigger problems now than I did last week, but they're my fault—everyone else got blindsided.

Especially Maddie.

"That sucks," I say to Steph. "I've never seen a storm like that before."

"It was really scary," she agrees. "I heard the hail broke some kind of record."

"It was so huge! And the lightning was crazy *bright*."

Steph nods, her eyes wide. "I went to volunteer yesterday, and I kept crying. I was afraid they were going to send me home." She bites her lip, obviously wondering if she should have confessed that to me.

But suddenly I want Steph to trust me. Whatever she might've heard about Gabe's party, this right now is so easy, so normal—like *I'm* normal. Like I know how to just have a regular conversation with someone, with a girl.

"I do that on a regular day," I tell her. "I cry at commercials and stuff all the time. It's so embarrassing."

She nods again and looks surprised, but relieved, too.

"Were you with the St. John's group?" I ask.

"Yeah. We went over to the Emery streets for a while, but parts of it are still too dangerous, gas lines and stuff, so there wasn't much we could do. There's gonna be a clothes drive this week at school, though, if you have anything." She glances down at my shorts. They're at least three inches shorter than hers.

"I have *way* too many clothes," I say, trying to skip past any discussion of our wildly different tastes in attire. "And my sister grew like a foot this summer, so I bet she could just give you her whole closet."

Steph smiles. "We're trying to use the gym to organize everything, but I don't think they'll let us. Student council says there are too many other things going on in there."

"I could talk to Maddie," I say. "I know she'd want to help."

But you can't talk to Maddie.

The voice is back. Terrific.

"Yeah—oh." Steph nods quickly, then turns to smile at the people who've just opened the door, making the little bell *ding-ding*. "That would be great," she adds quickly before practically shouting, "Welcome to Dairy Queen!"

It's a dad and a girl, about nine, obviously getting out of the house after dinner. DQ isn't the only business that's been able to maintain normal operations since the storm, but I've still been surprised to not have more customers tonight. You'd think people would be craving comfort foods.

The dad looks tired as he puts a hand on his daughter's shoulder. "What do you want, honey?" She squints up at the board, then comes closer to the glass cases to look at our hard-serve flavors.

"You guys seem to be holding up fine," the dad says to us. His eyes flick over to me, away, and back again, and I feel my chest get tight. I know that look.

"We were spared," Steph says with a little laugh. "Even Mother Nature loves ice cream, right?" She's smiling at the girl, who's too old for the joke but smiles back anyway. Steph is really good at this job.

But the dad looks right at me when he says, "You know what, I'll get a cone." He's grinning and standing up straighter, trying to show off how tall he is. You can tell he was good-looking, back in the day, but no one looks good when they're trying that hard. "Swirl in a sugar cone." And then he *winks*.

I turn around fast so he can't see me cringing. There's no good option here, though—as I grab the cone and start filling it from the machine, I can feel the guy staring at my ass. The girl orders something, too, and thank God Steph starts making her order, because all I can hear is the blood rushing in my ears. I just want to be invisible right now. It's a truly shitty feeling.

Besides, it's extra gross when older guys look at me. This isn't the first married or married-with-kids man I've noticed trying to flirt, but it always makes me feel vomit-y. The first time it happened I'd just kissed a boy—one my own age—the day before. Tom Mueller, at a sixth-grade party, playing a totally juvenile game of seven minutes in heaven. The kiss was awful and way too public, but I *loved* it. I was so happy when my name came out of the bowl of little paper slips and Tom's eyes lit up. I was so happy to be the girl he wanted to be "forced" to kiss.

And then the next day at the pool, some man I'd never seen before kept staring at me. And it felt like—it felt like he knew, somehow. Knew I liked attention. Which made me wonder if maybe I liked it too much. And I couldn't explain to him, or anyone, that I didn't like *his* attention. He wasn't Tom Mueller. He was a creep.

Just like the guy standing behind me. I've forgotten about the ice cream and suddenly it's pouring all over my hand, spilling out of the cone and onto the grille under the machine.

"Shit!" I yell, and everyone goes silent for a beat.

"Sorry," Steph apologizes for me. I don't even have time to feel grateful because I'm too busy grabbing a towel and a new cone and trying to finish this stupid order so I can get out from under this asshole's eyes.

"Shouldn't talk like that in front of kids," the dad says as I turn, finally, and hand over the ice cream.

My hand twitches and I'm genuinely afraid I might slap him. I really could—but then I see the girl, standing just out of her dad's line of vision, roll her eyes. Steph hands over the Blizzard, rings them up, and says, "Sorry again—it's been a long weekend for all of us."

The man's expression softens. He nods at her, takes another look at my boobs, and they leave.

As soon as the door *ding-dings* closed I sit straight down on the floor, on the gross rubber mat, and start to cry.

"Wha— Rosie! Are you okay? Don't worry about it, you just spilled a little ice cream! I think we get a couple of screw-ups waived for every shift, right?" Steph seems to realize she's babbling because she goes abruptly silent and squats down next to me.

I'm not *sobbing*, exactly, but I'm crying hard and I can't stop. My nose is running, and my eyes are all scrunched up. I'm ruining my mascara. I look like a psychopath.

Steph puts one hand on my back, gently. She doesn't pat or rub or anything, just sits there for a while. When my outburst finally slows down, I hear her sigh.

"This is exactly what I was like yesterday," she says sympatheti-cally. "Just these little breakdowns every once in a while."

I nod. If she thinks I'm having sympathy pains, maybe she's right. Obviously I'm upset about Maddie and the storm and . . . I don't know.

But the truth is, I don't know why I'm crying right now. And I don't know why that scares me so much. But it does.

"Now, I know these don't match your outfit, *but*." Ryan holds out the work gloves, and when I don't take them right away, flaps them around a little. "They will save your manicure."

I make a face, but I take the gloves and put them on. They're as scratchy on the inside as the outside.

"You don't have to put them on yet," he says.

I sigh and take them off again. I'm tempted to give Alex an exasperated look. He's standing right next to me, so he's the only person seeing what a jerkface Ryan is being, but I don't think we've achieved the knowing look–exchange level quite yet.

It's just the three of us. Actual set building won't start for a while, apparently, but Ryan asked for helpers to clean out the backstage area and start prep work. He's going for Greatest Drama Club Member of All Time, or something. And wants to hang out with the famous new kid, too, I guess.

I thought I might be alone with Ryan and finally find the nerve to ask about his mystery hookup at the football game. But I guess this is fine, since I had no idea how I was going to do that, anyway.

"Safety goggles," Ryan goes on, holding up two pairs of the most hideous plastic glasses I've ever seen.

"Are we supposed to be keeping all this stuff somewhere?" Alex asks. "In our lockers or something?"

Ryan lets out a big, snorty laugh, then looks horrified. Ha, so I'm not the only one who still can't be normal around Alex Goode.

"No," he tells Alex. "It's all theater property, so it stays, you know. In here." As Ryan turns back to the rest of the "theater property" he flares his nostrils at me and bugs his eyes. Definitely not keeping his chill.

I smirk at him, feeling slightly smug. I'm not that bothered by Alex anymore. Or anything. My head has gone all light and airy, and everything that's happened since I got to school today has felt distant, removed. It reminds me of last year when I accidentally got a contact high in Paul Maziarz's car. Same kind of fuzziness, minus all the random giggling.

Even seeing Cory this morning didn't do anything. He ignored me; I avoided him. He never wrote me back, so when I saw him and Maddie together, clearly *together*, I didn't freak out at all. I started to text Ryan, *So she dates cheaters now?* but stopped myself. First, I know he wouldn't answer because that would be picking sides. And second, no one needs a reminder that I was the other cheater. Especially me.

Maybe we can all just not talk about it.

And now I'm thrown together with Alex again and—I don't know. I should probably apologize for never showing up to volunteer. Somewhere in the back of my mind, I think I still want to impress him, but I've forgotten how to try.

If I had the energy to think about it, I'd probably think I'm acting strange.

"I have to go over the safety rules first, before we talk about anything else," Ryan is explaining. "Because if you get hurt we're basically all screwed. But I'm sorry, this part is incredibly boring."

"Yeah, no, it's cool. Do your thing, man."

Ryan and I both look at Alex.

"What?"

For the first time all day, I smile. "You just sounded so . . ."

"So *Midcity*," Ryan finishes.

"Is that bad?" Alex asks. It sounds like he really wants to know our opinion, and I can feel Ryan getting as flattered by that as I am.

"Not exactly—" I start, but Ryan's already saying, "Just be careful. Pretty soon you'll be punctuating every sentence with *bro*."

"Or *dude*," I add.

"You say *dude* all the time!" Ryan cries.

"Dude! Don't rat me out to the new kid!"

Ryan points at me and stares at Alex, as if to say, *See what I mean?* Alex laughs.

That's the . . . huh. I've lost track of how many times I've made him laugh. That's probably healthy. Even if my own laugh sounds more like a raspy kind of bark.

"Okay, okay," I say to Ryan. "Can you show us some of the stuff we're supposed to be safe around? You know, the *cool* stuff?"

"Is there *cool* stuff?" Alex deadpans.

"He *said* there was, but I don't know," I mutter.

"There is!" Ryan's face is getting pink with annoyance. "Oh my God, I'm going to need to ask Mrs. Walsh for some *less insolent helpers*, aren't I?"

As if we'd rehearsed it, in perfect unison Alex and I shrug in the same exaggeratedly innocent way.

Ryan jerks his head back and goes, "Okay. That was. Cree-ee-eepy."

And *that's* when Alex and I share a look. A smile.

Ryan leads us into the actual backstage area, where there is, in fact, some decently cool stuff. In a Home Depot kind of way. Pulleys and bags of sand, huge planks of wood and particleboard waiting to be turned into sets, dozens of cans of paint and power tools and serious-looking ladders.

Soon we each have planks we have to move around—"Ridiculous fire hazards," as Ryan calls them—and for a while Alex and I fall into a wordless routine. It's calming and I think again, vaguely, that things are kind of just . . . *okay* when we're together. It's not like he's easy to be around. He's intense and intimidating and he refuses to flirt with me.

But I don't know, it's peaceful. It's dark backstage, and no one is looking at me, making me talk. Even Ryan had to go somewhere else, so he's not doing that supportive-friend thing where he asks, again, why I haven't made more of an effort to talk to Maddie. Which means I don't have to think about that.

Alex hands me another plank, and I move it, and that's all. It's enough.

13

"I DON'T UNDERSTAND what that is."

"It's supposed to be a kitten."

Alex angles his head to the right, then the left. "Nope," he says. "It's a manatee."

"So it's an ocean kitten."

He nods in that way I'm getting used to—that *I acknowledge your joke and I'm taking it under advisement* way.

"Kitten of the sea," he offers.

"Right. Now why don't you keep your eyes on your own clay," I tell him, pointing to his side of the art table. "Make a mermaid for this . . . 'manatten.' She can adopt it as a pet."

Alex pretends to get right to work on that, but of course he's already halfway through a really impressive—

"Wait, weren't you just making a hand?" I ask.

"No," he says, and I can't tell if he's joking anymore. "I mean, yes. But it was bad."

"It wasn't bad. It was really good."

"These probably aren't the words we're supposed to be using

in a serious art class," Alex says.

"What words? *Kitten? Hand?*"

He folds his clay carefully, constructing something that definitely isn't a hand, but doesn't really look like anything else, either. "I meant *bad* and *good*. Aren't those terribly binary, outdated judgments? Aren't we to *strive* for more specific *language* in our pursuit of *fine art*?"

I glance up and notice that Mr. Kline is hovering nearby, eavesdropping. I open my mouth to tell Alex that he might not want to make fun of our art teacher right this second, but then I see that Mr. Kline is smiling slightly, then walking away to help someone else. He's a cool teacher, but I can't help wondering if I just saw Alex get away with something. On account of being a hero and everything. I'm pretty sure if I openly mocked the exaggerated way Mr. Kline lectures us about *fine art* within his earshot, I'd at least get a warning look.

"Well," I say, leaning a little closer to the thing Alex is trying to sculpt. "Throwing around fancy art terms probably isn't a requirement in Intro. Technically."

"Why don't you do something that speaks to your experience?" says the other girl at the table, Fiona. I've been calling her Fiona Freshman in my head and mostly forgetting that she's here, mainly because she never, ever speaks to us and only wears black, even on her lips.

"Oh, uh." Alex is obviously as surprised to hear Fiona's voice as I am. He looks up at her with a confused expression. "My experience?"

She glares at both of us from under her black bangs. I think she's trying to look intense, but instead she just sort of looks pissed.

"With gun violence," she growls.

I don't gasp, but only barely. Instead I check Alex's face again to see if he's all right—and to my surprise, I find him staring at me. And he seems . . . amused. His lips twitch ever so slightly, and I realize that we're sharing a moment. Knowing-look level: unlocked.

I twitch my lips back, almost as an experiment, and one of Alex's eyebrows moves very slightly upward.

But to Fiona, he is all sincerity. "I think art always exposes the soul, don't you?" he asks her.

It's the perfect thing to say. Not only does she stop scowling for half a second, she nods so wholeheartedly that I feel this huge surge of affection for all her goth-emo nonsense. And I can tell that Alex—whatever he thinks of some random freshman bringing up gun violence in the middle of seventh period—really wants to be nice to her. He really is the guy who will bring bagels to your church relief effort at 6:00 a.m. on a Saturday. He really will stop a gunman and save an entire high school.

Fiona opens her mouth to say something else, but then, from the front of the room, Mr. Kline tells us it's time to put away our "works in progress" because there are only five minutes left.

I sneak my phone under the table, just to check. I know there won't be anything—if Maddie was going to text back to any of my messages, she would have by now. The *let's talk* texts; the all-emoji lists I thought might make her laugh; the #tbt photo of us from the eighth-grade dance with our stupid pink-streaked hair: none of it has moved her.

So much for her getting a boyfriend making our friendship better.

I don't even try to time my movements to Alex's, I just end up walking out the door with him naturally. It feels good—lucky. Even Ryan is starting to seem distant, despite the fact that we spend every lunchtime together in the theater. I didn't know how much I was going to need a friend like Alex this year.

It doesn't even bother me anymore that he never looks at me the way boys usually do. I sort of haven't been thinking about boys that much lately.

My heart beats a little faster, though, afraid I might ruin all the easiness when I say, "I'm sorry about that girl. Fiona? You must get that kind of thing a lot."

"Not very much," he says, chill as ever. "Most people don't actually say the word *gun*, but pretty much everyone is thinking about it whenever they talk to me. I get it."

Olivia and Annabelle walk by right then, and Olivia does this weird thing where she glares at me and then looks back over her shoulder, like she's worried she left something behind. That's when I see Maddie leaning against a locker, talking to Cory, at the end of the hall.

"Don't you just want to not have to *think* about it all the time?" I ask. My voice sounds sharp, desperate, and I try to laugh but that sounds even worse.

"Yeah, of course," he says, either not noticing my strange tone or letting it slide on purpose. "All I do every day is try to forget about it."

This confession surprises me so much that my head jerks around toward him, and away from Maddie.

"Exactly," I whisper.

"It's not healthy, I mean," Alex adds. "I have this therapist— bleh, never mind, you don't want to hear all this."

There's an awful moment when I almost say something right, something like *Of course I want to hear it, you can talk to me*, but then the words don't come out. And the moment passes.

And then we're right next to Maddie and Cory, and she looks over and sees us, and her face—God, her face. I might as well be walking along, holding her heart like an apple, taking a bite, laughing at her.

Cory doesn't look at me at all. He juts his chin at Alex, holds out his fist for a bump, and says, "Practice?"

"Yep," Alex says.

"Cool."

Alex gives me a little smile and peels away with Cory, leaving me there next to my betrayed best friend.

"You really have a thing for other girls' boyfriends now, huh?" Maddie says.

Okay, so I'm not the only one who noticed the girl on Alex's social pages. I'm sure Maddie also saw that he hasn't posted any-thing new in like ten months, but whatever, I get the dig.

I get that I'm the one who messed up here.

"You know I'm really sorry, Maddie. The whole thing was just this giant misunderstanding—"

Her whole face contorts. And still looks beautiful, radiant. "Yeah, except remember, I'm not stupid. I'm pretty sure I *understand* what happened."

"Come on. I'm the one who wanted you guys to get together! Why would I go and mess that up?"

"You *didn't* mess it up," she snaps. "We're fine. Cory explained, and obviously I already know how you are. I wish you would just look at yourself, though. I mean, you didn't even like him that much, and you still needed to, what, know that he liked you best? What even *is* that? I'm sorry, but how pretty do you have to be to not be so *insecure* all the time?"

The words stick themselves into my skin like splinters, and I know they'll hurt like hell later. But right now all I can register is her eyes, and how they flash from angry to righteous to—to pitying. To superior.

I need to say something. My heart stutters in my chest, aching at how much I miss the Maddie I had a week ago. Or maybe a summer ago. Any version of Maddie who wouldn't be like this—who wouldn't forget everything we promised each other about friendship being more important than boys. The Maddie who would *listen* to me.

"It was dark, he just started kissing me." My stomach turns completely over and I'm not sure how to say the rest without vomiting. But before she can interrupt I add, "I'm sure he thought I was you!"

Her forehead wrinkles. "Seriously? Jesus, Rosie."

I open my mouth, but nothing else comes out. It was a mistake. Wasn't it? Or it was Cory trying to hook up with me one last time, and I was too drunk to get him to stop. But I was stopping him—why can't I just say that?

Because I *did* flirt with him, didn't I? I did feel jealous of Maddie and Cory, together.

Maddie takes a shaky breath. "I just can't believe you lied to me," she says, her eyes filling with tears. "You think I'm so helpless without you, but I'm not."

I can't breathe. I want to scream that of course not, of *course* I know she's not helpless—of course I didn't lie—of course I'm the helpless one, the one who doesn't know how to make this better, the—I don't know, I—

I can't get my mouth to *move*.

"I guess I should've known that the only thing that makes you happy, Rosie, is being the girl everyone wants. But everything in the world isn't actually about you. You'd know that if you knew how to be a *friend*."

And then Maddie whips her hair around and walks away.

And I stand there, staring at the ugly orange lockers, wondering how I can still be alive if there's no air inside me. No life.

She's right, you know, says that awful voice that's still stuck in my head.

Yes. I know.

"So it's this whole thing at halftime, and we're taking donation bins, and it's basically huge. I mean, they had record-breaking crowds there last week to see Alex Goode; can you even imagine how much money we're going to raise if that happens again? It could make such a difference. There're so many people who don't even have houses anymore. Not just in Emery Woods, but over in South Omaha? Where all the power is still out? There are help centers and stuff but a lot of them are at schools, so the kids can't go to classes, and it's a total mess. So Father Matt said we have to do more, and this is totally going to be so much more. And there's not a lot we can do at night, so I really want to be there. To help. Okay?"

Mom and Dave stare at Ayla with their mouths open. I might be staring a little bit, too.

That was more words than my sister has said at one time in . . . months.

"So?" Ayla prompts. "Can I go to the game on Friday?"

Our mother finally shakes herself out of her shock and nods. "Of course, sweetie. Of course."

"You know," Dave says, glancing at Mom and then back at Ayla, "we really should make it a family night out. Show our support all together. This is such a terrible time, and we're so lucky—Ayla's right, this could be a huge fundraising opportunity. It's the least we can do to show up."

"That's a great idea," Mom says, brightening. "I don't have a shift until Saturday afternoon, so I can definitely be there."

Ayla smiles at them both—actually smiles! With her teeth!— and then takes another drink of her water. Probably so she can be ready to give another monologue about civic involvement or something.

"Rosie, you can get us all tickets at school, right?" Dave points his fork at me. "So we don't have to buy them at the door?"

"Oh, I forgot," Ayla jumps in, "they're going to charge more for tickets, too, and give the extra to the Red Cross!" She smiles again, triumphantly this time. I wonder if it was her idea, the pricier tickets.

But it doesn't really matter either way. "I'm not going," I tell Dave. "But sure, I can buy tickets for you guys."

Now our parents are staring at me—but not with openmouthed wonder. With serious irritation.

"Rosie, you know we let you skip Ayla's banquet last week. For a football game." Mom's keeping her voice even, and I'm sure she's thinking she can get what she wants without ruining Ayla's good mood.

But she's asking too much.

"I'm sorry I didn't go to the dinner thing," I say, and I really mean it. I would love to go back in time and skip the game, skip seeing Ryan kissing some mystery dude who he's obviously never going to tell me about. And I would *kill* to not have been able to go to Gabe's party. I'd do just about anything to have been forced to leave that stupid church-basement dinner an hour early, due to the terrible storm, and never have to hurt my best friend so much that she won't talk to me. Whenever time machines are invented, I will be the first in line, and I will see my moody sister get some dumb certificate for being such a good Catholic, and I won't ever know what it's like to sleep in an armchair in Gabe's parents' fancy sitting room.

But in this version of history, Mom is *not* winning this argument.

"I'm really not going, though," I say. I catch Ayla's eye and add, "Sorry. I'll give you a donation."

"I'm not sure this is actually a debate right now," Dave says gently. Mom's hand is pressed on the table next to her napkin, and he places his fingers over hers. United front and all that. "Last week we let you go to a party, and this week we're asking you to do something as a family. It can't be about you all the time, Rosie. Sometimes you have to do things for your sister. I'm sure whatever party you want to go to this week is really—"

"Party?" I yelp. "Seriously? You don't even know why I can't go. You don't even ask me, you're just like, 'Nope, Rosie, your life is dumb, do what we say now.'"

"Hey," Mom snaps, but I've already stood up from the table.

"Whatever!" I yell at them. Ayla jumps in surprise, but I don't care. She's not the only one who can dump a tantrum all over everyone. "I'll go to the fucking football game with my *family*! For *charity*!"

Dave starts to get out of his chair, too, saying, "That is not an appropriate way to speak to your—"

"And by the way, no one has parties *during* the game, *Dave*. Obviously I'm the only one here who's ever had a social life, but whatever, let's all wear matching sweaters to the goddamn field on Friday! Go, Fuller family!"

Dave's face is so red I think he might burst a blood vessel, and frankly, as mad as I am, I'm afraid to even look at my mom.

"I want you to apologize for that language right now." Dave manages to keep his voice level.

But I don't. "I'm SORRY!" I shriek. "I'm very fucking sorry for my language!"

And with that, I turn and run out of the kitchen—literally run, all the way to the stairs and up to my room, where I slam the door as hard as I can and fall to my knees on the carpet, panting.

That was . . . clichéd.

Awesome. More input from the *voice*.

I lean over so I'm on my hands and knees, still trying to get my breathing under control. It *was* a cliché, I guess. And it came out of nowhere, like the other night when I cried at work.

My chest tightens again as I lower myself all the way to the floor, trying not to be scared.

After a minute I'm able to roll over onto my back and stare at the glow-in-the-dark stars Maddie and I put up in seventh grade. She wanted to make the whole solar system, but in the end we just scattered them everywhere and did a Big Dipper in the middle. They're all so old that the color has turned a pukey yellow, and even though it's already pretty dark in here, they aren't very bright. They lost whatever it is that makes them glow years ago.

There's a scratching sound at my door that might be a knock, and then I hear, "Are you in there?"

Ayla shoves her nose through the doorway and looks around, not finding me right away.

"Do you want a light on?" she asks. It's obvious from her tone that I *should* want a light on. Probably to do my homework or plan the next great storm-victim fundraiser.

"Go away," I say.

I expect her to argue or at least say something mean, but she doesn't.

She goes away.

And it's just me, alone, with the stars that won't shine.

14

"I SEE SOME room all the way up there, does that look good?"

"Sure! Let's go and then I'll come back down to get snacks. Or do you want to just save me a seat?"

"Yeah, why don't we do that? Can you get me a diet whatever?"

"No popcorn or anything?"

"Nah, I figure we can go out after the game—girls?"

Mom and Dave turn back to look at us, and Mom's eyebrows raise in surprise.

"What?" she asks.

"Can we just *sit*?" I hiss, and at the same time Ayla moans, "The seats are gonna be *taken* by the time we get *up there*."

Dave rolls his eyes. "Nice to see you two agreeing on something, for once. Snacks?" He points at us, but we're already shaking our heads impatiently.

"All right, let's go," Mom says, and starts climbing the bleachers.

I can feel eyes on me, but I keep mine pointed down, staring at the metal stairs clanking under my wedges. Off to my right I hear Olivia's voice say, "Oh my *God*!" but it doesn't sound like she's talking about me. Then I hear Maddie laugh, and that *does* sound personal, somehow.

Finally we're up past their rows and sidestepping over to some of the last free spots left. It's not as crowded as last week, but almost. And it's even more intense. Groups of parents were huddled around in the parking lot and down at the edge of the field, trading horror stories about last week's storm. The charity tables were set up two hours early for a kind of bizarre tailgating thing. Ayla's already been here since school let out, helping Father Matt with stuff. I went home after school and then drove here with Mom and Dave, because apparently *I'm* now the twelve-year-old in the family.

We sit and I finally let myself look around, carefully figuring out who, exactly, is here. The week has only gotten worse by the day. A bunch of the football players have grabbed my ass in the hallways, even the ones with girlfriends, and not in the funny, friendly way they used to. Or maybe it just feels worse to me now, I don't know—each time it happens I try to laugh, then end up in the closest bathroom, sure I'm going to puke.

And Olivia seems to be on a mission to make every other girl in school hate me as much as she does. I know there was that stupid kiss with Annabelle's crush, but otherwise I honestly don't know what I ever did to Olivia. Besides being prettier than her, which obviously I can't do anything about.

God, I'm being a bitch. But Olivia *always* is, and no one ever seems to care. I never cared, either, because I had whichever boy I wanted. And Maddie. And Ryan. And that was enough. More than enough, actually.

I look down and to the left, where Olivia's blond head is bobbing around between Annabelle's black hair and Maddie's high, messy bun. They look like a book cover, all girly and happily chatting and perfectly matched without being identical. Maddie leans in close and says something that makes Annabelle gasp and look toward the field excitedly, and Olivia shakes her head in this exaggerated way that sets my teeth on edge. I wish those two would just go cheer, already. They must love sitting in the stands in their stupid uniform skirts, acting like they own the whole school.

I feel like a creep, spying on them like this, but as I watch I'm slowly reminded of freshman year, when the four of us hung out sometimes. A lot, actually. We'd all been at the same dance classes when we were kids. And then in ninth grade we all had the same lunch period, so we became kind of a group. I'd forgotten all about that, I realize now. It was always a little stressful because Olivia had all these rules about food—no gluten, no soy, no sugar—and she'd constantly list off all the toxins the rest of us were eating and probably dying from. Plus, she obviously wanted to be Maddie's favorite friend and resented me for hogging that particular honor.

Toward the end of the year I started hanging out with this junior named Ethan, and Maddie was spending more time with the other girls on the soccer team, and we both sort of drifted away from Olivia and Annabelle, who were all into cheerleading and not much else.

It occurs to me now, way too late, that Olivia was probably *thrilled* when Finn Kramper stuck his tongue down my throat and broke Annabelle's heart. She'd hated me all along, but when that happened she had an ironclad excuse to hate me in the open.

Suddenly everyone is standing up, and all the cheerleaders still in the stands are running down to the field. It's already time for the national anthem. It's weird, hearing my mom sing next to me, with Ayla's high-pitched voice on my other side. It feels like old times, going to church together. Except now I can also see Dave climbing the bleachers, holding a whole armful of drinks and snacks. He reaches us right when everyone is sitting down again, and before I know it I'm holding a giant Sprite and a bag of pretzels.

"I didn't want—" I start, but Mom elbows me gently.

"Just eat some of it," she says. "It'll be a while until dinner, right?"

I glance over at Ayla, who doesn't seem fazed at all to be the new owner of a Sprite and a bag of Twizzlers.

"Split those with me?" I ask. She hesitates, so I add, "Here, you can share these, too."

The sharp sting of the sugary drink and then biting down on the candy makes me feel better for a while. Dave keeps leaning over Mom to ask me who people are or what grade they're in, but even that isn't so bad. It keeps me from staring at Maddie, at least. Charlotte and a few of the other student council kids have replaced her cheerleader friends.

Right before halftime, I see Ryan come in. His hair is gelled back and he's wearing another nice button-down, plaid this time.

He scans the bleachers and then waves to Maddie, walking toward her row.

My stomach does a big rise and fall, like a little kid on a swing. I can't believe he's picking sides. *Her* side.

As if he can feel my humiliation from all the way down there, Ryan suddenly looks right up at me. He's still climbing the stairs, but he pauses long enough to give me a *You're HERE?* look.

I shake my head, just once, trying to tell him—I don't know. To forget it, I guess. Then he sees the rest of my family, and his face turns apologetic, like he can tell I'm here against my will. And then he looks away, squeezing onto the end of the bleacher next to Maddie.

What a wonderfully awesome night this is. I suck on my straw so hard I get brain freeze and have to tense all my muscles just to keep myself from throwing the cup out over everyone in front of us in a fit of rage.

"You okay?" Mom asks, I guess noticing that I have one hand pressed to my forehead.

"Mmph," I mutter.

"I have to go to the bathroom," Ayla announces importantly.

"Okay, let me get my bag—" Mom starts, but Ayla stands up and lets out this huge sigh.

"I can go to the stupid bathroom on my own, Mom."

I wait for our parents to react, for Dave to tell Ayla to be more respectful or Mom to say something about how it's dark and crowded here and neither of us is as mature as we seem to think. But we're technically having this nice family night, and I can feel that neither of them wants to be the one to ruin it.

I kind of want to say something bitchy myself, but instead I stand up next to her and say, "I have to go, too. We'll be back in a few minutes."

Mom gives me a grateful look, but I'm too mad at myself to even smile back. Why did I just volunteer to parade around in front of everyone again? If I were smart, I'd be hiding behind my parents until the end of the game.

Ryan looks over his shoulder at us as we're making our way down, and when we pass his and Maddie's row he holds out his hand, just long enough for me to brush his fingers with mine. I don't want to forgive him for this, but it's not like I asked him to come to the game, either. It didn't occur to me, even after what I saw last week. Maybe Maddie asked him to come. Maybe he already told her about his mystery football boyfriend.

My stomach lurches again with jealousy, but I know I'm being completely self-centered. As we circle around the bleachers I see all the tables set up for the church and some other groups helping the storm victims, and I feel like I could probably try a *little* harder to have some perspective on my miserable life.

"Which one is yours?" I ask Ayla.

She raises her eyebrows at me, surprised I'm talking to her, I guess. But then she points and says, "That one. And that one. It wasn't that much work. It's mostly the coordinating stuff, after the money comes in, that'll be hard."

"Oh," I say. "I could probably help out, if you need people." As soon as I say it, though, I think of all the show-off posts right after the storm, everyone making sure they could be seen being good. I sort of don't want to be seen at all lately, not even for a good cause.

Ayla shrugs as she walks. "If you want. We'll have a lot of stuff to fold, after the clothing drive. I think Alex is getting the whole team to volunteer, so that'll be cool."

It's funny, I've barely thought about Alex tonight. He's been right in front of me this whole time, playing or sitting on the bench with his sweaty hair shining under the lights. I can see him every time I look at the field.

But I've been trying to *not* see Cory. It's been easier to stare at Maddie and feel bad than it has to just watch the game. Because the more I look at Cory, the stranger I feel. Bad, obviously. But also just really, really confused.

Why hasn't he messaged me back? What happened last weekend, exactly? What did he tell Maddie—that's what I'd really like to know. But even more, I want to know what he was thinking that night at Gabe's.

Because the more *I* think about it, the more I wonder if I'd really flirted with him that much. Did I really do anything that said, *Sneak away from your new girlfriend and have sex with me?* I mean, really?

I keep thinking that I was drunk, I was stupid. I'd hooked up with him like that before—we hadn't had sex yet, but we were probably going to. Ironically—sort of—I probably would've had sex with him that night, if we'd still been hooking up. If it hadn't been for Maddie.

And then a big part of me wants to believe what I tried to tell

Maddie in the hall that day. Because it could be true—he could've just gotten confused in the dark. Maddie and I don't look alike when the lights are on, but we're about the same height, and my mom says we have a lot of the same mannerisms from spending so much time together. Or he could've been so drunk that he forgot he wasn't hooking up with me anymore . . . which isn't a great excuse, but it sort of makes sense.

"Isn't that Paul?" Ayla asks, shaking me out of my pointless, gerbil-wheel thoughts.

"Where?"

She points and I see him—and he already sees us. Paul Maziarz is striding across the lawn on those long legs of his, grinning at me like I'm water in the desert.

"Rose Parade!" he yells from a few paces away. And then he's close, scooping me up, spinning me around in a big hug.

He smells the same, like a mix of CK One and weed, and his arms are still strong even though his chest feels a little softer. I hang on and let him spin me, but about halfway around I start feeling dizzy. And kind of annoyed, actually. Almost . . . angry.

I used to love when Paul would scoop me up. And now I just want down, away—why do I—

My stomach plummets again, worse than before.

Cory ruined this, I think.

Am I always going to feel shitty now, when a boy grabs me? Am I always going to panic a little, wondering which girl I'm hurting when a boy touches me instead of her?

Paul sets me down and goes, "Whew! You look like a delicate

flower, but you got some *weight*, girl!"

I do my best to arrange my face into a smile, but it might not be working. In fact, it probably isn't, because Paul's bushy eyebrows suddenly furrow.

"Not like you're fat, baby. Like *muscle*." He flexes one arm, then the other, gun-show style.

"Yeah, I know," I say, finally finding my voice. I want to turn and run to the safety of the bathrooms, but I force myself to be polite. Normal. "How *are* you? Why aren't you in Kansas?"

"Big game!" he booms, pointing toward the field. "Big storm!" He points the other way and makes a face. "Crazy shit, right? Oh, sorry." He glances at Ayla, hovering close to my elbow.

"No, it's fine," she says quickly. "Totally crazy shit."

I give her a look, but she's gazing at Paul. Then she flips her hair over one shoulder, and I have this vicious flashback of Maddie and Cory that nearly knocks me over.

"We were just going to the bathroom," I tell Paul. "My little sister had to go, so I'm taking her."

I grab Ayla's shoulders and smile like the selfless elder sibling I am.

"You guys are super cute," Paul says, smiling at me but *winking* at Ayla. God. "We should hang out, yeah? I'm here all weekend."

I pause, wondering if he just asked *me* to hang out, or me *and* Ayla. Not that it's possible he wants to hang out with a seventh grader, but the way they're still smiling at each other, who even knows what he's thinking?

"Awesome," I say. "Text me!"

And then I shove Ayla away so hard she yelps.

"What the hell?" she asks, stumbling out of my grip. "Could you be more *embarrassing*?"

"That guy is in *college*," I say. "And stop swearing all the time!"

"Oh my God," she spits. "Who cares? What is your problem, even?"

We reach the end of the incredibly long line at the girls' room—everyone is trying to beat the halftime crush, apparently—and I finally stop and get a good look at Ayla's face.

She looks genuinely, sincerely confused.

"You were flirting with him," I say slowly, wondering how she doesn't get why I'm mad.

"No, I wasn't," she says. I open my mouth to argue, but she cuts in. "And even if I was, who cares? Like you said, he's old. I'm not going to *do* anything with him."

I blink at her a few times. When I was Ayla's age, all I thought about was *doing* things with boys. Hell, I was two years younger than her when I got into that closet with Tom Mueller.

But I haven't even noticed Ayla getting older or looking at boys. There are the boy-band posters, of course, but she doesn't *flirt*. She's a *kid*.

"Okay," I say at last. "I'm sorry, you're right."

Ayla's eyebrows shoot up and she laughs. "For real? I'm *right*? Someone take a picture! What a time to be alive!"

"Hey, shut up, I'm trying to be nice."

She studies me for a minute. "Why didn't you talk to him longer? It seemed like he was trying to get back together with you."

I shake my head. "We're just old friends." She doesn't look convinced, but she doesn't say anything else. The line inches forward, and I know I should let it go, but after a minute I say, "You should wait until you're older to, you know. Be all flirty and stuff."

"Okay, *Mom*."

"Whatever, you know Mom *would* say that."

"And *you* know that you and Mom are the pretty ones, so it's easy for you to give lectures on boys and whatever."

Ayla turns away, her mood suddenly shifting again. Now she's—mad? Upset?

"You're pretty, too, Ay," I tell her.

She's standing perfectly still, her arms wrapped around her waist.

"Ayla, come on. What did I do now?"

"You don't even know if I already *have* a boyfriend," she says quietly. "You think just because everyone likes you, that no one else even has a life."

"That's crazy. Of course I don't think that. I just think you might want to wait for the boyfriend thing until you're older, is all."

The line keeps creeping forward, and we've finally reached the side of the building. I move over so I'm leaning against the wall, forcing Ayla to face me. She *humph*s and tries to turn away again, but I reach out to hold one of her arms.

"Wait, *do* you have a boyfriend?"

She hugs herself even tighter and doesn't answer, which seems like a pretty clear *no* to me. "You didn't wait," she says softly.

"No," I admit. I didn't know she'd noticed, but I guess all those lectures from Mom about how I should be less boy crazy haven't exactly been done in private.

"Not everyone is, like, a guy magnet." Her voice is tight with the tears she's not crying yet, and I don't know whether to hold my breath so I don't laugh or bite my lip so I don't cry, too. It's overwhelming, getting slammed with all these feelings at the same time.

"Ayla, seriously. You're gorgeous. You look *just* like Mom, way more than I do. And being a 'guy magnet' isn't that great all the time. Actually, a lot of the time. And look at all the cool stuff you're doing—you're so *involved*, you know? It's amazing. You're amazing. I'm just saying that that's the most important thing, okay?"

The line moves again, and we step inside the door. Fluorescent lights glare down on us, and across the room a wall of mirrors feels like it's staring. We're visible again.

"See?" I tell my sister, putting an arm around her shoulders and turning toward our reflection. "We're both pretty."

She scowls at first, and I give her a little shake.

"Plus, not for nothing, but being pretty and guys liking you are totally not the same thing."

"They are with you and Mom," she mutters.

"Maybe," I say. "Sort of. I don't know, but I do know that there are tons of girls at school with really nice boyfriends, and they're all just okay-looking."

"Are their boyfriends cute?"

I laugh. "The point is that looks aren't that *crucial*, kid."

She stares at me in the mirror, her mouth twisting in thought.

"But everyone thinks you're pretty, so you can say that," she insists.

"Damn, you're stubborn."

The last woman ahead of us disappears and a stall opens up, so I push Ayla toward it.

Turning back to the mirror, I twist my long curls a little bit and think about what she said. I know I'm right—I know looks aren't everything. I guess I'm lucky, getting to look a way that people think is pretty. That even I think is pretty, usually.

But it hasn't really *gotten* me anywhere. It's not like I'm a supermodel or the most popular girl at school or anything. It maybe gets me into trouble, like what happened with Cory.

What if it was like Maddie said—that I needed to know that Cory still liked me that way, because if he didn't, then what?

Maybe being seen as pretty has gotten me into a lot more trouble than I've realized. Maddie wants Cory because she likes him, she feels a way about him—he's really her first solid boyfriend and I'm missing it.

But maybe I'm missing more than that. Maybe I'm missing the thing where I like a boy, too. And not just for the attention. For him.

I turn away from the mirror and wait for my turn. But I can feel my own reflection in the corner of my eye. Like it's waiting for something, too.

15

I WALK AYLA back to the bleachers, but I can't make myself climb up. Glancing quickly, I see that Ryan isn't next to Maddie anymore, so she's right on the aisle, and I just can't. So I wave to my parents and say to Ayla, "Tell them I'm going to talk to some people for a minute."

"Like Paul?" she says with a smile.

"Sure," I lie.

After a few minutes of pretending I don't know where I'm going, I wander all the way to the edge of the dark soccer field and sit on the empty bleachers there. To my left are the deep shadows near the back door, where I could see Ryan and the mystery boy kissing last week. And if I stay very still, no one can see me unless they really try.

No one else is creeping around, it seems, not even Ryan. Maybe he went home, or found a new halftime make-out spot. Probably it's insane that I'm even trying to catch him again, not that I've admitted I'm doing that. My official story is that I want to find him and talk.

Or you're hiding.

The voice is almost nice tonight, almost like a friend.

Because you don't have any real friends anymore.

Maybe not.

I focus on the noise of the game behind me, the announcer's muffled voice and the steady chanting of the cheerleaders. I look up at the black sky, which almost has stars tonight. None of the ominous clouds we had last week. It's even a little bit chilly, enough that I'm glad I have on a light sweater. Not that I felt like wearing anything more revealing, anyway.

I think about Paul's hug and wonder, again, why it felt so bad. I guess the thing with Cory was just . . . upsetting. It must have thrown me off more than I realized.

Or maybe it scared you, the voice offers.

I pull my feet up onto the bench, sitting sideways so I can stare at the dark hulk of the school at the top of the hill and wrap my arms around my knees.

It did sort of scare me. All week I've been hoping to talk to Cory, to fix everything—on the one hand, I know I should just be apologizing to Maddie, over and over, and not worry about anything else. But on the other, I feel like I'm not sure what to apologize for. Because, I mean . . . what was Cory doing, exactly? Did he think I wanted to hook up?

Or was he just doing what he wanted, whether or not . . .

Yeah, right. The voice is laughing at me. *Like anyone has to force you to do anything.*

I dig my chin into my knees and tighten every muscle, trying to block all the feelings I might start having. I can't start sobbing here in the dark, it's too pathetic.

You know—

The voice starts again, but I jump up and start walking, fast, toward the main road, away from the football field. I reach the sidewalk and keep going, so quickly that the wind whips my hair back and I almost feel free.

I'm not far from the Dairy Queen, so without thinking I head in that direction. It feels good to have somewhere to go, even if I don't really have a reason to go there. At least it'll probably be empty right now. The game crowd won't be showing up for another half hour at least.

When I can see the glow of the tall sign a few blocks away, I pull out my phone to text Mom. *Getting a ride home with a friend*, I tell her. Maybe it'll end up being true. If not, well, I've walked home from here before.

Then I realize I might not know who's working tonight—and it might be Hadley, the super-uptight manager. Joel would be good, but I stopped paying attention to his schedule a while ago. I walk more slowly, watching as the windows of the restaurant come into view, and sigh with relief when I see Steph standing behind the counter.

The door *ding-ding*s and I step into the cold, brightly lit store with a real smile on my face.

"Rosie!" Steph says. "What are you doing here?"

I shrug. "Game was boring."

"Oh, crap, I forgot about the game . . ." Steph looks past me with a worried expression. "It's going to get so crowded."

"Isn't someone else coming to help with closing? Joel or Hadley?"

Her eyes get big and almost guilty when she says, "No. They said I could close."

It takes me a minute to figure out why she seems nervous—she must think I'll be hurt, that they trust her to close, but never let me do it. Instead I laugh out loud as I walk over to the counter and lean against it, across from her.

"Well, you picked a terrible night to get promoted," I say.

Her eyes stay wide for another second, but then she laughs, too. "Oh my God, please tell me it's cold outside?"

I wave my hand like, *sort of.* "It's chilly, but you'll still probably get some sweaty football players."

Steph lets out a moan and leans her head down on the counter. That's when I notice there's a huge book open in front of her, with a notebook next to that.

"Oh, come on," I say. "Are you upset that you'll be slammed or that you won't be able to do more homework on a Friday night?"

She looks up at me from between her fingers and narrows her eyes. "It's for my internship. Which might start paying me, which would be *amazing*, since it would get me away from sweaty football players and sticky kids and stupid chocolate sprinkles everywhere . . ." She moans again and then stands up straight, slamming the book shut. I see something about art history before she whisks it into her backpack.

"What internship?" I ask. "You're leaving me all alone with the sticky kids?"

"At the art museum. They have this program for high school students, but no one from Midcity ever gets in. Mr. Kline has been helping me, and it's really cool—I can maybe go to Italy next year and getting into a good art school will basically be automatic, and—"

She stops suddenly and reaches back, tightening her mousy-brown ponytail. Her round cheeks are flushed and the wholesome smattering of freckles across them disappear in the pink. She looks like an adorable farm girl, like maybe she milked the cows that made all the ice cream in here.

But she also looks really serious about this plan. So maybe I don't know much about Steph Barnes at all.

"That sounds incredible," I finally say. "I'm jealous. I can't even make a kitten sculpture."

She opens her mouth like she's about to say one thing, but hears me a second later and changes her mind. "Wait, kitten sculpture? What?"

I wave my hand again, dismissively. "I'm in Intro. For arts credits or whatever. Mr. Kline told us to pick something we thought we could stick with, just to get the feel of the clay?"

She smiles. "Yes, he's a big clay-feeler. God, that sounds so *nice*."

"Ha, I bet you totally miss hanging out with the wannabe-goth freshmen, drawing bowlfuls of fake pears."

"'You don't draw the *pears!*'" she says, throwing her arms up just like Mr. Kline does. I catch on and together we practically yell his favorite line together: "'You draw the *light!*'"

We both laugh and she seems to relax about a thousand percent. I feel a lot better, too, which I guess is why I hop up onto the counter and swing my legs over.

"What are you doing? No free samples!" Steph squeals.

With a snort I brush past her to the back room. I find an extra shirt in a box on the desk. Before Steph can argue, I've swapped my sweater for the horrible uniform and come back out, sweeping my hair into a ponytail.

"I'm helping," I say. "The game's gotta be over by now or really soon."

She starts to speak again, but I just point at her book bag.

"If you go into the office now, you might get a little more studying done before the hordes descend and crush your dreams of Italy."

She snaps her mouth shut and grabs the bag.

"You're a saint," she tells me.

"Yeah, or the opposite of that." We both smirk as if I'm actually joking.

Just before she disappears into the back, she stops. "Wait, did you clock in? Are you—I don't know if you're allowed to clock in, are you?"

"Yeah, no, this is completely not legit," I say, realizing I might really be breaking some kind of law even as I'm saying it. "But who cares? I don't really need the twenty bucks or whatever it would end up being, anyway."

"Well, I'll split my hours with you. And testify at your trial, you know, when you get arrested."

"See, *that's* saintly. But seriously, don't worry about it. I totally owe you after bailing last weekend."

She looks at me with something that sort of resembles surprise mixed with respect, but I don't have time to quite figure it out before she nods and disappears into the back.

And then there's just enough time to drink half a Diet Coke before the people start coming. At first it's just a few fans, their pink cheeks and warm orders—a lot of hot fudge toppings and one random coffee—a clear indication that the temperature is dropping fast.

But then there are kids from school, and *more* kids from school, and soon I have to yell back to Steph that I can't handle the orders alone.

All four picnic tables outside are covered in Midcity students, and I'm starting to regret my decision to help out—especially if it means hosing those things down when we finally close—when the door *ding-ding*s again and in walk Cory and Maddie.

They're with a ton of other juniors, Gabe and Olivia and Annabelle and even Ryan, toward the back, but all I can see is the happy couple. Cory has his arm around her shoulders, and she's wearing his letter jacket.

Oh, God, I'm going to throw up. *She's wearing his letter jacket.*

Steph literally shoves my arm, and I stumble to the side, over behind the hard-serve flavors. "Hey, guys, what can I get you?" she trills, smiling right at Maddie.

I haven't even regained my balance when Ryan and Gabe circle around to me, acting all innocent about their obvious interference running.

And here I thought no one cared how I feel about this whole situation. Or, okay, I guess they might be protecting Maddie. Either way, at least I don't have to look at Cory's smug face.

"We both want Blizzards," Ryan says loudly. "Butterfinger."

I nod and get to work, grateful for an assignment that forces me to turn my back on the room. Whose idea was it to come here? It couldn't have been Maddie's, right? She's barely seen me at work; maybe she forgot I even have this job. Or maybe Cory suggested it and she agreed so . . . she could show off? That isn't something I thought Maddie would do, but the world is full of goddamn surprises. Especially lately.

After an eternity, Steph and I get everyone's orders made. Olivia, of course, just wants water, but to my shock, Annabelle looks almost friendly when I hand over her dipped cone. And then they're all out the door, shoving some sophomores away from a table and taking it over. I can still hear them, sort of, but they're just a blur of color on the dark side of the windows.

When the counter is suddenly deafeningly vacant, I sigh.

"Thanks for that," I tell Steph.

"No worries. I figured it might be awkward."

She goes to wash her hands, so I wait until she turns the water off to take a deep breath and ask, "What did you hear, exactly? About . . ." I angle my head toward the door, trying to be subtle in case anyone's watching us from out there.

She opens her mouth and shuts it again, which I'm beginning to realize is just how she forms a sentence before she speaks. Another open-close, then finally, "Not much, really. Mostly it was just from—ugh, I'm sorry, I don't want to get him in trouble. But I was talking to Ryan, and he said you and Maddie had, like, a thing."

"To Ryan?" I ask stupidly.

"Yeah, you know, we're friends." When I don't respond, she adds, "From theater? I do all the sets every year? Okay, maybe I'm the only one who thinks I'm famous." She laughs lightly and shakes her head.

"I'm on tech," I say. "So I see Ryan every day now—I guess I'll see you, too?"

"Oh, yeah, you'll be totally sick of me by October! I've been away with the—"

"Internship stuff," I finish for her. "Right."

We just sort of nod at each other a few times, not sure how to keep the conversation going. I want to ask again, find out what exactly Ryan told her. But that feels kind of pathetic, and besides, Ryan wouldn't have told her anything that bad.

"Oh, we can start closing!" she says, looking up at the clock. "Quick, go lock the door!"

In a flurry of activity we lock up the front and wipe down all the counters. Employee of the Year that she is, Steph already washed the windows, so after ten minutes of work, all that's left are the tables outside. I change back into my sweater and grab my purse so I can leave right after we're done with the hoses.

It's cooler and much quieter when we step out the back door, locking it behind us. I help Steph unwind the hose, but she waves me off when I try to carry it. "Stop, you've done enough. And you're wearing real clothes. Go home!"

I step aside, grateful. But I feel a little lost, too. I wonder if it would be weird to ask Steph for a ride. I know she appreciated my help tonight, but it was also kind of needy, me showing up like that. And then she helped me with Maddie . . . and I just can't ask for anything else.

So, with a wave, I walk around to the front of the store, heading toward home.

But as I step into the parking lot, I see a silver car. With someone leaning against the hood.

"Rosie," Alex calls softly.

I hold my breath, waiting to feel . . . I don't know. Nervous? Annoyed and a little sick, the way I felt with Paul?

But there's none of that. I just feel happy, really happy, to see a friend.

"Hey," I say, stepping closer. "What are you doing here?"

He smiles. "I heard you might need a ride home."

I breathe out, long and smooth. "Yeah," I say. "But let's go somewhere else first."

16

"HAVE YOU BEEN talking to Ryan about me, too?" I ask once we're in the car.

"Uh, no. Why?" Alex turns on the engine, but doesn't start driving yet.

"Oh, you said you heard I needed a ride . . ." I feel silly, assuming he's been talking about me with anyone. Maybe it was just an expression.

"I ran into Maddie on her way out," he says. His voice sounds totally neutral and for a minute I'm stuck, trying to figure out what that might mean. Was Maddie trying to help me? Is she less mad now?

Or she could've been making a mean joke about me not having anything to do tonight, and Alex didn't realize? It's hard to picture, but at this point I'm not sure I know Maddie as well as I thought. After all, before Cory came along, I thought that no matter how much I messed up, she'd at least give me a chance to explain.

"So . . ." Alex drums his fingers on the steering wheel and watches me.

"Right, okay, you want to go somewhere?"

"I have until one," he says. The clock on the dashboard says 10:23.

Too late, I realize I've been thinking of places that other Mid-city kids go—the old elementary school playground, or the big park in Omaha where people smoke weed sometimes. I don't want to run into anyone, not after serving all of them stupid ice cream, but I also know that a bunch of places farther away might be tricky. Dave said that half of downtown is still blocked off because of storm damage to the river.

Here I have an actual chance to impress Alex Goode, and I'm completely blowing it.

"Sorry," I say, after too much silence has filled the car. "I guess maybe the park? I don't know if it's just a bunch of fallen trees right now, or what . . ." I trail off, feeling awkward. The park is two blocks away, and I haven't even seen it since the storm.

Alex nods. "It is," he says simply. Of course he already knows where the worst damage has been done. He's probably been cleaning it up all week, in between school and football.

"We could probably just—" I start, but he's already saying, "I have a place."

"Oh." I nod quickly. "Okay."

He pulls away from the DQ, and I lean back in my seat, watching the dark storefronts go by. There are almost no other cars on the road—it's late and this is a pretty residential area—but for once the sight of empty streets doesn't fill my chest with that ache I usually get. That deep-down loneliness that comes from living in a small town a million miles from anything interesting or important. That desperate void that opens between my lungs and can't be filled.

It can be quieted, though. A new crush, a party hookup. A new guy who thinks I'm hot and tries to make me laugh.

Alex isn't that guy, and yet, I'm okay. I guess it's because he's interesting and important, just as a person. Alex is bigger than this town. He's not from here; he's not stuck here. A whole new kind of panic balloons under my lungs, but it's more like excitement than stir-craziness.

"So I guess you know my sister," I say as we pass St. John's.

"Yeah, Ayla, right? She's a great kid."

"Not sure she'd agree with the 'kid' part," I say. "She's gonna be *thirteen* in a few weeks, you know."

He smiles. "Junior high was the worst."

"Ugh, I know. I tried to cut my own bangs."

Alex snorts a little, glancing over at me like he's checking to make sure my hair doesn't still look ridiculous. "And it didn't work?"

"Are you kidding? My mom literally screamed when she saw me."

"Oh, man." He shakes his head sympathetically.

"I'd totally forgotten about that until just now, isn't that weird? Anyway. Why was it bad for you?" I ask. "Junior high, I mean, not my bangs. I know why those were bad."

This time he laughs, a real, out-loud laugh, and I get that buzzing feeling I get at school whenever I make a joke that really gets him. Somehow the buzzing feels a lot more intense now, alone with him in a dark car on a dark street in the deep, quiet night.

And it's more intense with Alex than with other guys. The way he doesn't flirt with me but still seems to see me, to really listen—it's not the kind of attention I'm used to.

But I could get used to it.

"Got in a lot of fights, I guess," he's saying. "Kind of a troublemaker."

"You?" It sounds like I'm teasing him, but I'm genuinely surprised.

He shrugs one shoulder, his eyes fixed on the road. "My parents split up when I was eleven, and, I don't know. I did the standard acting-out thing, I guess."

"It couldn't have been that bad," I say, still trying to imagine Alex having any strong, out-of-control feelings. Or hitting someone. "You seem so . . . level."

"Do I?" He sounds surprised. "My dad says I act like I'm too good for everyone."

There's a painful heat to his words that I don't know how to respond to. I hold my breath as he turns down an unlit street, and then again onto a dirt road between two soybean fields. For a second I bother to notice that we're really alone—really out in the middle of nowhere, and not a part of nowhere that I recognize.

The car bumps along the road for a while and then I see a dim light ahead, shining over a garage door with an old basketball hoop barely hanging on to it. Alex drives past the house, so I don't get a very good look except to see that it's about as badly kept as the hoop and there's a truck in the driveway.

A short distance past the house is another dirt road that leads to a small barn. More like a shed, I guess, but big enough for a tractor.

Alex pulls all the way up to its weather-beaten door and stops the car.

"Is this the part where I find out you're a serial killer?" I say. My voice jumps around, betraying the fact that I really do feel nervous all of a sudden. Not in an entirely bad way, though. Maybe a little excited.

But it's not like I'm the most trustworthy person in the dark, either.

Alex laughs again, quietly this time, like he's afraid of waking someone up. "Sorry," he says. "I guess it does look pretty creepy, huh? I didn't even think of that. It's just—there's actually a hell of a view on a good night like this. I wanted to show you."

We look at each other in the dim light of the dashboard readouts.

"Then I want to see it," I say.

The slamming of our car doors is the only sound besides a few crickets and the wind moving through the grass and crops next to the road. I have to jog to keep up with Alex, who's hurrying around to the side of the shed-barn. Just before the car's automatic lights switch off, I see the ladder.

"Oh, come on," I say. It only feels *pitch*-dark for a second—there's still enough light from the city out here that my eyes adjust almost immediately—but I'm still not sure I want to climb an old, metal ladder up to the roof of an old, questionable outbuilding on a cold Friday night.

"You go first," Alex says. "So if it breaks you'll fall on me."

I widen my eyes at him.

"Kidding! Seriously, I come up here all the time. Like,

daily. Nightly. It's fine—you only need to go first because I'm a gentleman."

The buzzing feeling trickles down my spine as I grab the rusted ladder and lift my foot up onto the bottom rung.

It's trickier to climb than I thought, and by the time we scramble onto the roof itself, I'm wondering if I should start going to the gym for arm exercises. Plus, the roof is pitched just enough that I have to stay on all fours, scooting out of Alex's way and then carefully turning myself around to sit. I feel wildly uncoordinated.

But then—then I see that he was right.

We're not that high up, but the view is perfect. Along the horizon you can see the glow of the city, then another little sparkle where our own suburban downtown area is still lit, the car dealership signs poking their heads into the night sky. But the fields below us are as black and vast as an ocean. Short stands of trees break the horizon line like ships, and the noise of the bugs could be the rhythmic splashing of waves. Or a giant heartbeat, filling the night air.

"Look up," Alex says, his voice barely a whisper.

We lie back at the same time, and there are the stars.

"They're so bright," I breathe.

"This is a good night," he says. "It's usually hazy out here, especially in the summer. When my dad first moved back he used to drag me up here every night, and half the time you couldn't see anything but the Dippers, if you were lucky."

He doesn't say it, but I know we're both thinking how lucky we are to be here right now. You can see the whole *universe*. The sky is inky black behind the sparkling stars, and though I don't know any of their names, I stare at them like I'll never get enough. Like we've been reunited after a long, long time apart.

"The Milky Way is over there," Alex says, pointing. I follow his hand and blink at the white smudge. I feel impossibly small and incredibly perfect, all at the same time.

I let out a long breath. "What you were saying the other day— about, you know, therapy and stuff? We can talk about that, if you want."

Alex doesn't say anything for a minute, and I bite my lip. What the hell happened to my ability to flirt, anyway? He's brought me out to look at the stars, and I'm talking about therapists?

I feel him sitting up next to me, but I don't move. I know I've ruined the moment but I can't face it yet.

"I'm sorry, I was totally just joking." My voice is small, whiny.

He stays silent, and I keep staring up, but finally I sit up, too. He's hunched over his knees. Doesn't look at me.

Damn it. Maybe he's flirting, maybe not—either way, I could just be a friend. Right? I could try.

"Listen—I know you probably get sick of talking about what you did, but you don't even know . . ." I hunch, too, trying to catch his eye. Suddenly it feels very important, to make him see what everyone else sees when they look at him. "Most of us go through every day and make things *worse*. Like, my entire life is a mess because I'm an idiot, you know? And you did this thing that was so big and brave and helped so many people, it's just—"

"Rosie, come on. Don't." He keeps his elbows propped on his knees, his face in his hands.

"I just think you should know, it's amazing, the way you help people—the way you helped your whole *school*—"

"It wasn't *like* that." His voice is angry but not scary—just insistent. "You know, I went to school with Brian for *years*. Everyone knew he was the fucked-up kid with the shitty house, right? His dad drank and his mom would disappear for weeks, and all of them had all these guns and stuff, like serious *weapons*, way beyond the normal stuff. Brian was mean to everyone, and we were mean to him right back."

I stare at him, thinking of all the news stories that showed Brian as a troubled kid with access to a lot of firearms. I never really thought about where he was before that day, though. I never imagined that he'd *known* Alex. And the other kids. The teachers.

"We played football together when we were kids, and he never had the right gear, you know? So we'd all laugh at him. And then he dropped off the team, and not one of us cared or asked why or even thought about what he might be doing. Everyone basically ignored him—it was just easier."

Alex throws his head back again, looking up at the stars, but not seeming to see anything but his memories.

"There was this post on the school message board, like, one of those anonymous ones?"

I nod. Midcity had a real-names-optional online board until last year, when all the bullying got so bad they took it down.

"And someone said they were going to shoot themselves in the head. And then someone else said they hoped it was Brian Hinckley."

I inhale sharply, and below us the crickets pause their song, like even they're shocked by this.

Alex nods. "It wasn't me," he says, as if there's any way I would've thought it was. "But I didn't say anything back, either. I saw it and I just . . . left it."

"You didn't know," I whisper.

He shrugs. "Maybe not. But my dad gets depressed, you know? And whatever, I'm not a *complete* asshole. Aren't you supposed to reach out? Isn't that what those goddamn assemblies are for? *Don't be a bystander*, et cetera?"

I sigh. Those assemblies make it sound so easy, and then everyone goes back to class and tries to survive. The kid who actually tries to talk about whatever antibullying message just got handed down? They're the biggest joke in school until the next assembly.

"You didn't know," I say. "You couldn't know he'd try to—to kill *other* people."

"See, there's the thing." Alex lets his arms fall straight out, so his elbows are still on his knees but his palms are open to the night sky. He stares at his hands for a long minute before he goes on. "Brian came to school with some guns. And I had to be there early for a team thing. And I happened to run into him."

I can feel my heart pounding in my chest. I can't imagine how scared I would be, to have been where Alex was that day. I'm terrified just hearing about it, so much that I kind of want to jump off the roof and run away through the fields.

But I wait, and Alex keeps talking.

"I heard these weird noises in the sophomore lounge. We had

these rooms—you guys only have the senior lounge, but at Sioux Crossing all the classes got them. I don't know why he was in there. It was always crowded in the mornings, but like I said, it was early. And the weather was really bad, snowing. Anyway. I was just walking down the hall and I heard this click, and it sounded like a gun being loaded."

Alex pushes a long breath through his lips. I've never heard him talk this much. I've never seen someone who seemed to *need* to talk this much.

"And I just went in. I just waltzed into that room, like some kind of goddamn Clint Eastwood shit. And there's Brian, all suited up, fucking Kevlar vest and the whole thing. Ammo, rifle. He looked like he was joining the army. He looked like he *was* the army. He's sitting in this stupid plastic chair, next to a bunch of beanbags, like a goddamn video game character."

"Jesus," I breathe.

"I know, right?" Alex looks over at me, and for a second I see something glimmer in his eyes. Regret that he's telling me all this, maybe. Or maybe just regret.

He shakes his head again, looking back out at the horizon.

"I wasn't scared, though. I got really *pissed*. I called him a loser and pathetic and all this shit—I don't even remember. I said only a real shithead had to hide behind his dad's guns. And I said he should just get it over with and kill himself and leave the rest of us alone, and everyone would be a lot better off."

The crickets don't go silent this time, but everything else does. My heart stops beating, and Alex doesn't move a muscle, and the world probably stops spinning, too.

And then he takes a gasping breath, like a sob, and lowers his head again. I don't need him to say anything else. Everyone knows how the story ends. Brian killed himself. Right there in that room, while Alex watched.

Everyone knows it was a miracle.

But until right now, I didn't even think about how it was a tragedy, too.

I'm already sitting close to him, but I slide across the scratchy roof tiles until my body is pressed to Alex's, and I put both arms around him. He falls into me, not crying but shaking, trembling. His head rests on my shoulder, and his arms are tucked between us, gripping his sides. Holding it all together as best as he can.

A long time goes by. We don't move—in fact, Alex gets calmer, more still, his chest rising and falling in a smoother and smoother rhythm. He sits up, but we keep our shoulders together, leaning equally so you can't tell who's holding who up.

I've never sat with someone like this, just being sad together. I've only even been to one funeral, for the little brother of a girl I didn't know very well in junior high. And I guess there's a lot of silence at church, but it's different. Everyone at church is thinking about their own thing—their own problems, their own prayers.

Alex and I, on the other hand, just sit in the awful truth of what happened to him that day in March, and we don't talk, and we don't move, and the stars above us are beautiful and useless but at least they're silent, too.

Finally it starts to feel like maybe we're actually getting close to curfew, so I take a deep breath and look for something to say.

All I come up with is "I'm really sorry that happened to you."

"Yeah," Alex says. "I'm sorry it happened at all."

"That, too. It sounds like he really did have a lot of problems."

Our shoulders move as Alex nods.

"Thank you for telling me everything," I add. "I didn't—I don't know, I guess I never would've thought it was that complicated."

He lets out a little half laugh, half snort. "Isn't everything?"

It's not the same at all, and I'm ashamed when the thought comes, but immediately I think of Cory and Gabe's party and Maddie's feelings. And my feelings.

"I guess so, yeah."

"Anyway." Alex leans away and stretches his arms over his head, then lets them fall back onto his knees. "I'm sorry I unloaded everything on you. It's kind of nice, though. I mean, you're easy to talk to."

No one has ever said that to me before, and I want to hold on to it, but I'm stuck on the part where he's sorry he told me.

"You can tell me anything," I say, not at all sure that's true. Not at all sure I could handle more than what he's just said—but oh my God, I want to. I want to be the person he opens up to, about everything.

He smiles, but it's sad, and he turns away again. "Thanks. But it's not really fair. I just haven't talked to anyone in so long. . . . My mom had me seeing a therapist, but that's not my dad's thing at all, and it just seemed easier to skip it. But I guess I needed to get it all, you know. Out."

I feel our moment slipping away. I'm still on the roof, still almost touching him, and the night is still heavy over our heads, but it's all coming loose—the one good thing I have right now, the one solid, exciting, interesting thing. I think about going home to my empty text messages and Maddie's smiling face next to Cory's smiling face on my social feeds, and I feel that yawning sense of nothingness creeping back in. It's like I'm hungry, *starving*, but not in my stomach. Not for anything as simple as food.

And even worse, I can hear the awful *voice* murmuring somewhere in the back of my mind. Mumbling about how I don't deserve this rooftop, this boy. I'm not someone he can trust. I'm a cheater and a liar and a . . . well.

Before the voice can call me names, I sit up straighter and turn to Alex.

"I really am here, if you ever need to talk. About anything," I say.

And then I lean into him. I reach across and put my hand on his opposite shoulder. I drop my head close so my hair falls like a curtain around us, and I kiss him.

17

THE KISS IS long enough for me to think, *I've never kissed a boy before*.

I mean. Obviously I've kissed boys. A lot of them. But I've never been the one to do it first—to move in first, to make it happen.

It's amazing.

It's nothing like Paul grabbing me at the game or like Cory last Friday—actually, it's nothing like Cory on any night, in any situation. It's nothing like I've ever had at all, and besides being so new and surprising, it's *good*.

Alex smells like a mix of pine and soap, and his lips are soft but not too soft, and when we touch he breathes in through his nose in this dramatic way that makes *me* breathe in and feel so full of air that I might just float away. Behind my eyes there's a pure, white light, not fireworks like you read about, but *light*. The inside of my head is lit up. And every other part of my body is warm and desperate to get closer to him. I'd crawl into his lap except we'd probably slide down the roof. But maybe it would work, maybe I could just wrap my arms—

He pulls away.

He pulls all the way away, puts his hands on the roof, and moves back toward the ladder.

"Rosie, I can't. I can't."

His feet are over the side and he turns, ready to climb down. My lips are still parted, one of my hands still hovering in the air, and he's halfway to the ground.

"Let me take you home. Please."

I don't know what else to do, so I nod. I follow him down the ladder and walk as fast as I can to the car, though he practically runs, so he's already starting the engine by the time I'm opening the door. The insect sounds are instantly muffled, and the lights from the dashboard feel too bright.

You idiot. The voice sounds happy to be back. *You can't do anything right, can you?*

I think I hear Alex open his mouth to say something, but I'm too afraid to look at him. I'm too embarrassed. So I stare out the window, careful to not catch my reflection in the glass. Careful not to think too clearly. The voice keeps reminding me of what an insecure loser I am, how I can't be happy unless I make out with every boy I see. But I stay very, very still, hoping it'll leave me alone.

Last Saturday morning comes rushing back—that need to hide under something, to get under all the leaves and just wait for the world to forget me—and I focus my thoughts on my bed at home. On the fact that everything I just did happened in the dark, so maybe Alex won't remember. Maybe I can hide under my covers and it'll all go away.

There's a thought hovering at the edge of my mind, just behind the voice, that I can't quite focus on. Something about how hiding won't help anything—

Of course it won't. Everyone knows what you are. Even the new guy! And he doesn't even want you.

Plus, it was dark when you let Cory kiss you, too.

I go back to thinking about my room and force everything else out as much as I can.

A lifetime later, Alex pulls up to my driveway. I start pulling on the door handle before he's even stopped completely, and finally he says something.

"Hey, hang on."

I wait, but I still can't face him.

There's a sigh and the sound of him running his hands over his face.

"Listen, I just—gahhh." His voice is low and frustrated, and I want to scream a thousand apologies, but then I might cry, so I don't say anything. "Listen," he says again, more calmly. "I should have told you. This is my fault, it's all—it's my fault, okay?"

I feel my head shaking, and I don't even know what I'm arguing with.

"Rosie, I have—I have a girlfriend. Back home. Selena."

My head slows down and I drop it, staring at my lap. *Of course.*

I want to ask why the hell he took me out to a roof in the middle of nowhere on a dark night, but all I can think about is Maddie's voice in the hall the other day. She was right about this, about everything.

About the way I just *am*, without even trying. Slutty. Desperate.

"I should have told you," Alex says again. "I'm sorry."

I realize that my chance to scrape up some of my dignity—if I have any left—is right now. So even though it kills me, I raise my head and turn back, looking right at Alex.

God, how did I ever not think he was handsome? He's beautiful.

"Don't apologize," I say. "I shouldn't have—assumed. I'm the one who should be sorry."

I know I should say that I *am* sorry, but the words just won't come out. I wait for them, and they never come.

Alex is shaking his head anyway, not accepting my taking responsibility, and I can feel us getting stuck in this awful loop that might not ever end if I don't just get out of the car. It's 12:52, so I point at the clock and say, "I should go."

"I'll talk to you—?" He wants to say *over the weekend* or *tomorrow* or something, I can tell, and he stops when he remembers we're not that kind of friends.

Thanks to me, we might not be any kind of friends at all anymore.

"Yeah," I say simply, and open my door. The dome light is blinding for a second, just long enough that tears spring to my eyes, but I'm safe now. I'm out of the car, hurrying up the driveway. I pull my keys out of my bag and wave a hand over my head without looking back. Alex's car is silent, waiting. He's watching to make sure I get inside safely.

I remember the last time Cory brought me home, one of the only times actually, and how he drove away while I was still standing on the sidewalk. I was laughing, watching him go. It was funny and fun and meaningless.

I twist the key in the lock and wonder how my life suddenly

became this thing that is the total, worst opposite of *fun and meaningless.*

And then the door is closed, and I slide down the wood, leaning over my knees, and let myself cry.

My eyes pop open so early on Saturday morning that I can't remember what day it is. I stare at the clock on my nightstand—7:33—and let the week come crashing back over me. I feel like I've been hit by a truck, but at least I'm not late for school.

Normally I'd try to go back to sleep, but for some reason I get up and take a shower. I take a long time with my hair, and I'm extra careful with my mascara. All the dumb rituals of getting ready are sort of soothing. It's like when you're sick and taking a shower fools you into thinking you feel better, at least for a little while.

Downstairs I get a yogurt out of the fridge and lean against the counter, eating, wondering what exactly I think I'm going to do today. I don't have a shift, and I'm not sure I want to see Ryan, even if he's free.

So when Ayla comes down and gives me a suspicious look, I actually smile back at her. She's dressed, too.

"What are you up to?" I ask, trying not to sound too eager.

"Um . . ." I can tell she's looking for something sarcastic to say, but finally she just opens the fridge, gets out the milk, and says, "Volunteering."

"Where?"

"St. John's. All the sorting I told you about—we're supposed to get started today."

I nod and throw my empty yogurt container in the recycling. "Is Mom taking you?"

"I think so—"

"Maybe she'll let me." I start to leave the kitchen, but Ayla's yelp stops me.

"You want to go? Why?" Her suspicious look is back.

"Am I not allowed to volunteer?"

Her eyes stay narrowed, and she doesn't say anything. Finally, though, she turns back to the fridge, and I run upstairs. Of course Ayla's right—I'm acting weird—but suddenly I have this urgent, choking need to get out of the house.

But I swear to God, I am not posting a volunteering photo online.

Ten minutes later we're driving to church, the windows down and the radio probably too loud for the early hour. Ayla doesn't object. And when she fiddles with my iPod until a Band of Horses song comes on, I don't say anything mean about her liking Dave's music. Sometimes I like Dave's music, too.

The St. John's parking lot is mostly empty, which gives me a little bit of hope. There's definitely no silver car, so that's good.

"Did you say the football team is coming?" I ask carefully, switching off the engine.

"Tomorrow, I think. If *any*one from Midcity shows up today, I don't think they'll get here this early." Ayla doesn't look back at me as she hurries to the side door that leads to the big church basement.

My resolve to be cheerful today is shaken when I see the

rows and rows of tables covered in plastic bags of stuff. Clothes, housewares. Along the far wall are boxes that seem to be full of nonperishable food.

"Holy—crap," I say, remembering just in time not to say something worse.

"I know, right?" Ayla says, surprising me. "It's going to take forever."

I look at my sister, and it's crazy, but I feel like I've never really seen her before. Her light brown hair is pulled back in a ponytail, and she has on just a hint of lip gloss but no other makeup. Her nose is just like Mom's, but her blue eyes have gotten darker over the years, and around her mouth you can see Dave's features. Not that she looks like a boy at all—more that she looks like someday she'll grow up to be one of those people who smiles all the time.

Not yet, though. Right now she's scowling with a determination that I don't think I've ever felt about anything. She's glaring at all the work sitting in front of us, and there's this intensity, this willingness to dive in and do the hard thing . . . and in that moment, I can really see that my sister is beautiful.

She turns and finds me staring at her.

"What? Are you going to bail?"

I raise my eyebrows. "Is that an option?"

She sighs. *"No."*

"I was just kidding. I'm totally gonna help. How long are we here for?" Now she's glaring at me, and I hold up my hands. "I'm just asking because we could have a *race*."

Racing was our favorite thing when Ayla was little. When we

had to do chores, I'd challenge her to see who could finish first. It was easy when she was really small. All I had to put up as a reward was, like, a single cookie, and I almost always won. As she got older, the stakes got higher—borrowing each other's toys, picking the movie on movie night, that kind of thing. I don't know when we stopped, exactly. I guess when we both got too busy with the rest of our lives to ever be home at the same time.

For a second, I'm not sure Ayla even remembers what I'm talking about, but then I realize she's just trying to decide if she's too cool for racing now. Like anyone is actually too cool for hardcore competition.

"I told Father Matt I'd stay until lunch," she says slowly.

"So, about three hours?"

She nods.

"I can get five whole tables done in that time," I say. When her eyebrows go up, I smirk.

"No, you can't . . ." she starts, but I've already run to a pile of garbage bags a few rows away. "Hey!" she yells after me. "I haven't told you what to do!"

"I'm beating you!" I singsong back.

That's all it takes—she goes running, tearing open a box. Father Matt walks in and sees us both frantically folding clothes, and without a word he goes over to the food boxes and starts methodically unloading them.

Time starts moving pretty quickly, and I'm sort of feeling like a genius, except that new people keep showing up, taking over the tables I want to work on next. I stay in the zone, though. I don't look up except when I get something gross—don't people know you can't donate old *underwear?*—and need to hold it up for Ayla to see. It doesn't embarrass her like I thought it would. Instead she just sticks out her tongue or yells, "Ew!" across the room.

It's fun. Actually, honestly *fun*.

But as lunch gets closer, the room is a lot more crowded, and I know I'm annoying the older women at the end of my row. They keep glancing over at me and shaking their heads, like they've never seen someone sort sweaters into piles on the floor, then attack them like a sweater-folding machine. I'm tempted to invite them to the race game. They definitely wouldn't get it.

Around ten thirty, Ayla yells, "Bathroom!" and we both sprint off, practically side-tackling each other to get to the one free stall first. I let Ayla win, but I'm not happy about it. While she pees, I look back at her latest stack of folded shirts and wonder if I could knock it over. . . .

But we play fair, and by eleven thirty I've made it through a solid four tables of old clothes, shoes, books, and toys. Ayla's done three tables, though she would've gotten closer to four if a few other volunteers hadn't accidentally started helping her. I've been so focused, I've barely had time to wonder if Alex is going to show up. And even less time to think how messed up it is that I want him to see me here, doing something worthwhile.

"I beat you!" I cry, holding my hands up in victory until I realize I'm sweating. I put my arms down quickly and do a little dance instead.

Everyone looks up from their work to see the jerk who's

celebrating a local tragedy, but Ayla just rolls her eyes.

"Barely," she argues.

"That was some impressive work by both of you," Father Matt says, striding over to us on what Mom always calls his long bean-pole legs. "I don't think we can match that enthusiasm, but I hope everyone will try."

Ayla flushes with the compliment. "We didn't mean to be disrespectful," she says.

"Not at all," he tells her. "I mean it—I wish everyone would find their own motivation. It's hard work, and getting out of your own sadness is a great way to lighten the load."

He smiles down at us, and I feel that familiar mixture of pride and creeping shame that I always get at church. There's just something about a priest—it's like a cop. Even when you know they're supposed to care about you, you're wondering if they can read your mind. If you've done something wrong that you just can't remember.

And I *have* done something wrong. Quite a few somethings.

"I'll be back after Mass tomorrow," Ayla says. She cuts her eyes to me, but I ignore her. I might not have the energy for any more of this. Maybe I'd see Alex at church, but I'd almost definitely see Maddie and Cory and everyone else, too.

Back in the car, I turn the stereo back on. Ayla doesn't touch the iPod. An old Jay Z song comes on, and I start to sing, but she's staring out the window at the sparkling blue sky. It's one of those days that pretends to be autumn—right before it either goes back to eighty degrees and humid or just skips ahead to winter and we get an ice storm.

"I don't feel like going home," I say as I pull out of our parking space. "Can we go get lunch?"

She throws her head back onto her seat and groans.

"What? Ayla, *what*? What did I do now?"

"I just don't understand why you're being all *nice*," she says. It's definitely an insult.

"Sorry," I snap. "I'll just take you home, Your Highness."

"Ugh, you know what I mean! You just left the game last night without even saying anything, and then this morning you're all—" She waves a hand at me, indicating the fact that I'm here in Mom's car with her, I guess.

I want to say something mean back, but suddenly I'm just too tired.

"I miss you. I miss hanging out. We never have time anymore, and that's—"

"You're the one who doesn't have time!" she cries.

"Yeah, that's what I was *saying*. I was going to say that I know you're busy, and obviously that's okay. I'm busy a lot, too."

"But now you're fighting with Maddie, so you want to hang out with your dumb little sister again?"

Her voice is quiet, almost gentle, but the words still slice through me.

"It's not like that," I whisper.

"Um, okay."

I turn the car away from our neighborhood, toward the strip mall with the Chipotle. I'm not really hungry anymore, but I still don't feel like going home.

"For the record," Ayla says, "I had a huge fight with Emily."

"You did? Wait, Emily *H.*?"

She nods. Emily Hambrecht has been her best friend for basically all eternity.

"What happened?"

"She likes all her jock friends better now," Ayla says.

"That probably won't last," I say. "Maddie has a bunch of jock friends, too, but we're still . . . you know." I can't quite finish the thought.

"So what happened, then? Why are you guys fighting?"

"A boy."

We're both quiet as I find another parking spot, right across from the restaurant. Ayla turns off the radio and looks at me.

"You're not supposed to fight over *boys*," she says matter-of-factly.

"It wasn't my idea," I tell her.

"But did you tell her you're sorry?"

I open my mouth but close it again without answering. I said I was sorry. But I still haven't had a chance to *explain*.

I try to picture it—calling, or texting, or emailing again. Or just walking up to her at school. What would I say?

I'm sorry I flirted with Cory but it was just a habit—no.

I'm sorry Cory didn't understand that I didn't want—crap, no, not that, either.

I'm sorry you couldn't even listen to my side of the story before you marched off in a righteous huff and drove home in the middle of a storm just to get away from me, even though I was the one trying to be a good friend by letting go of a guy who'd been mine first, and whether

I liked him wasn't even the point, it was supposed to be me and you, Maddie. We're the ones who count, right?

And by the way, your new boyfriend is kind of a dick.

Oh.

I stare out the windshield, a little stunned by my own thoughts.

"It's really complicated," I whisper. "You have no idea how messed up stuff gets in high school."

"Whatever. That's just what people say when they don't want to deal with the truth."

She gets out of the car and slams the door behind her, and I sit, watching her cross the parking lot. She's so tall. She has such great posture, such a confident walk. She's a good person.

And as much as I hate to admit it, she's probably right.

18

"Psst, Rosie. Come back here."

Joel's head disappears back behind the door to the office, and I look over at Steph.

"Do you think I'm fired?"

"No?" she says, then makes a face. "No way," she tries again.

I sigh. "I actually have a shift today. It's not like I'm going to come in for fun every weekend."

She looks nervously at the door with Joel behind it.

Whatever. If it really is illegal to work when you don't have a shift, I can find another job. If Mom and Dave would get me a car, I could work anywhere. Even around here there's a McDonald's and a gas station.

I sigh again, then jam the door open with my shoulder and walk back to my doom.

Except Joel isn't sitting in the tiny office—and he's not going through the boxes in storage or checking inventory in the big walk-in freezer. He's not back here at all, and for a second I'm completely confused, until I smell the smoke. The back exit door is propped open with a cinder block, and marijuana smoke is drifting through the gap.

Stepping over the block, I join Joel against the back wall, leaning against the painted bricks. He's staring at the Dumpster thoughtfully, his whole face seeming to concentrate on the small, hand-rolled joint in his hand.

"What's up?" I ask. I wonder if he's allowed to fire me while literally breaking the law at the same time. Maybe it doesn't matter, technically, but it would be annoying. Even if he does look kind of hot, with his shaggy hair falling over his eyes and his big tattoo of a tree poking out from the cuff of his store-manager shirt.

"You smoke?" he asks, squinting at me and holding out the weed.

I open my mouth and point back at the door at the same time, but words don't come out. If he can read unofficial sign language, he can probably tell I'm trying to say, *I think I'm supposed to be working right now? So . . . no?*

His face breaks into a slow, lazy grin. "Makes the day go faster," he says with a shrug. "Or slower, depending. Easier, definitely."

I'm not quite following, but I shift on the wall so I'm leaning on my right side, facing him. He's always flirting with me, at least whenever he's actually here, but I've never really been alone with Joel. Maybe this is what I need—maybe my problem is all those high school boys, with their high school girlfriends and their high school issues. Maybe a college guy, a guy with a job and a car, would be better for me. At least it wouldn't ruin my reputation at school.

Joel rolls to the side, too, so now our chests are only a few inches apart. Holding the joint in two fingers, he traces the rest of his right hand along my arm. Shivers trickle along the line he draws, but I keep my face perfectly still.

"Girls didn't look like you when I was in high school," he says. It sounds like something from a movie, but not necessarily in a bad way. "Hell"—he takes another puff, holds it, and lets it out in a smooth stream over my head —"they don't look like you in college, either."

He taps the tip of the cigarette against the brick between us. We both watch as it slowly loses air and goes out, and then he tucks it behind one ear. And then he moves in.

First he holds my jaw, moving his hand back under my ear to the base of my skull, as his face gets closer and his lips meet mine. He's still braced against the wall, but then we're turning, and I'm pinned back against the cool bricks. A panicky feeling pinches the back of my throat, but I swallow it down. This is easier, like he said. *Makes the day go faster.* Slower and faster at the same time.

But then his tongue snakes between my teeth, and I'm not ready for it and I jump a little. He doesn't seem to notice. He tastes kind of like dirt, or gross beer, but there's not much time to think about that before he juts his hips forward and pushes more of me against the wall. His other hand finds the hem of my shirt and starts untucking it.

My hands are trapped behind me, pressed between my lower back and the wall. I want to push Joel's hands away from my shirt. I want to stop doing this before Steph finds us out here.

And that's when it hits me, how embarrassing this feels. I feel *gross*. Joel's tongue tastes bad, and his hands have this dead weight to them. He can't seem to get under my shirt, even, and I guess he must be really stoned but he's *heavy*, too.

I try pushing away from the wall, but he's pushing back, and suddenly I can't breathe. Every part of my body starts moving at once—my head twists to the side, my hands shove against his arms and his chest, my knees start to buckle. My feet scrape on the rough concrete underneath us, and I think I might accidentally scream if he doesn't get off me *right now right now right—*

"Whoooa, what the fuuuck?" Joel stumbles back, blinking like he just woke up.

I'm still moving, convulsing like I have a spider in my shirt. I shake out my arms and skitter closer to the door, my head swinging back and forth the whole time, *no no no no no.*

"Jeez, girl, calm down. You epileptic or something?"

I let out a shuddering breath, and for a second I'm afraid it's happening again—I'm going to crumple to the ground and start sobbing. Steph will have to sit with me again, and I'll have to feel all those feelings again, and I *can't. Joel is just a bad kisser,* I tell myself. *There's no need to fucking lose it.*

"Sorry," I gasp. He's just staring at me. He doesn't seem mad or annoyed or anything. Just dumbly staring. "Sorry," I repeat, and I take off.

I'm halfway home before I realize that I didn't finish the last half hour of my shift, and I didn't clock out, and whatever goodwill I'd built up with Steph is probably ruined now that I've bailed on her for the second week in a row.

But at least if they fire me now, I won't really care.

"Don't forget to buy your tickets to the Homecoming Dance! All the proceeds this year will go to tornado relief. And don't forget to vote! Ballots for the Senior and Junior Courts are with your home-room teachers right now!"

Maddie's cheerful voice cuts out briefly, and there's a sharp crackle of static through the PA system. Then, suddenly, she's back.

"And go Lions!"

Everyone in Mr. Richnow's room laughs a little, except me. I don't even recognize Maddie's voice anymore. She sounds manic, hyper, just like Olivia—

Or she just sounds happy, now that she doesn't have to deal with you.

I glance over at Alex's chair for the fifth time, wondering why he's not in it. Mr. Richnow drops a ballot on my desk, and when I turn back around, I find Finn Kramper staring at me.

"What?" I say, before I have a chance to think better of talking to him. Suddenly I remember how Maddie used to call him Finn Creeper, and I want to laugh. Or cry.

"You going to the dance?" he asks. He almost sounds normal, but I'm not fooled.

"Probably not." As soon as I say it, I realize with a sick feeling that it's probably true.

Finn purses his lips and studies me. I dip my head back down, letting my hair fall around my eyes, and study the empty paper in front of me. Three spaces for boys, three for girls. Kings, princes. Queens, princesses. What a bunch of bullshit.

All around me, people are whispering and giggling. Mr. Rich-now, as usual, doesn't seem to care. I wish he would at least tell Olivia to stop talking—it's like her voice is inside my head.

Ryan Tucker, I write on the first space under *King*. I pause for a long minute, then add *Gabe Richmond*. At least Gabe is nice to me. He's the only one of Cory's friends who still says hi to me in the halls like nothing happened.

And *Alex Goode*.

Under *Queen* I write fast: *Madelyn Costello*.

Then *Stephanie Barnes*.

And then, because what the hell, I write *Rosie Fuller* in the last space for Queen.

Because apparently I live in a fantasy world now.

By lunchtime I still haven't seen Alex anywhere—not at our lockers, not in English. I'm still disappointed when he doesn't show up in the theater, though. This was going to be my chance to act normal. Or to apologize. Or to apologize and *then* act normal, so he'd know I'm not jealous of his girlfriend. I'm not a crazy fangirl who'll swipe through every single photo he's ever put online, then all the way through again. Obviously I'm not that girl at *all*.

"Where is he?" Ryan snaps at me.

"How should I know?" I don't even try to pretend I don't know who *he* is. I'm dying to talk to someone about where Alex might be today.

"Well, *I* don't know! Is he sick?"

I just stare at Ryan for a minute. "Why are you mad at *me* about this?"

He throws up his hands. "Steph can't start until next week and the stupid crew doesn't get assigned until auditions! I'm not running some shitty community theater, here—we need *sets*! And don't even get me started on the *costumes*!"

"Hey, okay." I step closer to Ryan, trying to pat him on the shoulder. But my hands are full of my lunch—a Diet Dr Pepper and a pack of Bugles—and instead of comforting him I sort of thwack him with the chips.

"Thanks," he says, taking the bag. I don't bother correcting his mistake. I don't feel like getting yelled at anymore.

"We finished that whole platform thing on Friday," I remind him. "And I can probably make the table. The small one, I mean."

We're standing backstage, surrounded by boxes and paint cans and big slabs of plywood. It's a huge mess, no doubt about it. I don't know how a "shitty community theater" would look six weeks before a show, but this definitely isn't great.

"We can make it until next week."

Ryan is throwing Bugles into his mouth one at a time, snapping down on them so loudly the sound echoes around us. "This is no way to operate," he says.

"Yeah. Sorry," I say. I open the Dr Pepper bottle and take a drink.

"You know something about Alex that you're not telling me." Ryan keeps his eyes fixed on me as he pours the Bugles crumbs into his mouth.

I'm not sure what to do with my face. Since Saturday morning,

I've been pretending my night with Alex just didn't happen. I hate that this means I can't think about how magical it was, sitting on that roof with him. Or how close I felt to him, how special.

But if I'm going to forget what a sad, needy loser I acted like at the end of the night—when I was trying so damn hard to be the exact opposite—I have to ignore all the good stuff, too.

In fact, if I could just erase everything about the last two weekends from my memory, that would be ideal.

I shake my head at Ryan. "He's probably sick."

"Huh." Ryan doesn't look like he believes me, but he crumples up the chip bag, throws it out, and turns to me with his all-business face back on. "Well, he's a lot better than you with the power tools. So let's paint, yeah? Mr. Klonsky got us some backdrops, so we can start on those."

I glance down at my sweater and jeans. I didn't feel like dressing up today, so I should actually be fine if I splatter paint on myself. I haven't felt like dressing nicely in a while, actually. I think Ayla's basically cleaned out my closet by now, and I haven't even noticed. Maybe if I could get my own boyfriend, instead of accidentally kissing everyone else's, I'd feel like wearing something cute.

Yeah, look how well it worked out with Joel. You started shaking like a big baby.

"You'll be fine," Ryan says, misinterpreting my wardrobe check.

On my way to my next class, my hair is so full of fumes I think I might be a little bit high. Everything feels lighter, like my thoughts were too heavy before and now they're lifted off my shoulders. Maybe I should try to use industrial painting supplies every lunch hour, just to take the edge off.

I'm so hazy, I don't hear Cory's voice until he's right behind me.

"I'm telling you, we're fine without Goode," he's saying. Shouting, practically.

"I don't know, man, he's been your go-to for—"

"Shut it, Richmond," Cory snaps. "If Alex wants to skip town, fuck it."

I've stopped walking, confused and stunned. What does he mean, Alex skipped town?

Then I feel Cory's hand. On my butt.

He grabs me, hard, and squeezes. It hurts, and it knocks me off balance. When he lets go—as fast as he grabbed on—I've spun halfway to the lockers on the right side of the hall, dizzy and breathless.

Cory keeps walking with his entourage of football guys and doesn't look back. The only face I see, as I stare stupidly at the backs of all the tall, wide boys taking up the entire hallway, is Gabe Richmond's. He looks over his shoulder with something in his eyes—pity? Apology?

I can't tell. There's a free space along the wall next to me, and I fall against it, my shoulder connecting with the cement blocks hard enough to bruise. I stay there too long, long enough to watch Maddie walk by with Annabelle. She's not trying to ignore me, she's just genuinely laughing and talking and doesn't see me.

I have to move, but Cory's in my next class. That's why we were walking in the same direction—we're going to the same room. The same small, closed, cramped room.

Suddenly all my limbs move at once.

I push away from the wall and fight through the sudden crush of underclassmen to the back door. Mom didn't need her car today, so it's in the parking lot—maybe I can just sit in it for a minute. Just to be alone for a little while. Just to push down this rush of vomit trying to get out of my throat and the tears trying to drown my eyes. Just somewhere I can breathe for a goddamned second.

No one sees me leaving, or no one cares. I throw my backpack onto the passenger seat and collapse behind the wheel, feeling exhausted and wired at the same time. I still have paint on my hands. I still smell like a new house.

I still haven't done anything right, not even apologized to any of the freaking dozens of people I owe apologies to.

And I know, now that I'm here, that I'm not just sitting in Mom's car. I'm leaving.

I've never skipped school by myself before, but it just feels like nothing. The car slides out of the parking lot as easily as it would at two forty-five. The wheel practically turns itself around the familiar corners all the way to our house.

But at the end of our street, I stop at the curb. I don't really want to go home—and I've run out of other places to go.

Unless . . .

Getting out my phone, I scroll through my contacts until I find the one I'm looking for.

Did you go somewhere?

I wait. And wait.

Five eternal minutes later, the phone buzzes.

Had to come back to my mom's for a while. Sry.

I stare at the words, not touching the keys. The screen goes half dark, then shuts off, and I throw the phone onto the seat next to my bag and shift the car back into drive.

And point the car toward Iowa.

19

THE LAST TIME I crossed the Missouri River was for one of Paul Maziarz's away games. It was just in Council Bluffs, basically two minutes from Omaha. And I guess there's that weird stretch of road on the way to the airport, where you're technically in Iowa and then back in Nebraska again. Dave always laughs about that. He was born in Iowa so he likes to make these loud *I'm home!* jokes every time we go somewhere or pick someone up. I guess I forgot about that when we picked up Maddie at the end of the summer.

God, I wish I could go back and do that all over again. Or go back even further, and never hook up with Cory to begin with. Maybe not hook up with half the guys I have . . . except, I don't know. They were fun. I was just having fun.

There's a lot of traffic driving toward downtown, but I don't know any other routes east, and now that I'm moving I don't want to stop to get my phone out. Plus, it's easier to pretend I'm just going shopping or something. Or for a drive. I turn on the radio and flip around for a while. I roll down my window, but the air outside has turned colder, so I roll it back up. Dark clouds are starting to gather in my rearview mirror, too. Crap. I hate driving in the rain.

In the passenger seat my phone buzzes a few times, new texts making it scoot around on the upholstery. I ignore it, telling myself I'm just being a good driver by not texting. And actually, Mom is always threatening to take away my license if she ever catches me texting and driving. How she'd catch me, I don't know, but it's okay because it freaks me out, too.

Finally the main road turns into an off-ramp, then a bridge, and then with absolutely zero fanfare, I'm in another state. I pass the big welcome sign, and a good Katy Perry song comes on the radio, so I sing loudly, but inside my heart is thudding around in my chest, beating against my lungs and it feels like my stomach, too. I don't want to think about how this is probably a terrible idea . . . but, I mean. It probably is.

I keep singing, song after song, and watch the boring road fly away under my wheels. There's nothing to see out the windows and the clouds are getting heavier, but for a long time I manage to not think about anything but the cars around me and the white stripes ticking by between the lanes of traffic. Just hurtling through space. Like you do.

I didn't tell Alex I was coming. I don't even have his address, but I know it's Des Moines, so basically I just have to take the highway east. For a couple of hours. And then . . .

And then he'll really *know what a whack job you are. Good work.*

No, then I'll apologize. Make something right. Just one thing.

My argument with the voice in my head is immediately,

mercifully drowned out by a deafening crack of thunder that sounds like it's going to split the roof of my car in half. An instant later, everyone on the highway has slammed on their brakes as a freaking monsoon's worth of water comes hammering down on top of us.

I've been driving for an hour and a half already, and I have no idea where I am. Especially now that I can't even see any signs or move faster than fifteen miles per hour. I lean over the steering wheel, trying to see through the wall of water, and ease forward whenever the giant SUV ahead of me does. We all creep along, and I'm sure I'm not the only one who lets out a little half sob of relief when an exit sign appears on the right. I join another line of cars pulling over, but I don't park along the ramp like a bunch of them are doing. I keep going until there's a turn, then a gas station, and I ease into the parking lot.

The rain is even louder with the car stopped, and for a second I wonder if it's going to start hailing again, like last weekend. Or something worse.

My hands are shaking, but I manage to open my texts, which all seem to be from Mom and Ryan. I'm too scared to read what either of them wants right now—too scared and too far away and too determined to see this stupid trip to the end. Especially since I'm a lot closer to Des Moines than I am to home, thanks to my dumb ideas.

I have to try three times before I successfully click through and dial Alex's number, and even then I'm not sure if I'll be able to hear him. If he even picks up. It rings once, twice, three times, four times—

"Rosie?"

"H-he-ey!" I'm stuttering and yelling at the same time. "I'm sort of in Iowa?"

"What? I can't hear you at all, is everything okay?"

I take a deep breath and put it all behind my sad little voice to shout, "I'm in Iowa! I need your address!"

There's a silence, and I can practically *see* all the confused thoughts going through Alex's head right now. But after a few seconds he yells back, "I'll text you!"

I realize I'm nodding and almost laugh at myself. "Thanks!" I yell and then he's gone. The phone vibrates in my hand a moment later, and as much as it scares me to get back on the road, the map says I'm only twenty minutes away, even with the current traffic. I turn the radio back up and take a few big inhales.

I could turn back around. It's not too late.

I keep going.

The rain is slightly less downpourish when I pull back onto the highway. I can see more than one set of taillights ahead of me, and I can drive closer to forty miles per hour now. The annoying GPS voice alerts me to the exit I want about six times, and I yell back at her every time, and eventually I almost feel like a normal person again.

Alex's neighborhood—or his mom's neighborhood, I guess—is kind of old and run-down. The houses are all really small, a few of them bordered off by ugly chain-link fences and the rest just sitting on plots of weedy, toy-strewn lawns.

The GPS robotically nags me to turn right onto Fort Road, and as soon as I do, the rain stops completely. Everything goes weirdly quiet for a second, until the phone announces, "Your destination is on the right."

There's a cute, tiny, yellow house on the right. Lights glow through the windows, and an old swing hangs from a tree in the front yard. The number 112 runs diagonally on the narrow stretch of exterior wall next to the front door, and there's just enough space in the driveway to pull in.

Too late I realize I haven't checked my makeup all afternoon, or brushed my hair, or bothered to scrape the paint splatters off my jeans. *You probably look exactly like the psychopath that you are*, the voice says gleefully.

I start to check my hair in the rearview mirror, when the front door of the house opens and Alex steps onto the small top step of the concrete stairs. The car fills with silence, and everything feels lighter, weightless, as I look at him.

He's in jeans and a gray, long-sleeved T-shirt. His hair is messy, like he just woke up, and he's standing barefoot on the rain-soaked stair. He watches me with so much . . . *concern*. My heart does a flop, and my hands are trembling even harder than before as I fumble to get my phone and my purse and open the car door.

"Hey," he calls as I step out.

"Hi. Sorry to just . . . drop by."

He smiles. "It's nice to see you."

I shut the door and carefully, methodically tuck my keys into my bag, which gives me a second where my hair falls around my face and hides my blush.

I'm doing a selfish thing right now, I know it. I told myself I came here to apologize, but I really just want to see him, want to change his mind about Friday night, and it's crazy and also very, very *selfish*. But it feels amazing. It feels better than anything I've done in a long, long time.

"You hungry?" Alex calls.

I circle around the car and climb the steps. He backs into the house, holding the door open for me, and as I step inside I smell lavender soap and something smoky and the piney scent that I know is Alex himself.

"I'm starving," I say, and he closes the door behind us.

"Okay, Mom. I know. . . . Yeah, I saw that. I'll tell her. . . . See you soon. . . . You too. Bye."

Alex hangs up the phone and rolls his eyes at me. "My mom's worried about the storm. She made me promise to keep you here until she gets home from work, and you have to call your parents."

I glance back over my shoulder at the front windows. We've been sitting at the kitchen table eating chips for a few minutes, and the rain looks like it's stopped for good.

"If the storm was over I could just go . . ." I don't want to leave, but I'm not sure I'm ready to meet Alex's mom, either.

He shakes his head. "There's another thunderstorm behind this one, I guess. Not another tornado or anything, but pretty bad. You might—" He stops, clearing his throat. "You might need to stay here tonight."

I laugh. "I can't do that. My mom's already going to kill me!" I pick up my phone, look at it, and set it back down. I can call her in a minute. "So are you, like, sick? Is that why you weren't—I mean, why you're here? And not at school?"

"No," he says, sitting down across from me and staring at his can of Coke without opening it. "I came out for the weekend, and I just—wasn't ready to come back."

"Oh," I say. I stare at my Coke, too.

"Weren't you . . ." He looks at the clock hanging over the kitchen sink and then at me. "When did you leave?"

"I sort of skipped out of school early," I admit. "It wasn't the best day."

"It's crazy you're here."

"I know—I don't know why I came, I . . ." I stop myself, bracing my hands against the table. "Actually, no. I felt like I owed you an apology for what happened." I sneak a look up at him and try not to laugh at his bewildered expression. It's not that it's funny, he just looks so *surprised*. "I didn't mean to make you talk about things, and then try to turn it into something it wasn't. I don't know, I just . . . I'd like to be friends."

He blinks at me a few times, then shakes his head. "We're definitely friends, Rosie," he tells me. "I mean. Do you know the last time someone came to my *house*?"

I shake my head lamely. My skin prickles with electricity. It's the storm, I think, changing the air. Already we can hear rain starting to tap against the roof again.

"Even—even Selena," he says softly, like he doesn't want to bring up his girlfriend's name. "After everything with Brian, no one knew what to say. No one wanted to be around me."

I must look baffled—I definitely feel confused by that—because he nods.

"I know, I'm this big hero, right? But there's this *force field* around me. No one can get in, and I can't get out. I forgot what it felt like to just talk to someone until . . . "

Until me, I think.

And Alex says, "Until you."

My hands soften, slide off the table into my lap.

"I wanted to see you," I say very softly.

"I wanted to see you, too. I'm sorry about Friday."

I shake my head. "I'm the one who's apologizing for that." I smile shyly at the unfinished bowl of chips. Somehow this is a completely different place than I was just sitting a minute ago.

"I came back here to . . . do a lot of things, actually. But I also wanted to break up with Selena. In person," he says. "We're still friends, you know? But I met you and I realized it just wasn't fair. I've changed too much. Everything's changed too much."

My whole body is frozen so I can listen as closely as possible. My heart doesn't beat, my eyes don't blink, my hair doesn't grow.

"I know we just met, basically," he goes on, and a warmth starts crawling up my spine. "But I mean. I hope this makes us . . . after I talk to her, you know, maybe you and I could . . ."

My head nods for me, without even checking in with my brain first.

"Okay." Alex sighs, leaning back in his chair like he's relieved. "Okay."

I'm not sure what to say back. I twist the strap of my purse between my fingers, staring down at the blue and gold polish on my nails. For Lion Pride, of all things. I'm so happy, but suddenly I feel terrified, too. What have I done? What have I convinced Alex to do? Am I actually ready to be who he wants me to be? I'm not even sure who that is, exactly.

He clears his throat. "And just so you know, I wanted to kiss you. I should've been more honest about the situation."

I lift my face and find him staring at me, his face on the verge of a smile. Before I can open my mouth to ask all the rest of the questions I have, there's the sound of a car outside.

"Oh, shit, my mom's home," he says, reaching over and grabbing the bowl. "She hates when I snack too close to dinner, sorry." He pauses and grins at me. "That is definitely the most embarrassing thing I've ever told a girl."

And then he's flying around the kitchen, putting the chips away and pulling out stuff that looks like it's for dinner. I stand up again, awkwardly, and turn toward the door.

Alex's mom comes in like her own little tornado, all flushed cheeks and wild, curly hair, shaking an umbrella behind her.

"Hey, there!" she calls to us, still propping the door open with her hip and half leaning outside. Finally she throws the umbrella down on the small entryway mat and laughs. "You must be Rosie!"

"Hi," I say, taking a step closer to her. I'm terrible at meeting parents, especially mothers, and I feel almost sick as I reach out a hand for her to shake. Moms can always see right through me. Or they don't care what I'm doing or who I am, and they just hate me on sight. One night last year I was hanging out at Paul's house and his mom wandered in from the next room, clearly drunk, and swung her empty wineglass my way. "You are *too damn pretty*," she'd slurred. "I was pretty like you. Believe it or not." She said the last part like it was a curse or something. And then she left.

But Mrs. Goode is definitely sober and definitely just smiling at me. Just truly, kindly smiling. And when she sees my hand she doesn't shake it—she grabs it and pulls me in, wrapping her damp arms around me.

"You're so tall!" she exclaims, still hugging me. "Alex, you didn't tell me how tall she was!"

"Mom," he says warningly.

She lets me go and holds my shoulders, looking up so she can study my face. I feel like she's trying to memorize my features, maybe so she can pick me out of a lineup later on.

"And beautiful," she says thoughtfully. "Really beautiful."

"Mo-om."

"Alex, honey, I think this girl knows she's beautiful. Don't you?" she asks me.

I make a face and she laughs again.

"Yeah, you know. She knows, honey!"

"You're only supposed to embarrass *me* to death," he tells her, coming out of the kitchen to kiss her cheek. It's such an easy, loving thing to do that it nearly takes my breath away. Effortless.

"Sorry about the house," Mrs. Goode says, taking off the cardigan she's wearing and throwing it on a chair next to the TV.

"It's really nice," I say.

"Yeah, it's really not," she says matter-of-factly. "But it's in the right school district, if you can believe. Fat lot of good *that* did us."

Alex is still hovering nearby, and now he turns pointedly to look at me. "Tacos okay?" he asks. "That's what we have on Mondays."

"Taco Mondays!" his mom yells. "It's actually *margarita* Mondays." She winks at Alex and hurries toward the fridge.

"I'm sorry," Alex says to me in a low voice. "She's really . . . high-energy."

"And she can hear you!" Mrs. Goode shouts. "Plus, she has a name!"

"Right, sorry." He widens his eyes for a second, like he's gathering his strength and I should, too. "Rosie Fuller, please meet my mother, Jillian Nolan."

"Nice to meet you!" she calls from the kitchen, where she's holding up a bottle of margarita mix.

I do a quick mental fix of her name and smile. "Nice to meet you, too, Mrs. Nolan."

"You should just call her—" Alex starts, but his mom is already yelling, "Jill!" over her shoulder as she pours herself a drink.

"Seriously," Alex whispers. "I'm so sorry."

"Are you kidding?" I ask him. "This is amazing."

And it is. Even when Jill forces me to call home and get yelled at by my mom—but only for a minute, because then Jill grabs the phone from me and has a loud, laughing conversation with, it sounds like, my entire family. Then she makes me and Alex virgin margaritas, and then we all sit down and watch two reruns of *SVU* together. Which is embarrassing, what with all the prostitutes who get killed, but somehow Jill manages to make jokes through-out the whole show—jokes that are actually hilarious—and then, when an episode of *Seinfeld* starts, she declares, "Not funny!" and switches off the TV. Before I know what's happening, I'm helping her unfold the couch we were all just sitting on and catching the opposite end of a fitted sheet she's helping me wrap around it.

Alex disappears down the hall, I guess to the bathroom, and Jill hands me a pillow with a pillowcase, taking the other one to fix up herself.

"I'm really glad I got to meet you, Rosie. Alex has talked about you a lot."

"He has?"

"I can see why," she says. At first I think she's going to talk about my looks again, but then she shakes out the pillow, throws it on the sofa bed, and smiles. "You seem like a really kind person. Maybe a little, you know, reckless? With the driving?"

I blush, looking down at the pillowcase I'm still wrestling with. She holds out her hands, and I give it over.

"But he needed someone to show him that they cared. You got here just in time, kid, and I'm grateful." She throws the second pillow down and holds up one finger, asking me to wait for something.

I stand next to the bed, feeling both too far from home and incredibly warm inside. A few seconds later, Alex's mom hurries back in, carrying a bundle that turns out to be pajamas and an extra toothbrush. She brings them all the way to my side of the couch so she can press them into my hands and grab my fingers, squeezing a little.

From the hall, Alex gives me a little wave and disappears back to his room, and his mom kisses me on the cheek and follows. And just like that, I'm sleeping in a strange room again, trapped by a storm. But it doesn't feel like that night at Gabe's at all.

I crawl under the thin blanket and listen to the rain. It sounds like a million tiny feet, dancing.

20

I WAKE UP in the darkness.

Outside there's a dog barking, and it sounds like a big dog, and then I hear a person shout and throw a bottle. It shatters. The dog is quiet for a minute. I don't even have time to worry that someone maybe threw a glass bottle at a dog before the barking starts again, filling the night air and coming through the walls of Alex's house like they're made of paper.

That's not what woke me up, though. I fell asleep happy, but it didn't last.

The mean voice, at least, is quiet. But I can't stop worrying about getting home tomorrow and what Mom's going to do. I know what she's *not* going to do—she's *not* going to let me borrow the car again for approximately twelve thousand years.

And Cory. Why did he grab me like that? He used to be nice. I swear, he was . . . maybe not nice, actually. Maybe he was always grabby.

I should have told Ryan I was leaving. Except I can't tell what kind of friends we even are anymore. He's kind of the only person I've got, but then I see him hanging out with Maddie, laughing, and I don't know how to feel. Why hasn't he told me that he has some secret hookup on the football team? Does Maddie already know?

Maddie. I don't understand how she just disappeared from my life, just walked right out. Because of Cory Callahan, of all people.

But it can't be because of Cory. It's because of me. It's because I've always been a crappy friend, and she finally figured it out. I wasn't there for her before she went to Spain, and then she came back and she was beautiful and I was jealous and I couldn't let go of a guy, even though I thought I could.

That has to be it. If she doesn't want to be friends anymore, it's because *I* messed up.

I roll my head to the side and stare at the green light of the clock on the cable box. After midnight already. I can't believe I came all the way here by myself. I can't believe Alex wants to be with me. A few weeks ago, I couldn't understand why he wouldn't flirt or stare or try to impress me like guys usually do.

But then he laughed at my jokes. And talked to me. And now I think maybe I get it, what it's like to want to be with someone because you know them. Because they know you.

And I'm here.

Silently, slowly, I move the blanket back and swing my feet out onto the carpet. The couch hinges squeal and I stop, listening— but the house is still quiet, the dog is still barking. I stand up and make my way slowly toward the short hallway. I'm just going to splash some more water on my face in the bathroom, but when I get closer I see that there's a light on under one of the bedroom doors. I didn't see Alex's room earlier, but the door has a huge poster with a dragon on it. It looks old and loved and it makes me grin.

My hand hesitates midair for a second and then, *knock*.

I'm trying so hard to be quiet that I'm not sure if he heard me, so then I'm scratching my nails lightly on the dragon's face, and when the door opens I gasp kind of loudly.

Alex doesn't look very surprised to see me, but his whole face is pantomiming *shhh*.

"Sorry!" I mouth.

He steps back and I step through as fast as I can, waiting for him to gently close the door before I let myself breathe again.

"Sorry," I say again, audibly this time. "I saw your light."

"No problem."

"But I mean, I don't want to keep you up—"

He waves a hand at me, turning to sit down at his desk. "I don't sleep."

"Really?" I say, looking around his room. There's art everywhere, all kinds of it—posters from museums and postcards of real places and paintings, plus a whole wall of what looks like original drawings. "Always, or just since—you know . . ."

"Always," he says, unoffended as usual by my clumsy insistence on bringing up his traumatic past. "My parents got me tested when I was a kid. They thought I had, like, adenoid problems or something. But no one could figure it out. So I just learned how to keep busy."

He swivels back and forth in his chair, watching as I slowly pick my way around the room. I'm staring at the walls, at the floor. There aren't any bookshelves, but there must be two hundred books, piled along the baseboards in towering stacks.

"It's a total fire hazard in here," I say, picking up a paperback by someone named Connie Willis. "But I guess if you're not asleep, you'll probably be okay."

"Yeah, that's the theory."

Finally I turn to look at him. He's wearing a T-shirt and sweatpants, and I'm just in an old shirt and pajama pants of his mom's. We're not at all naked—not even touching—and yet I feel more naked with him than I've ever felt with anyone else.

"Rosie?"

"Yeah?"

"Did you really come all the way here to say sorry?"

"Yeah?"

He nods, and right at that moment we hear a distant roll of thunder. More of the storm moving in. "I just thought—I've done my share of runinng away from stuff. So I thought maybe that's what you were doing."

The only other place to sit in the room is on his bed, so I try not to think about it too much as I perch on a pile of blankets, facing Alex.

"Maybe that was part of it," I finally say.

He nods as if that makes sense, which is nice of him. "Did something happen?"

I sort of huff and laugh at the same time, but I'm not smiling.

"It's been kind of a bad couple of weeks," I admit. "Except for you. So I guess I just wanted, I don't know. I wanted the thing that wasn't bad?"

He raises one eyebrow as if he's trying not to grin. "I'm flattered."

I can't help smiling, rolling my eyes at him.

"I'm going to be so embarrassed about this tomorrow," I tell him. "Your mom was so nice, and I can't believe you guys let me stay. . . ." I feel my smile fading. "You have so many other things going on. I have these stupid problems that are just . . ." *Pathetic. Pointless. Small and insignificant,* the voice chants helpfully. "I should just get over it."

He lifts up his chin in a half nod and stares out the window, off to my left, like he's remembering something. Outside the rain starts, hitting the roof like fingers tapping impatiently on a table. I can't hear the barking dog anymore, and I hope someone brought him inside.

"You know . . ." Alex trails off, still watching the window. It's too dark to see outside, and for a second I wonder if I'm reflected in the glass. I shift uncomfortably, wishing I could see what he's seeing.

"You know," he says again. "No one tells me anything. Like you said, I have all this—all these *other things*. My mom doesn't talk about work, my friends never post funny shit on my Facebook wall. Not that I ever go on Facebook anymore."

He goes quiet again, and I sit very still, watching him. Finally I clear my throat.

"That sucks."

He smiles and his eyes meet mine. "I like that you come right out and talk about stuff, you know? You just *ask*."

The back of my neck burns with a confusing mixture of pride and humiliation. All those stupid things I've said to him come rushing back.

He shakes his head. "But seriously, we can't be friends or . . . whatever, if we only talk about me and the terrible shit that happened to me last year."

It's not funny at all, but I find myself sort of smiling at him. Then he leans forward, his forearms on his knees, and looks me right in the eye.

"Tell me something about you, Rosie. Tell me whatever you want—it doesn't have to be whatever made you drive to the middle of nowhere, Iowa. Just tell me something that doesn't have anything to do with me."

A burst of thunder cracks right over our heads, making me jump. Alex sort of shivers, but he keeps looking at me, and I wonder how this happened. How the guy who was always so quiet became the only person I want to talk to.

"You know Maddie Costello, right?"

He nods.

"And you know Cory, obviously."

Alex's mouth twitches very slightly, like he's not sure he wants to know Cory. But maybe I'm imagining it. Either way, he nods again.

"I was hanging out with Cory a lot over the summer. And Maddie was at this soccer camp in Spain—I mean, she was learning Spanish, too, so it was a whole thing."

I don't say anything for a second, and Alex goes, "That sounds cool."

"Yeah. Yeah, I guess it was. I don't know—I've been friends with Maddie for so long, but all of a sudden she has a million things I don't get. Like she's basically perfect, but then last year she had all this . . . her parents are getting divorced and this guy broke up with her and . . ." I sigh, shifting on the bed so my feet are tucked under one of the blankets. I fix my eyes on my hands as I twist the soft fabric around my fingers. "I wasn't a very good friend, and I thought, when she got *back*, you know, *this* year, I could be better. And then it turned out she really liked Cory."

"Okay," Alex says when I pause again.

"And I didn't really want to be with Cory anymore." I let the words hang between us. "I mean, in a way, I did. I don't know. How do you actually know?" Without meaning to, I glance up at Alex. His face is unreadable. "Anyway. Maddie liked him, and she totally needed something good in her life."

I stop talking and smooth the blanket between my hands.

"And then you figured out you still like Cory?" Alex's voice is tight.

"What?" My head snaps up, and he's got that same super-intense look from the first day he was here, the first time I saw him. "No, not at all. Really. At that party—no one even let me explain. Cory kissed *me*. I know that sounds shitty, like I'm so irresistible or something, that's not what I mean—but I don't like him anymore. I don't know if I ever did."

We're staring at each other. There's an expanding feeling in my chest, a balloon of something like hope that's filling up in there, pressing on me with an aching realization.

All the boys I've been with, hung out with, made out with . . . Alex really is the first boy I've *talked* to.

He's watching me, waiting for me to say something else. And this is my chance. I have to say it out loud, the thing I don't want to say.

He's going to think you're a slut. He's not going to believe you. He's already heard about that party, you know he has, being pathetic isn't going to help.

Shut up.

"I tried to make Cory stop kissing me that night. Stop—everything. And he wouldn't. He didn't stop until Maddie caught us. I was so scared and then it was over and I didn't even know what happened."

Alex's face shifts. I think he's about to say something, but I have more; words spill out of me now, like when you can't stop crying even though you know it's no use.

"I wanted to think he was confused, like maybe I was Maddie, because it was totally dark—the power had gone out. But that doesn't make any sense, does it? Because he'd already kissed me before, right, so wouldn't he know the difference? And we were both really drunk, and I'd been, like, hanging out with him at the party, we drank and stuff. But I was drinking with everybody, and Maddie was *there*, she was at the party, too, and when the lights came back on she was standing there, just *seeing* us, and I honestly thought—you know, I *honestly thought* she would know what was happening. I thought she'd see my face, and I wouldn't have to explain. But maybe my face didn't look like anything."

I stop to breathe, my fingers twisting around and around.

"I feel *horrible*. I didn't want to hurt her. If I were a different kind of girl, Cory wouldn't have done that, right? They always say you can't blame yourself, but what if you really are to blame? If my best friend thought I wanted to hook up with her boyfriend, obviously *he* wasn't going to know . . . like, why would he think I didn't want . . ."

I'm breathing too hard now, and the words fade under the fall of real tears, crashing down onto my palms. I stare at my hands without seeing them and I don't know if Alex has even understood what I've said. It feels like the rain is falling straight through the roof onto me. Not loud anymore, just insistent. Just pushing me down.

The bed shifts as Alex moves next to me, and then his arm is around my shoulders. "Don't cry," he says softly.

I nod. I don't *want* to cry. I don't want any of this.

"I was really scared," I whimper, and then I'm sobbing. I'm turning my face into his shoulder and shaking. The bed shakes and we shake. But under all the bad feelings I can feel the softness of his T-shirt, the strength of his shoulder underneath it.

I manage to catch my breath, finally, but I keep my face down so he can't see me rubbing my nose on his mom's shirt. We both take a big breath, and I think I'm done, *hope* I'm done, being such a freak. But then I'm talking again.

"I don't know what would've happened if the lights hadn't come back on. If Maddie hadn't found us. It was—I don't think it had anything to do with her, you know? Like, obviously I didn't want to kiss Cory if he was supposed to be together with my best friend. Like, that was a reason to stop. But it wasn't just that. He was actually hurting me."

Alex and I sit very still, almost like we're afraid Cory can hear us. That's what I'm afraid of, at least.

But I'm all the way in Iowa, so.

I sit back up, running my hands under my eyes, across my cheeks. "I'm sorry. This is so stupid."

"It's not." Alex's hand is still on my back. Just the right amount of pressure.

"I swear I'm not trying to be one of those girls. I'm fine. I'm not saying Cory was, you know . . ."

"Okay."

We're quiet again. Outside, it sounds like the storm has turned to regular rain.

"If you were, though. Saying that." Alex shrugs. "I'd believe you."

I let out a long, shuddering sigh. "Oh."

Even though you're such a slut? The voice sounds like it's laughing at me. *You should stop talking forever. You're just ruining Maddie's life, and Cory's, and being a big drama queen.*

I look over at Alex, and then suddenly he's pulling me into a hug, holding me.

The voice doesn't have anything to say about that.

I don't know which one of us pulls away first, but we both get off the bed and walk toward his door like we know it's time for me to go.

I put my hand on the doorknob and then turn, not quite able to meet his eyes. "Maybe we could drive back together?" I ask in a half whisper. "Tomorrow?"

"Oh," he says, a little startled by my question. "That would be amazing. But, I mean. I can't go back yet. I need more time."

I nod, but I don't try to open the door.

His hand hovers near my shoulder, but he lets it drop again.

"Thank you for talking to me, Rosie."

I almost laugh, despite everything. As if I've done him any favors tonight.

Finally I lift my gaze to his. I point at the opposite wall, the one with all the original drawings. "I don't think you should be in Intro anymore. Those are really good."

"You're standing all the way over here," he says. "If you don't get any closer, you can keep thinking that."

My face will only smile halfway, but it does that much. "I should actually go. Maybe I can take a closer look another time."

"I'd like that," he says quietly.

I can feel the heat from his body. I can feel the weight of everything I said, and as I ease the door open and step into the cold hallway, the weight shifts. Some of it stays in his room, with him.

I carry the rest of it back to the lumpy sofa bed and sleep.

The rain stops, and the silence wakes me up.

It's still dark, but there's a thinness to it. That feeling of light that comes just before dawn.

Very carefully and quietly, I take the sheets off the bed and fold them. I manage to get the couch put back together without waking up the whole neighborhood, too, and I change into yesterday's clothes in the bathroom, leaving Jill's pajamas on top of the sheets.

I leave a note in the kitchen saying thank you. I apologize, too, for sneaking out, and my pen hovers over the notepad for a minute while I try to come up with some reason. I guess *I have to get back to school* is basically true. But instead I just say sorry again.

Outside the world is wet and heavy. The sky is turning a soft blue, but otherwise I'm reminded so much of the morning after Gabe's party that I almost go back inside Alex's house, just to make this daybreak different from that one.

But this time I have a car. This time, I find a Dunkin' Donuts on the way back to the highway, and I get a big, sugary coffee drink.

This time I have a plan. Not a stupid plan, though it's maybe a little *reckless*, as Alex's mom would say. And the plan only works if I get on the road right now, when the sun is barely skimming the horizon, and race away from the sunrise as fast as I can.

I set the address into my phone and head back west. Back home.

21

"ROSEMARY. HI, THERE. It's so early! Are you—uh, are you picking up Madelyn, sweetie?" Mrs. Costello stands in the doorway to their big, boxy mini-mansion, not inviting me in. She's dressed for work already, all crisp suit and blown-out hair and huge coffee mug. Mrs. Costello always makes me feel kind of *wrong*, and this morning is no exception.

I just smile at her. I'm bouncing on the wide front steps, wishing I'd stopped to pee or just not guzzled an iced vanilla latte the size of my head on the way here. As nervous as I am, it's surprising how the need for a bathroom can make you brave. Or something.

"Yeah, no, I just needed to talk to her? And maybe use your restroom, if that would be okay? I'm sorry to barge in like this, I know it's early, but Maddie's always leaving around now for her SGA meetings or whatever, right? Or does she not have one today? I'm sorry, I don't really know, that's why I wanted to talk to her; can I see her? Is she home? Maybe I could just come in for a minute?"

I would definitely keep babbling except Mrs. Costello finally steps back into the house, an alarmed look on her face, and lets me jitter into the entryway. There's a guest bathroom on my right. She and I both point at it at the same time with matching question-mark faces. I laugh crazily and then rush inside, accidentally slamming the door behind me.

This wasn't part of the plan, to start off by emptying my bladder. But there's a kind of comfort in all the familiar things, the old smells. The shell-shaped soaps on the sink that look like they've never been used; the cornflower-blue hand towels folded perfectly on their brushed-platinum hangers. Everything clean, in its place, reminding you that some people's lives are more orderly and also way better than yours.

I wash my hands with one of the seashells and mess up a towel, then mess it up even more when I try to refold it. Finally I take a good, long look at myself in the mirror.

I don't look great. My hair is falling out of the bun I put it in this morning, and the top strands are a little greasy. Yesterday's mascara is pinching half my eyelashes together. I have a lip balm in my pocket, so I put some on, but still. I look pathetic.

Maybe that'll help.

Stepping out of the bathroom, I stop to listen. Mrs. Costello is in the kitchen talking, and then I hear Maddie's voice. I can't tell what either of them is saying. It's obvious they're bickering, though.

I creep through the big entrance area, past the sweeping staircase that spirals down like some kind of Disney castle. There's a short hallway with a regular ceiling, and then it opens up again when you reach the kitchen, which has these massive two-story-high windows looking out at the woods behind the house. I used to be really jealous of this house, and then for a while I wasn't, because I practically lived here, too. Now I wonder why Maddie and I never, not once, tried to slide down the banister. We easily could've fallen to our deaths on the marble tile floor, of course, but we should have at least *thought* of it.

"Because I want to, Mom. It's basically *rude* to say no."

"I don't see how this helps your résumé at all—"

"It does! It's school participation!"

Mrs. Costello snorts. In a very prim sort of way, of course. "You have more than enough *school participation* at this point. If we free up your time, I think I can get you into another class at UNO, and we need to talk about taking at least two in the spring."

There's a very thick silence. I lean against the wall, between a photo of Maddie as a baby, sitting up and smiling perfectly in a little bow headband, and one of those everyone-wearing-white-on-the-beach shots of about fifty Costellos. I can't see into the kitchen, but I can hear Mrs. Costello's mug being set on the granite counter-top, a spoon scraping a bowl. A sigh.

"Maybe we could just talk about this later," Mrs. Costello says, her voice soft and conciliatory.

"I have to tell them today. I'm *going* to tell them today." Maddie sounds as mad as I've ever heard her, and my heart sinks pain-fully. My plan is not going to work. And from the sounds of it, Mrs. Costello doesn't approve of Maddie being nominated for Home-coming Queen, and Maddie is super upset about it. So my timing is basically a nightmare. As usual.

I've just resigned myself to turning back around and sneaking out when Maddie comes storming into the hall and sees me.

The first thing I think is, *She looks weird*, which isn't very nice, but is kind of true. She has on a long, flowy skirt and really dangly earrings and what looks like a handknit sweater on—all of it seems chic and expensive and European, but also like a total disconnect from the whole house around her. It's like she's trying out a Rebellious Daughter costume for Halloween, but wasn't quite brave enough to go full-on goth.

And the next thing I think is, *Oh, shit*. Maddie really hates feeling like she's been spied on.

"What are *you* doing here?" she yelps.

My eyes dart past her toward the kitchen, wishing that— what? That Mrs. Costello would come out and explain? Like that wouldn't make this a million times worse?

"Wh—" Maddie stops herself. "You know what? Who cares? I have to go."

"Wait!" I finally say, though she's already stomping upstairs. "Wait, I just need to talk to you!"

"Now?" she spits, not even bothering to look down at me or pause for a second. I start chasing her up the stairs and even that doesn't get a reaction, though she does keep yelling at me. "How are you even *awake* this early?"

"What is that supposed to mean?" I cry.

She doesn't answer me, just runs into her room and slams the door in my face.

I forget everything in my desperation to get her to listen. I start pounding on the door with all of my strength and yelling, "You have to let me talk! You never even let me *explain what happened*!"

The door flies open again, and I nearly fall onto her.

"Then *explain!*" she screams.

From downstairs I hear Mrs. Costello calling up, wondering what's wrong. I guess Maddie hears it, too, because she grabs my wrist and, with surprising strength, pulls me into her room. The door slams again and she whirls on me, her arms crossed and her cheeks bright red with fury.

It's crazy. It's all extra, insanely crazy, and I'm still a little hopped up on latte, and that's the only reason I can think of for the fact that I start to laugh. Just a little. But I definitely crack up.

"You have *got* to be kidding me," Maddie says, her voice dangerously low.

I hiccup, covering my whole face with my hands, and hold my breath. "Sorry," I whisper from behind my palms. "Sorry."

"I have to go."

I let my arms fall and nod. "I know. I'm sorry. I thought if I came over first thing—no, hang on, that's not it. I just couldn't wait any longer."

Maddie leans back against the closed door and glares at me. "Seems like you waited a pretty long time to me."

I nod again. "But I didn't know, before. I didn't—I didn't understand."

"That you're pathetic?"

I feel my face crumple, betraying how hurt I am. For a moment Maddie looks like she regrets saying it, but then she seems to decide that she has to be strong, and her jaw sets in a hard line again.

My legs go all rubbery and I look around, wondering if I should just sit on the floor. That's the first time I notice that Maddie's room is a mess. It looks like *my* room, it's so messy. Clothes and books everywhere, the bed unmade, one set of shutters open and the others still closed.

"Wow," I murmur. "Your mom must hate this."

I catch Maddie's smirk before it disappears, but otherwise she doesn't react to me at all. Finally I just sink straight down, cross my legs on the carpet, and sigh.

"I didn't want to kiss Cory that night," I say. I can feel Maddie stiffen, and I know she's going to interrupt, so I rush to get everything out. "But I flirted with him a little. I think it was just a habit, sort of, or it was that I was jealous of you." I hear her snort, much less gracefully than her mother, and I shake my head. "You got back from Spain all, like, *amazing*. I didn't know how to be around you anymore. I know it's not fair!" I hold up a hand, stopping her from interrupting. "I know that was shitty. I know I shouldn't have flirted with him, or anyone you liked, just to feel . . . better. About myself."

I'm staring at my knees, but out of the corner of my eye I see Maddie slide down against the door, sitting down across from me. My breathing gets more even, just knowing that she's listening, but I still have to close my eyes to get the next words out.

"So I just want you to know, I wasn't lying when I said I wasn't into him anymore. And he was being so nice to you, and it made me happy to see you happy. That was all true. And then at the party, I guess I hung out with him a little, but we weren't sneaking around or anything. I barely even talked to him, I swear."

I pick at a speck of dried paint on my jeans. It pops off, disappearing into the carpet, and I force my hands to be still. Maddie is being completely quiet, and I know I have to keep talking, whether I want to or not.

"It was after the power went out, and the house was dark. I was drunk and upstairs, I wanted to get my stupid shirt, and Cory started kissing me. I don't know why. We didn't have some plan, I didn't ask him to. I wasn't kissing him back. And he—he pushed me onto that couch, and I couldn't get up. I—"

My voice just stops. I lift my eyes, checking Maddie's face. She's watching me. Most of the anger and suspicion is gone. She looks like she just wants to hear what I'm saying.

If it had been anyone but Cory, I realize, I would've run to Maddie a long time ago. She might've even understood that night—maybe she wouldn't have assumed I was hooking up with him on purpose if she hadn't been so angry, so convinced I was betraying her.

But it was Cory. And the person who listened to me was Alex. More than anything else, this is the thing that makes me realize how much it's all changed. My friendship with Maddie, my whole world. I'm not the same anymore. I'm braver. Just a tiny bit, maybe, but I think it counts.

Still. I wish so much that I didn't have anything else to say. For both of us, I wish so hard that the end of the story was something about a drunk mistake that I could just apologize for. Maddie's version of the story is wrong, but God, it's so much easier. I wish it was really that easy.

"He hurt me. Not, like, a lot. But I couldn't really breathe. And when I tried to, um, push him away, he didn't—he wasn't stopping. I don't think he would've stopped if you hadn't come in. And I wanted him to. I was trying to stop him."

I swear I see Maddie's pupils dilate from here. I feel prickles of sweat break out on the back of my neck, a nervous reaction to what she might say to me now. I'm suddenly so sure that she's going to accuse me of lying. It's still just my side of the story—what if I'm wrong?

Why should anyone believe you?

But I know I'm not wrong about this. I've been trying to believe a different version of this story for days, and it's not working. Because Cory didn't care whether I wanted to kiss him or not. He didn't care that I wanted him to stop taking off my clothes, he didn't care about Maddie, and he still hasn't apologized.

"I'm sorry," I say again.

"Stop saying that."

I blink at her.

"Jesus, Rosie. Is that really what happened?"

I nod. She rocks forward onto her knees, then stops.

"So the lights came back on, and I found you, and that's—that's what I walked in on? Was he *raping* you?"

"No!" I yelp, but hot, fast tears burst out of my eyes at the same instant. Maddie starts moving across the floor to me, but she's just a blur. The tears *hurt*, they're so hot, and everything behind my eyes feels like it's burning, too. "No," I say again, and Maddie has her arms around me.

"God, Rosie," Maddie whispers, patting me on the back while I cry. "I'm sorry."

"No," I sob. "*I'm* sorry. He's so nice to you, and I ruined everything." The words spill out with the tears, and I don't know if she can even understand me with my head tucked into her elbow, ruining her fancy sweater.

"Just stop," she says softly. "Just—stop."

I hold my breath, trying to make the tears shut off, and her arms tighten around me.

"Don't stop *crying*, you weirdo. Stop apologizing."

The tears keep coming, but I force myself to gulp down some air and sit up. Water is streaming down my face in total free fall, but I can look at her now. I can see her.

"I didn't want to hurt you," I say.

"You didn't hurt me. He did. I was just too stupid to see it—and he hurt you, too, by the way, so stop apologizing for him."

Exactly.

The voice in my head is a whisper. It's a gust of wind lifting my chin just a tiny bit.

Maddie sits all the way down on the floor with a big sigh. She runs her hands through her hair and stares at me, her eyes getting big. "This is really bad," she says. "I knew he was kind of—I don't know. Pushy. Entitled. But this is bad."

"Not anymore," I say. "Not if you forgive me."

Her face softens into something that looks like pity. "He

assaulted you," she says slowly, like I might not understand.

"No," I say automatically. "It was just—"

"God, Rosie, stop!" She looks up at the ceiling and laughs without any happiness. "You know what he told me? Well, I mean, first, at the party, he wanted to sneak up to one of the rooms. And I wouldn't go with him."

I remember Maddie saying something about Cory getting what he wanted, right after she caught us. It hurts, but now I guess I know what she meant.

"And then when he was, like, *explaining*, he said you were drunk and all over him, and he was trying to get away, but he'd been drinking, too, and . . ." She waves a hand in the air like, *etc., etc.*

"And you believed him," I say weakly.

She stares at me for a second, hard, right in my eyes. "I didn't *want* to. Or I did want to, I guess. I believed . . . I thought *you'd* changed. Over the summer. I thought maybe you were sick of me being this little Goody Two-shoes, always doing her homework on time and never going to parties and just being the least fun, least interesting person in the entire goddamn *world*. I wanted to go off to Spain and get interesting, or grow up, or *something*. And all I did the whole time I was there was miss you and Ryan and worry about my parents, and I still felt like a total fool around boys, and it was so embarrassing! I was still this sad, stuck-up loser, even a whole freaking ocean away from home."

I wrinkle my eyebrows at her. "You're not stuck-up," I say, confused.

"I know!" She throws her hands up in agreement. "I think I'm pretty nice, right?" I nod, but she shakes her head. "Apparently not in freaking Spain, I'm not. This one guy kept calling me 'Princess' and I thought it was a compliment for like three weeks. Some other girl had to explain it was because I wouldn't hook up with anyone. They were making fun of me and I didn't even understand it."

I feel like tiny parts of my brain are exploding with surprise and confusion. "But that's crazy," I say. "You're perfect. You're the opposite of a loser. I mean, you *are* a princess, basically."

Maddie takes a little, hiccupy breath and looks up toward the open window. Her eyes are shiny, but she doesn't cry. "I just didn't want to be your sad, single friend anymore. I don't want to be the girl who gets *balloons* at the *airport*."

I blink, stung.

"I don't mean it like that. They were really sweet. I just— sometimes, like around you, I feel like a little kid, you know? Like a permanent virgin."

"Jesus, Mads. First of all, everyone likes balloons, so stop being a crazy person. And second, do you even *want* to have sex?"

She looks at me, surprised. "Yes?" she says, though it sounds like a question. "Right?"

I laugh. "No, you don't! All the Midcity guys are way too lame for you!"

"The guys in Spain weren't," she moans. "They were really hot. And older."

"And jerks!"

She wrinkles her nose. "I should've just told you."

"Yeah, but I get it." I pause and look down at my knees. "I felt so

241

bad after everything last year. I've just been the most *useless* friend. The whole time you were gone I was trying to figure out how to be better. I thought this year was going to be so much *better*. And I made everything a million times worse."

"What are you even talking about? You're a great friend. Just because I sometimes feel kind of intimidated by your whole— *thing*, doesn't mean I don't love you."

Suddenly I'm afraid I'm going to cry again. "But I'm too bitchy. I mean, you're the only girl friend that I have. That's weird," I mutter.

"Okay, well, if you feel like that's a problem, we can work on that."

I peek up at her finally, wondering how she makes it sound so easy. "By the way, I'm not friends with you based on whether you like to *party* or not. I just like you. For you."

She gives me a *duh* look and shoves my shoulder with one finger. "I know that, you big doofus. I like you for you, too."

"Okay."

"But we still need to talk about what happened," she says. "We have to . . . I don't know, don't we have to report Cory?"

"Report him?"

"Yes. For *assaulting* you."

I shake my head. I mean, I know Cory hurt me. But the word *assault* feels so . . . legal. Scary. It sounds like something people will have to know about. It makes me feel embarrassed and ashamed all over again.

"Nothing even happened," I say.

"Yes, it did."

"I mean, he cheated on you, and I was stupid and drunk, and . . ." I feel myself backpedaling, and Maddie is shaking her head at me. "I just wanted to be friends again," I say.

"We are," she says. "Which is why I'm telling you, we can't just let this go."

But that's exactly what I want to do. I glance at the door, wondering why Maddie's mom hasn't reminded us to go to school. I feel like I could curl up on her floor and sleep for a day and a half, but I have to get Mom's car back. And I have to get out of here.

"I'll think about it," I tell Maddie, and she seems satisfied.

But I'm pretty sure I'm lying. Because all I really wanted was my friend back. I wanted a chance to explain, and I wanted things to go back to normal.

And now I can just forget that anything happened. Because I'm fine.

Yeah, sure. Totally fine.

22

DAVE RUNS HIS fingers along his nose, pushing his glasses out of the way. His elbows rest on the table on either side of his untouched chicken dinner.

"I'm still not understanding what the hell you were thinking," he says with a pained sigh.

"I'm really sorry, " I say to my plate. I can feel Mom's eyes burning a hole in my head. "I didn't know I was going to take the car, I just—it just happened."

"It just *happened*?" Mom sets her water glass down so hard that a few drops splash out.

"Beth—"

"No, Dave, let her talk."

Beside me I can feel Ayla smirking, eating her dinner daintily. She so loves being in the room for this. I want to burn the stupid book that convinced my parents to have important conversations at family mealtimes.

"I'm sorry," I say again. It's the latest stop on the Rosie Fuller

Apology Tour. Except tonight, no one is telling me to stop, like Maddie did this morning. This time I definitely need to be really, truly sorry.

Even if I'm just a tiny bit not sorry. The truth is, I feel better than I did yesterday. Something about driving that far just made the world feel bigger. And having Maddie with me in the halls at school again almost made me forget that Alex wasn't there.

And then as I was getting into Mom's car after the last bell, I got a text from Alex.

I don't have a girlfriend anymore. Can we talk later?

I didn't go out there to ask him to break up with anyone. And I feel a little guilty that he did, but my heart races just thinking about it. Plus, he said that it wasn't just because of me. So the least I can do is believe him.

He didn't say when he's coming back, though. I think I'm supposed to give him space and time, so I didn't ask. It's torture.

Mom stabs a piece of chicken with her fork but doesn't eat it.

"Rosie," says Dave, "we need you to get what we're saying here. What you did was seven different kinds of dangerous—you could've gotten killed by the traffic, or the storm, or—"

"I might still kill you," Mom interrupts.

I think I hear a tiny whisper-giggle escape my sister's lips, but I don't look over. Mom does, though. She points her fork at Ayla, even though there's still a big chunk of chicken on it. Now even I sort of feel like laughing.

"This isn't funny. The car could've broken down. We don't know Alex that well, he could've been living God knows where—so even when you *got* there," she says, swinging the chicken over to me, "how did we know you were safe?"

"Jill talked to you—"

Dave shuts me up with a look. Somehow I can never remember that interrupting Mom is only going to make things worse.

But she just sighs and throws the fork down on her plate again. "You showed a complete lack of judgment, I needed the car last night, and you're not driving again until I say so. And by the way, can I just point out that you're sending your sister a *terrible* message about how to act with boys."

And there it is. Of *course* Mom thinks I was just sneaking out to see Alex, because with her everything I do is about some guy. I take a breath and notice Dave's mouth forming a thin line, like he can tell this fight has moved past his powers to negotiate. Right before I have a chance to throw some choice words in Mom's face, though, Ayla speaks up.

"Oh my *God*, she's *fine*," she snaps. "Can we please just remember she went to see Alex *Goode*? What is the big deal?"

"Great, now neither of you is taking this seriously—" Mom starts to say, but Dave puts a hand on her arm.

"Ayla, let us handle this," he says in his calm voice.

"Whatever. All anyone ever does around here is yell at Rosie, but fine, I'll just be quiet like I always am!" Ayla's voice gets louder with each word and the rest of us sit back a little. Normally I might glance at Mom and exchange a look—*Ayla thinks she's always quiet??*—but we're all too shocked to hear her defending me to do anything.

My sister pushes her chair back and throws up her hands. "People like boys, okay? It's a regular thing! Stop acting like it's the end of the fucking world!"

"Language!" Mom yelps. Dave looks back and forth among all of us, probably wondering why his male-feminist approach to life isn't working out better.

"I did mess up, though," I say to Ayla. She looks at me, startled. "It's not like there's nothing to be mad about."

"Ugh, Rosie, you just have to make everything about *you*."

And in a spectacular huff—the kind I still couldn't pull off, four years older than her—my little sister storms from the room. We listen to her pounding up the stairs and slamming her door, none of us daring to meet each other's eyes.

I stare at my chicken, rice, and broccoli, turning cold and gross. Mom takes a sip of water and Dave sighs again. Finally I break the silence.

"I know I shouldn't have done that. At all. I just—something bad happened, and I needed to talk to my friend. And I made a mistake, taking the car. I wasn't trying to sneak out and see a boy, I swear. I was just . . . upset."

Mom takes a long breath through her nose.

"What happened?" Dave says. "What bad thing?"

Mom looks at him, then at me. I know she thinks I'm just being dramatic, but that's fine. There's no way I can get into the whole Cory thing with my parents—especially not Dave.

"Can we talk about it tomorrow?" I finally say. "I didn't sleep very well, and it's been a really long day . . ."

Mom rolls her eyes, and I know she wants to point out how my day was only long because I started it on the wrong side of the state line. Whenever she gets really mad it just keeps going and going— she can't seem to calm down until every single terrible thing has been said. Ayla's scorched-earth fighting techniques were learned from the best. Or the worst, I guess.

Dave puts his hand on the back of Mom's shoulders. "Tomorrow is fine," he tells me.

"It's her turn to do the dishes." Mom is still glaring down at her plate and her voice is quiet, like even she can see that she's being petty.

"I'll do them," Dave says quickly. Then, giving me a stern look, he adds, "Go to bed."

I don't need to be told twice. I take the stairs two at a time, grateful to find all my own familiar bath products right where I left them, next to my favorite toothpaste and my own toothbrush. I finish cleaning up and am practically running to my room when I hear music coming through Ayla's door. Sad music. Sad *Sia* music.

I stop midstep and consider my options. All I want to do is crawl into bed and text Alex a hundred pointless thoughts. I want to talk to Maddie, too. She broke up with Cory right after homeroom, and I got to hear the whole story about how he just said, "Whatevs," and she said, "You're a violent asshole, and I hope they kick you out of school," and everyone looked at her like she was nuts. She told me all this and then stared at me, like I should get excited about getting the star quarterback suspended.

I don't know if it's exhaustion or what, but I'm feeling sort of

numb about everything. I'm just wiped out, physically and emo-
tionally. I'm not sure I can handle whatever's making Ayla play Sia
on repeat right now.

But lately, it feels like she needs me. It's a good feeling.

I knock on her door.

"What?"

"It's me," I say, opening it a teeny tiny bit.

"Whoop-de-do."

Her room is as neat as Maddie's always is—always *was*, I
guess—and she's sitting up on her fluffy bed, holding her oldest,
dearest stuffed elephant to her chest. I lean against the doorjamb.

"Thanks for sticking up for me back there."

She shrugs, still scowling.

"I guess this means you have a boyfriend now?"

Her eyes go wide and nervous, which makes me laugh. I step
into the room and shut the door behind me, coming over to sit on
the end of her bed. Any other night she'd probably kick me onto
the floor, literally, but now she just tucks her knees up and stares
at nothing.

"That's good news, right? Boyfriend?"

"Until Mom finds out." Ayla buries her face in the elephant's
lilac chenille trunk. "Then she'll start yelling at me, too."

"Nah," I say. "Well, maybe."

Sia is still wailing in the background, so I take a minute to get
up and turn the volume down, then sit back on the bed.

"Am I a bad influence?" I ask Ayla.

"No," she mutters.

"Are you sure?"

She picks up her head and glares at me, which I don't understand at all. I guess I look surprised, too, because she says, "Figures. You don't even know. The *bad influence* is having you and Mom around, looking like freaking *supermodels* all the time."

"But—how is that—?"

"It's impossible!" she cries, throwing her hands up. "Dad keeps telling me to have confidence and not read magazines so I don't, like, die of *unhealthy body image* and he's basically forbidden me from *ever* watching reality TV *ever*, but no one cares that my mom and my sister are completely impossible!"

"Ayla, slow down. I have no idea what you're talking about right now."

"Seriously? If you looked like *me* and had to see *you* every day, living in the same house, looking like you should be on one of those *Bachelor* shows, it wouldn't make you feel just a tiny bit bad about how you look? I mean, for example, boobs! I don't have any!" She points at her chest with a grim triumph in her eyes. "I have *no* waist, I can't tan, my hair is, like . . ." She holds out her ponytail. "What *color* is that?"

It takes all of my remaining energy to not laugh. And it's not that I don't empathize, because I do—it's just that she's kind of funny when she's being indignant.

"You're twelve, dude."

"I'm thirteen in two weeks!"

"Yeah, exactly. Twelve, thirteen, fourteen—the worst. Everyone looks like a freak in junior high. And most of high school."

She's staring at me with an unreadable expression, and I realize what I've just said.

"Not that you look like a freak! *At all*. Just the other day I was thinking about how gorgeous you are! Really!"

"No, you weren't," she grumbles. And that's when I really feel bad, because it's just burning off her—the need for someone to tell her she's pretty. She's trying so hard not to believe me, but I can tell how much she really, really wants to anyway.

So maybe I'm a bad influence, after all. But for once I also know what to say.

I grab both of Ayla's hands and lean closer, forcing her to look me in the eye. "When we were at church over the weekend, and I was watching you working, I thought, *That girl is beautiful, and she's going to get more beautiful every single year*."

Ayla pinches her lips between her teeth.

"And it wasn't just because of your face, which, by the way, is *amaze*. It was your spirit—and hang on, I know that sounds like bullshit, but I swear it's true. And it's *important*. Your spirit is ridiculously pretty, okay? Like, Cara Delevingne–pretty. You are a *really good* person, especially when you aren't being crazy moody." I sit back again, still holding her hands, and stick my chest out a little. "And *trust*, you will get these. Mom has boobs and so do I, and have you gotten a load of Grandma Fuller lately? If you get those genes from Dave's side of the family, you are *set*."

Finally, this makes Ayla laugh. "Gross," she says, but she's smiling, and she hasn't squirmed away from me holding her hands yet.

"Now tell me about the boy," I say, stifling a yawn. I squeeze her fingers one last time, then take my hands away and use them to prop myself sideways on her bed.

"Ugh, no, it's too embarrassing."

"Sounds good already." I keep grinning at her until she grabs the elephant again and squeals into it. "His name is . . . ," I prompt.

"Henry."

"Good. I approve. He's in your class?" She nods. "Age appropriate, awesome. See, you're already way ahead of me, especially with Mom. She's going to be thrilled."

"He's kind of a science nerd."

I pick up one of her throw pillows and smack her with it. "Are you kidding me? Not fair! You were already the favorite daughter, and now you have a *science-nerd boyfriend*?"

She's giggling now, flinching away from my pillow attack. I smack her one last time and then launch myself up and off the bed.

"That's it, I'm going to sleep. You are *fine*. Put on some less mopey music and go Gchat Dr. Henry, okay? Sheesh."

She's still laughing when I get to the door and stop, turning back for a minute.

"And Ayla, seriously. I love you. I'm sorry if I've screwed you up or been a bad example of, you know, womanhood or whatever. But don't be screwed up. You are a very cool person, and Henry or whoever is lucky just to get to know you. And try to be nicer to Mom, okay? Just try."

She rolls her eyes at me, and I know I sound like Dave, or even Mom. But now I kind of understand all those self-esteem talks they've been giving us over the years. I still don't think they necessarily apply to *me*, but . . . maybe.

"I love you, too," Ayla says. "I hope whatever happened to you wasn't that bad."

I nod and slip out of the room fast. Somehow I managed to make that whole conversation go well, and I don't need to ruin it now.

In my own room I flop onto my bed and groan. Everything with Cory and being grounded and trying to get close to Maddie again—it'll all be there in the morning. I grab my phone and open up a text to Alex.

Want to talk but soooooo sleeeeeepy zzzz. Tmrw?

I don't even wait to hear back before I fall asleep, safe at home at last.

23

RYAN HANDS ME a hammer and raises one eyebrow. "So Cory's on Senior Court."

"Of course he is." I pull my hair into a ponytail, then take the tool.

"What if he and Maddie both get crowned?"

"Maddie will be fine, since she'll be *Junior* Queen and obviously *you're* going to win Junior King. So you'll be there to *shield* her."

Ryan rolls his eyes, but his cheeks get so pink that I can see the color even in the low light of backstage. It's just the two of us, a bucket of nails, some backdrops that need to be attached to wooden frames, and plenty of time to discuss the Homecoming Court announcements that were made this morning.

"I'm not gonna *win*," Ryan says.

"Dude, people love you. I voted for you already."

"You did?"

Now it's my turn to roll my eyes. "And for Maddie."

He gasps. "I can't believe you didn't vote for Olivia!"

I smirk. "Yeah, it was a tough call. You know how close she and I have always been."

We both laugh, and then we're quiet for a minute, and I wonder if he's feeling weird that the third Junior Queen nominee was Ashley Russo. And not me.

I don't know why I feel disappointed about the whole thing; it's a big school and I'm not a cheerleader or anything.

It's just another school thing that Ryan and Maddie are doing and I'm not.

But Alex is nominated, too. So basically there's no way to not feel left out. Maddie and Charlotte Lewis made the announcements during homeroom, and for a second, it felt like that day at the airport. Or the party where Maddie and Cory fell in love or like or whatever it was. Or the walk home from Gabe's party.

I guess *feeling left out* is getting pretty familiar. But not easier.

"I'm never gonna beat Mr. Better-than Goode, anyway," Ryan says.

"If he doesn't come back in time, though, you could win by default." I guess I sound as depressed as I feel, and Ryan swats me on the arm.

"He's not gonna stay away that long. Default, deschmalt." He gives me a look. "Maybe next time you go out to Iowa, you can stuff him in the trunk of your car. Like a balloon."

This makes me smile, finally, but I shake my head. "You know I'm so grounded I'm barely allowed to be at school right now."

He snorts. "Everyone thinks you're some kind of crazed groupie."

"Yeah." Skipping school to drive across state lines added an interesting wrinkle to my reputation. "I just needed to talk." I look up, realizing what I've said. "Not that—it's just, I know you hate picking sides . . ."

Ryan shrugs one shoulder, still concentrating on his edge of canvas. I don't know what else to say, and for a while we just work silently. I wish I'd noticed sooner that Ryan and I were turning into the kind of friends who just joke about stuff. I thought we were having real, important conversations. But maybe I never had anything important to say before. So maybe he doesn't think of me that way—like the friend he can talk to about his love life, or the things that might really be bothering him.

Alex talks to me, even from far away. About everything—except when, exactly, he's coming back. When I get the nerve to ask, he just says *Soon*.

This morning right after homeroom, I texted him to say *You got nominated for Junior Homecoming King!!!*

It took a while to hear back, and all he said was *Crazy!* Not *Go buy a dress, girl, so we can go to the dance together!*

I wish I could ask Ryan what he thinks that means. Or Maddie—if only she could talk about something besides going to the administration about Cory. She thought it was weird I went to Iowa, and even though we're friends again, she's still too busy to hang out very much.

If only Alex would just come back, everything would be fine. I hate so much, for so many reasons, that all the bad things that happened to him last year happened—and I hate that sometimes

I'm glad that they did, since that's the only reason I met him in the first place.

Ryan starts working on support beams for some flats, his drill a loud whine behind me. Suddenly it goes silent, and I look over at him. Sawdust floats around his head like sandy fog. "You know, if you got Cory kicked out of school before Homecoming, the dance would be a lot more fun."

My stomach rolls over. "You've been talking to Maddie, haven't you."

"She's not wrong. I mean, if he really did what you said he did—"

"God, Ryan, I really don't want to talk about it."

He flinches. "Sorry, okay."

"No, I mean . . ." Ugh. I'm making everything worse. I set down my hammer and wipe my hands on the back of my jeans. If I keep holding on to the big, heavy tool, I'm afraid I might start smashing things. "I don't want to talk to *authorities*."

I still haven't even told my parents. They asked the next day, and I just explained that I'd been in a big fight with Maddie but it was better now.

"I'm not saying I don't believe you," Ryan says. He sets down his drill and steps over the boxes of supplies and paint to stand closer to me. After hesitating a moment, he puts his arms around me and we hug.

I sigh into his shoulder.

"It must have been scary," he says softly.

I don't say anything, but I think, *It was.*

"Whatever you decide to do, you know I'll go along with it.

Even if it costs me a whole crown."

I laugh, dipping my face lower so my forehead is pressing into his collar. "Ryan," I say, my voice muffled.

"Yeah?"

"Do you have a boyfriend?"

His arms stiffen around my back, but he doesn't move. I don't move, either.

"Maybe," he finally says.

I smile. "Is he nice to you? All the time?"

"Yeah, I think so. Aren't they supposed to be?"

Tears sting the back of my eyes, but I'm still smiling into the dark space between my hair and his chest. "That's what I've heard." I turn my head and rest my cheek against his shirt so I can hold him tighter, hug him closer. I haven't held anyone like this in a long time, I realize. I haven't wanted to touch anyone—not even Alex—for more than a few minutes. But I never want to let Ryan go.

I feel better.

No, you don't. Everyone still knows you're pathetic. And you can't feel better yet, that's not how it works if something really bad happens to you, you're supposed to be—

But I do feel better. So shut up.

Ryan tightens his grip, too, and we practically squeeze each other breathless, until we're laughing and falling apart again, shaking our heads at what idiots we both are.

I can still feel the voice lingering off to the side, like it's waiting in the wings. But for now, I've silenced it. For now, even if I'm just pretending to not be pathetic, even if I'm feeling the wrong thing . . . I'm okay.

"I totally nominated you, you know."

"I nominated you, too! But wait—what?" Steph laughs. *"Me?"*

"Don't say it like that! Why not you?"

"Uh . . ." She looks down at her DQ polo, faded jeans, and beat-up running shoes.

"Stop. You would've been a much better queen than *Olivia Thorpe.*"

Steph goes back to spraying Windex on the front of the hard-serve case. "You don't like Olivia? Why?"

"Seriously?"

She looks at me, confused. "Isn't she, like, the nicest person at school, basically? Besides Maddie, I mean. Obviously."

I laugh. "I said Olivia *Thorpe*, right?"

"Annabelle is really sweet, too," Steph muses, ignoring me. "But in a much quieter way. Olivia's the one who can get stuff done. Back in third grade she completely saved my life. This guy Chris kept calling me 'Stuff,' like as a fat joke, and Olivia poured her milk on him. It was amazing. And it was strawberry milk, which was even *more* amazing. We weren't even that close—she's just kind of badass. Zero tolerance, you know?"

I stare at her. She finishes cleaning the hard-serve case and moves over to the toppings side, unaware of how shocked I am.

"I guess I ended up on her zero-tolerance list, then," I say lightly. "Because she'd definitely pour strawberry milk on me if she got the chance."

"Really? Yikes." Steph seems to be thinking—she does that opening and closing her mouth thing about ten times—and I smile, waiting to hear what it is. Finally she says, "What did you do?"

"There was this . . . I don't know, like, *thing* with Finn Kramper last year. But Olivia kind of hated me before then."

"She liked Finn?"

"No, Annabelle did. I don't know why—the guy is gross."

Steph nods. She finishes the toppings case and ducks under the counter and into the back room. I hear her putting the Windex and rag away. I spin a little, back and forth, on the one stool behind the cash register while she washes her hands and dries them with a paper towel. I can't believe how lucky I am that I always get scheduled with her. I guess it's even luckier that Joel is clearly too nervous to work with me lately—I haven't seen him since last weekend, thank God.

"I voted for Maddie, anyway," Steph says in a low voice. Like we might be overheard by the sum total of no people buying ice cream this afternoon.

"Yeah, of course. She's obviously the best choice."

"I noticed you guys aren't fighting anymore."

I nod, twisting the rubber band on my wrist so it lies flat.

"But you don't seem that psyched about it," Steph says carefully.

"Hey, what's going on with your internship?" I ask brightly. "Are you leaving me all alone here or what?"

She narrows her eyes, obviously aware of how blatantly I'm changing the subject, but smiles, too. "Yeah, sorry. I'm out of here in two weeks!"

"That's awesome." I hold up my hand and she high-fives it awkwardly, making us both giggle. "I'll still see you for theater stuff, though, right?"

"Yeah, I'll be there. And I'll be backstage as much as possible. I'm doing some crew stuff this year, but that new lighting and sound guy is a dick."

I laugh. "That's *exactly* what Ryan said!"

"Seriously, though, if you want to talk about Maddie . . ." Steph turns away, obviously wishing she had something else to clean, and shrugs.

"No, we're good. It's just that thing, you know, where people change over the summer and it's weird, and . . ."

I stop, realizing I'm about to apologize for Maddie getting so mad at me for what happened with Cory. But it suddenly occurs to me that she forgave me really fast, as soon as she thought it was *assault* or whatever.

What if I really had just made a mistake, though? Would she still not be speaking to me? Would she still be dating Cory, who, come on, was at least *half* to blame in any scenario?

". . . and just talking about horses *all the time*, totally not caring that I can't ride them because of my allergies, you know?" Steph is saying.

I make a face and say, "Sorry, I missed the first part?"

"Annabelle. When she got back from horse camp in sixth grade."

"Oh, right. Yeah, she was always wearing those boots."

"*Every*where! It was ridiculous!"

I smile and decide not to tell Steph the truth—that I loved Annabelle's riding boots and was insanely jealous of them pretty much throughout junior high. I made my mom buy me the closest version we could find at Target, but they weren't real leather, and it didn't really make my jealousy go away.

Half an hour later, my shift ends, early enough that I'll get out before the Friday-night traffic, if there is any. The Lions have a week off before Homecoming next weekend, and Hadley's going to close up after Steph goes home in an hour.

It's dark by the time I leave at six, but it's still warm outside and not that bad to walk. I'm kind of getting used to cutting through the neighborhoods like this, like I'm a little kid again. Except now I have to be careful to avoid the streets that still have trees down on the sidewalks.

My mind drifts back to Olivia and Annabelle as I walk. It's always been obvious that Olivia's the stronger one, so I guess I can see what Steph was saying about her sticking up for people. That's definitely what she did when I accidentally made out with Finn— or at least, what she *thought* she was doing. I wonder if her problem with me being friends with Maddie was like that, like she didn't think I was good enough for her.

You're not, says the voice, but it's pointless, because I already know that.

And yet. Maddie's been so nice to me since Monday, so *attentive*. Almost like she's excited to work on my problem. My near-rape, or whatever she thinks it was. Maybe that *is* what it was, but what am I supposed to do about it now? No matter what she says, I cannot imagine anyone at Midcity sitting down and being like, *Oh, so you were drinking and you had a confusing tongue-in-mouth scenario with a boy whose tongue you'd had in your mouth a million times before? And that boy happens to be our star quarterback? Why, yes, obviously we'll believe you, the girl who has to be forced to do any kind of school activity and has also hooked up with half the school. Right this way to the near-rape survivors' lounge!*

It's not funny, but the thought makes me snort, right there on the corner of Lincoln Avenue. I kick the dried leaves at my feet and wait for a car to pass, wondering if I look crazy, laughing to myself under a streetlamp. Probably—if anyone's looking at me at all.

Maybe you can't get near-raped if you're already kind of a skank.

The voice stops me cold with that one. I know that's what people will think if I try to tell them what happened.

I think it might even be what *I* think.

I cross the street, slowly, and wonder what someone like Olivia would say. If she liked me, I mean. If I was one of the people she defended. But I already have a friend like that—I have Maddie. Don't I?

Maddie's trying to defend me, and I won't let her. And not just because I'm scared to tell the entire universe my most embarrassing story. It's also because I hate this feeling, that she wants me to be a victim. That by being a victim, I deserve her forgiveness.

I've finally reached my house, and I can see the lights on inside, hear the sounds of some acoustic-guitar-heavy band playing through Dave's iPod speakers. I stare up at the glowing windows for a minute and then sit down in the grass, under the big poplar tree out front. The one that lost the most branches, but still looks pretty good. I'm so glad it survived; its roots are huge and form all these little circles that make perfect seats. I find my favorite one, on the left side, and sit.

I know I need to do something. Be my own defender. But it was so hard, pushing Cory away that night. So hard to get home the next morning, go through the days of Maddie hating me. To finally get her to understand.

I feel like this tree—basically intact. Lucky that nothing really bad happened to me.

But I know that's not good enough.

24

"I'M ONLY LETTING you do this because of Maddie and Ryan. But you are still absolutely grounded, make no mistake."

"Okay, Mom."

"Don't get all pissy with me, either."

I glance over, watching as she deftly twists the steering wheel and drives us into the mall parking lot. The good mall, even. Where she's letting me buy a Homecoming dress—with my own money, of course, and with her along for the ride. But still. For a minute next Saturday night, I will be ungrounded. I still technically don't have a date, but I'll be out of the house somewhere besides stupid Dairy Queen or school.

"I wasn't being pissy," I say as mildly as I can manage. "I was just saying okay."

We get out of the car and hurry inside, since it's finally cold enough to need a jacket, but not so cold that either of us brought one. The warm, cologne-scented air of the Von Maur men's department greets us, instantly soothing my frayed nerves. God, I love the smell of new clothes.

Neither of us talks as we ride the escalators up two flights. Mom keeps checking her phone, but I do my best to leave mine in my bag. I just don't feel like arguing with her today, and nothing annoys her more than when I'm constantly texting. Or texting even a little bit.

At the formal dresses a saleswoman beams at us and for a second, it feels like old times. When I was really little, going out with my mom always felt like an event. People would stop us at the mall, at restaurants, on the street, just to tell us how beautiful we were. Men were especially infatuated with Mom, but women loved me best, always complimenting my hair, my eyes, whichever crazy princess dress I'd insisted on wearing that day. And I could always tell that it made Mom proud.

As I got older, though, she didn't like the looks that guys started giving me. She wanted me to be careful. She wanted me to be worried and definitely *not* flattered.

But that was so confusing, because wasn't it flattering? And it's not like I was trying to get them to look. I was just *being*. In the world. Usually she seemed angrier at the guys than at me, but it was still really frustrating.

Now she heads in one direction and I go the other way, running my fingers along the rows of hangers. I hesitate at a black bandage dress with a sweetheart neckline. I love it, but Mom won't, I'm sure. It's black, for one—she likes color and thinks I should, too. It's definitely formfitting and short, and I can't tell for sure without trying it on, but it's probably pretty low-cut. It's obviously not a turtleneck, anyway. After a moment, I grab the dark blue one next to it. Compromise.

By the time we circle back around to each other, we both have an armful of dresses. Mom gives me a small smile and leads the way to the changing rooms, but instead of waiting in the hall she comes in and sits on the chair in the corner, across from the mirror. I want to snap at her that I know I'm still grounded—but then again. Maybe this sort of feels like old times to her, too. So I just wiggle out of my jeans and grab the first dress.

"I like that color on you," Mom says. It's a pink number, big skirt, sort of ballerina-ish. One that she picked out, of course.

"It feels a little . . . ," I start to say, wondering if I'm going to offend her. "Just maybe a little young?"

I hold my breath, but she doesn't freak out. She looks at me in the mirror and nods. "Yeah, it's kind of ballet recital," she agrees.

The next dress has a big floral print, which feels wrong for Homecoming, but I thought it was pretty. I turn to see the back and Mom watches thoughtfully.

"Probably wrong for the occasion," I say, and she nods again.

"Nice, though. Maybe I could get you that one for something else."

"Really?" I say.

She meets my eyes in the mirror, confused. "Yeah, why not?"

"Money. And grounded. And . . . I don't know." I smooth my hands over the soft fabric.

"It looks lovely on you," she says. "And, yeah, *everything* looks great on you, but I think we can afford one extra dress. Maybe Ayla will like it in a few years."

I'd be shocked if that were true, but I'm too excited now to argue. I take off the dress and hang it carefully on the definitely buying hook.

I'm not really paying attention to what I grab next, so I have the dark blue bandage one halfway on before I remember to worry about Mom's reaction. But again, she just watches me mildly, maybe pinching her lips the tiniest bit when I zip up the back and adjust my boobs under the—yep—low neckline.

"Probably not this one," I say experimentally. I love it; I feel sophisticated and sexy, and even though I would've picked black if I thought I could get away with it, I think the blue might look even better with my dark hair and pale skin.

"Why not?" Mom asks, looking confused again.

"Um, seriously?" I turn to face her. "Because it actually makes me look, you know, like I'm not a little kid anymore?"

"Jesus, Rosie, I know you're growing up. Is that what you think? That I want you to be little forever?"

I lift a hand like *Well, duh, yes.* The last time we went shopping together was freshman year, when a senior named Ben had invited me to the junior-senior Snowflake Formal. Every single thing I tried on was "inappropriate," according to Mom. But before I can remind her of all that, she uncrosses and crosses her legs again with a big sigh and keeps talking.

"You're getting older. That's *fine.* I haven't always been crazy about how *fast* you seem to want to grow up. I'm sorry, but when you look like you do, growing up fast isn't something you have to try at." She sighs. "It's just—I mean, bad things happen to everyone, but trust me, pretty girls don't get any sympathy in this world—and some of them get a *lot* more than their share of trouble."

I stare at her for a few seconds, then sit heavily on the tiny bench across from her chair. I don't know if it's the tight dress or what, but I can't seem to take a deep breath.

"You probably already know what I'm talking about," Mom says, her voice much softer and quieter than before.

"I—Maybe," I admit. "I don't think I get into trouble because I'm pretty." I picture that night in the car, driving to Iowa. And then I think about Cory.

He pushed me because he thought I could be pushed. It wasn't about how I looked.

At the same time, I bet it wasn't about me at all. Except that I was in the wrong place, at the wrong time, with the wrong amount of alcohol in my veins or . . . whatever.

Guilt slices through me, again, for being so stupid. For being so lucky that nothing worse happened. For sitting there in the path of whatever tornado wants to pass by and just blind lucky to come out unscratched.

"I was really proud of my looks when I was your age," Mom says. She stares down at her hands, at the perfect manicure she paints herself every week without fail. "And when you were little— I mean, when I was pregnant with you, I thought my life was over. But then I never really gained any weight, not the way you see some women do, and after you were born I was thinner than ever. My boobs were bigger . . ." She looks up at me and laughs self-consciously. "It was stupid, but I felt pretty again. And you were just gorgeous. Everyone would ask if we did mother-daughter modeling, and I don't even know if that's a real thing, but it made me feel . . . good. Your father was nowhere and my parents hated me for screwing up college, and I figured, what the hell. Feel good when you can, right?"

I nod, still stunned into silence. Mom never talks to me like this. She's either tired from her crazy shifts at work, or working a crazy shift, or actually sleeping. Or yelling at me to put on longer shorts.

"Anyway. I'm lucky Dave found me again, because I was all set to just repeat every idiotic thing I'd done in high school. Date the same kinds of guys, act like the same kind of fool. Dave, of course, was the thing I ran *screaming* from in high school."

We smile at each other because I know this part of the story: Dave went to the same school as Mom and always had a crush on her, but he was busy having acne and learning to play guitar and drums in his band, and she was busy being popular and gorgeous and dating—well, athletes and stuff. And then after college he found her online and asked her out, and he'd gotten taller, and she was a single mom, and here we are.

"I didn't know you got in trouble in high school," I say quietly.

She raises her eyebrows. "Oh, yeah. Girls don't typically get pregnant in college without some practice first, didn't you know? I mean, I'd only had one *serious* boyfriend before your father. But I'd dated a lot—you've seen my yearbooks—and drank too much, and all that. It was fun. And then it wasn't fun."

"Because of me?"

"No! God, no. I liked your father a lot. I thought I loved him. No, I mean—ohhh." She lets out a long sigh and looks down again, shaking her head. It seems like she wants to tell me something, but also doesn't want to talk about it.

Suddenly I get that feeling I had with Alex, the night on the roof of his shed. Like I want to be trusted, I want to hear the story—but at the same time, I really don't. I'm not sure I can handle it. After I know whatever she's going to say, I won't be able to not know it, will I?

"Listen," she says, and I tuck my hands under my thighs, tightening my muscles. Gathering my strength. "I don't mean to yell at you all the time. I know it's getting worse as you get older, and as Ayla gets older—I don't know. It's so hard, sometimes, having two teenage daughters. But I especially see myself in you, and it just kills me to think you're making the same mistakes I did."

"I'm not," I say quickly, but she shakes her head.

"You could be, honey. You go to a lot of parties. You are *stunningly* beautiful, and I see the way people look at you—everyone wants to be around you. That can really bring out the worst in people. But all teenage girls bring out the worst in certain people, no matter what they look like. It's awful, you know? I feel like I'm Bambi's mom, or something, watching these long-legged, innocent creatures just trying to find their way in the world, and there are all these goddamn *hunters* everywhere."

She looks so worried but I can't help but laugh a tiny bit. It's just kind of a funny metaphor.

Mom smiles, too, but only for a second. "I had this boyfriend when I was your age," she says. Her voice is stronger now. Determined. "He flirted with me at school for weeks, and then he finally took me out for a nice dinner, and I thought I was some kind of princess. And then after the date we were kissing in his car, and he . . ." She only pauses for half a breath, just long enough to look down at her hands again. "I barely understood what was happening, and thank God it was over fast. I don't think I even said no." She looks up again, meeting my eyes. "After that I drank and partied a lot, dated a lot, did anything I could to not think about it. It was just easier to be stupid. Because I knew that something awful could happen and you'd be too stupid to even know how to avoid it—because you couldn't. Sometimes bad things just happen. But it would kill me if something happened to you."

I feel sick. That's all I can feel, just this awful pit of nausea in my stomach.

"It hasn't," I whisper. For some reason I know she needs to hear that, and for a second the sickness lessens its grip when she nods, relieved. Then it's back full force, because I have to ask, "What happened to the guy?"

She shakes her head. "Nothing."

"Did you—what happened to *you*?"

"I didn't get pregnant, which was incredibly lucky. But like I said, I did a lot of reckless things. I met the one serious boyfriend, but he wasn't very nice to me. Your father wasn't very nice, either, though at least he tried to be."

I feel stifled in the bandage dress, but at the same time I'm grateful that something is holding me together. In one piece.

"So you worry about me," I say.

"Every second of your life, honey. When you took the car like that—I didn't know what to think. I didn't know if you were running away or with a boy or what."

I nod. I feel crushed. "I'm really sorry."

"I know." She leans over and pats me on the knee. She looks like she wants to say more, but I guess we're both sort of overwhelmed, because her face clears a little and she says, "I like this dress, too. You want to try on the others, or should we just take these and go share a Cinnabon?"

"That sounds good," I say, because it does. It sounds perfect.

The sugar must go to Mom's head, because on the way home she lets me drive. She says it's so she can see if I'm at least following the rules of the road, even if I'm ignoring the big, fat *don't go to Iowa* rule. It's kind of nice, chauffering her around. Especially since she doesn't yell at me about anything.

When we pull up to the house, though, I realize I don't want to leave the bubble of the car. The strange closeness that's suddenly wrapped itself around her and me. The feeling that will, with absolute certainty, evaporate as soon as we open our doors.

I slide the gearshift into park and take a breath.

"Mom, I did have a bad . . . experience. It didn't—you know."

Beside me, Mom is frozen in the passenger seat. I'm not looking at her, but in my peripheral vision I see her arm suspended, reaching to unbuckle her seatbelt. My hands are still on the wheel but they can't feel it. I can see my fingers, but they could be anyone's. They could be a photograph.

"A boy started kissing me, and—more—and—I wanted him to

stop. I couldn't get him to stop." The words just end, and I realize I'm crying.

Mom's seatbelt clicks open, and I feel her arms around my shoulders, holding me as awkwardly as Maddie did. As tightly, too.

"I'm sorry." The words heave out of me, the way you keep retching even after you've puked your guts out.

"No." Mom sits back abruptly, and I stop crying in shock. "Fuck that."

I look over at her, not sure I've heard her right.

"Fuck sorry. You're not sorry. You didn't do anything wrong." She thumps her back against her seat, glaring out the windshield. "God*damn* it." Her eyes shoot over to me. "Tell me the rest."

"That's it, basically," I say. "I kept pushing him. And then someone walked in on us, and he stopped."

"And you didn't punch him in the balls? Who is it? Because I am absolutely going to beat him to death."

A laugh bursts out of me, short but loud. Mom doesn't even smile.

"Probably nothing's going to happen to the little shit," she mutters. "Girls come into the hospital all the time, get their kits done, wait for some kind of goddamn justice that isn't coming. I don't know how my friends in the ER do it, I swear to God it would kill me."

I lower my hands to my lap, just watching Mom and staying as quiet as I can. I can't remember ever seeing her get this mad about something that's not . . . well, a thing that *I* did. It's kind of amazing.

She looks me straight in the eyes, and it's like her soul is on fire. The sad, calm way she told me her own story, back in the dressing room—that's gone. She's as furious as I've ever seen her.

"What are we going to do?" she asks.

My heart drops. Just like Maddie, Mom wants to do something.

I immediately think of Alex, the way he wanted to take care of me and forget the rest. He's the only person who seems to understand what it's like, to want to simply hide and think about things for a while. A long time. Forever, maybe.

"I don't know," I whisper.

"This is a guy from school? We need to tell the school. It's not like these assholes make one mistake and suddenly reform. There's always another party, another girl. You know, after what happened to me I was so embarrassed, it was *years* later before I thought that he might've done the same thing to other girls." She pinches the bridge of her nose and takes a deep breath, trying to calm herself down. "I should've run him over with his own car," she says, her voice softer again. Resigned.

But her words claw at the back of my brain.

Other girls.

"Shit." I don't even realize I've said it out loud until my mom nods again.

"Yeah, it's a lot of shit," she agrees.

We stare at each other, both of us almost smiling. It's another one of those not-funny moments where you feel weird and lightheaded. It's strange and kind of wonderful to curse with your mom.

"I don't know what to do," I tell her. I feel like I'm going to start crying again, but I hold my breath until it passes.

"I don't really know either, Rosie. But we're going to figure something out."

"I just wish it hadn't happened," I say, my voice very small.

Mom reaches over to hold my hand. "God, kid, so do I."

I hang my new dresses carefully in my closet. They each have their own garment bag, and they've carried a ton of lovely new-clothes smell home with us.

I unzip the bag on the blue dress and stare at it. It's so pretty. It looks pretty on me. It's the kind of dress that people will stare at. I thought I didn't want people staring at me anymore, but I picked out this dress, and I want to wear it.

Nothing about getting Cory in trouble makes me feel better about what happened.

But I can't just let him erase me, either.

I zip the bag back up and go over to my laptop. I hold my breath and open a new chat window to Alex.

Will you go to Homecoming with me?

A lightning bolt of power and pride and total panic rips through me, and I practically jump off my bed as soon as I hit Send.

I pace back to my closet and start hanging things up that were on the floor. I throw big piles of clothes into my laundry hamper, stack books, open the window to let in some air.

And then, reaching to put away a pair of shoes, I see something.

It's the blue scarf Maddie brought me from Spain. I hold it up to my cheek and feel how cool and soft it is. I wrap it loosely around my neck.

I'm still full of a sick kind of energy, but I force myself to check the computer—nothing. Alex must be out.

Okay. Not what I was hoping, but okay. I'm trying.

Maybe it's not what Mom or Maddie think I should be doing, but I'm doing something.

I turn around, looking at my suddenly cleaned-up room. Leaning against the wall near my bed, my sketchbook for art class catches my eye. I grab my charcoal pencils from my desk.

And then I grab the big notepad, and for the first time in as long as I can remember, I sit down at a reasonable hour on a Sunday and start my homework.

25

WHEN MADDIE PICKS me up on Monday, she's wearing a sweater I recognize from last year, jeans, and the small diamond-stud earrings her parents gave her for her sweet sixteen. No feathers, no wispy skirt, none of her new, post-Europe style.

We match, sort of. I'm wrapped in a bulky cardigan over my torn jeans. Of course, I'm not the one campaigning for Junior Homecoming Queen.

I guess I'm not the only one who wants to fly under the radar, either. My chest tightens as I realize that Cory might be erasing Maddie, too.

"How's art?" she asks, glancing back at where I've stashed my huge sketchpad behind my seat.

"Not that bad," I admit. "Messy, though. Charcoal gets everywhere. I might've accidentally stained my bedroom carpet."

She doesn't laugh the way I'm expecting her to, and for a while we just drive in silence. The car rolls smoothly past houses that aren't houses anymore, flimsy orange tape strung around toothpick stakes marking the edges of what used to be front yards. I wish she'd driven around this neighborhood, but it's the quickest route to Ryan's.

"When is Alex coming back?" she asks suddenly.

"Not sure." I still haven't heard from him. I'm glad I asked him to the dance, but it's confusing and a little embarrassing, not knowing more about his plans. I feel like the longer he's gone, the quieter he gets. I thought I'd tell Maddie about my plan to get him to Homecoming, but now it just seems silly. I stay quiet.

"I hope it's soon," she says thoughtfully. "He seemed like a really good guy. And not that I care about the football team anymore, but, you know. It'd be nice if Olivia and Annabelle would shut up about how screwed the Lions will be without him."

"Olivia just loves drama."

But secretly, that's part of what I miss about Alex, too—the drama. For all his quietness, he made things interesting. I miss him as a friend and as a person I want to kiss again, but I also kind of miss him as an *event*. Without him, school is just the same kids I've always known, being mean to each other in new ways.

And way down, in the most secret corner of my heart, I want Alex to be a hero again, for me. To save me from everything that's gone wrong.

Which, okay. Now that I think about it, that isn't just unfair, it's impossible.

As we're pulling up outside Ryan's house, my phone buzzes.

I'd love to go to Homecoming with you. But I have to figure some stuff out first. Talk soon?

"Hey, girls," Ryan says, making the car shake as he drops into the backseat. "Christ, what is this billboard back here?"

"Rosie's art," Maddie tells him.

"Right, right. So what'd I miss?"

Maddie perks up now that Ryan's here, and they start talking about some youth group thing they went to yesterday.

I squeeze my phone as we drive back through Emery Woods, stare out the window, focus on the boarded-up houses and work trucks. At the very last one, a guy is cleaning a yard. The house itself is missing most of its siding and several windows, but the guy is cheerfully raking leaves, putting them in a big paper bag, just like any other dad. Maddie slows the car at the stop sign on the corner, and there's a pause in her conversation with Ryan. The guy in the yard looks up at us. He raises his hand, waving. After a second, we all raise our hands back.

That's it, I think. It's not the voice telling me anything, it's just my own thought: *You fix what you can. You move forward.*

The car rolls on, and I turn to my two best friends.

"I'm going to talk to Mrs. Walsh. About Cory."

"That's awesome," Maddie says. "Do you want me to go with you?"

"Um—I don't know. Maybe? But maybe not."

She nods, her face lit up with a smile. It's not like it's good news—but I don't know. Maybe she's proud of me or something.

Ryan reaches up from the backseat and pats my shoulder, and then to my relief they go back to talking about church.

Just as Maddie's pulling into a parking spot at school, I unlock my phone again and text Alex. Just a quick *Yes, talk soon*, and then, after debating it, a heart.

"Let it *go*, let it *go-oh*, don't wanna think about it any*mooorrre*—"

I turn to Steph backstage. "How does anyone not know the lyrics to this song?"

"Shh!" Steph has her hands covering her face, shaking with laughter.

"I mean, wasn't she listening to the *twelve other people* who just sang it?"

From the other side of the curtain we hear, "*I* am the one who will *WIN the SKY*," the poor girl's voice creaking like an old staircase.

Steph falls to her knees next to the flat we're painting and gasps for air.

"It's like torture," I say. I can't even laugh—I'm so confused at how many people have brought in the *Frozen* sheet music to audition with, I'm just standing here with my paint roller midair, staring toward the back of the stage curtain. It's a good thing no one can see us.

"Oh my God," she wheezes. "It's so painful!"

"Poor Ryan," I say, and for some reason this sends her into another fit of giggles.

"I'm sorry," she says. "I know it's mean—I just—"

"Yeah, dude, you're kind of a terrible person," I tease her. She just shakes her head, too busy trying to keep her laughter silent.

Outside the curtain the music finally stops, and we hear a very faint "Thank you!" followed by some footsteps and the shuffle of papers on the piano. Mr. Klonsky and Ryan are running the auditions while the band director, Ms. Ribar, plays everyone's music. I feel sorry for all of them.

"Really, though, poor Ryan," Steph agrees, wiping her eyes on the cuffs of her sweater and turning back to the paints. "It was his idea to let people bring their own music. Usually they have a few songs to choose from, so Ms. Ribar doesn't have to sight-read a million different things."

"Well, she probably has 'Let It Go' memorized by now," I point out.

Steph's face starts to crumple again, but she shakes her head hard, determined to stop laughing, and gets back to work.

Out front I hear Mr. Klonsky call, "Olivia Thorpe!"

"I want to see this one," I tell Steph, setting my roller on the side of the tin tray.

Creeping around to the wings, I manage to stay out of sight as the first notes of Olivia's song begin to play. They don't sound like anything from a Disney movie, which is sort of disappointing. In fact, they're upbeat, and I think I've heard them before, maybe from Ayla's room—

> "*Whenever I see someone less fortunate than I*
> *And let's face it, who isn't less fortunate than I?*"

I stare at Olivia and feel my jaw drop open. She's in her cheerleading uniform because it's Homecoming week, and every day is wall-to-wall pep crap. But otherwise, you'd never know she was even in high school. Her voice is strong and confident, her face expressive without being cheesy. She sounds amazing.

By the time she sings the word "*Pop*-u-lar!" I find myself smiling, and I know Ryan must be practically fainting with relief. Olivia always has some kind of role in the student productions here, but this year she's obviously turned into a star. The lyrics are funny, and she really sells them. After a while I wonder if she's still wearing her uniform on purpose, since it makes the whole thing even funnier.

I'm so focused on watching her that I don't realize I should get backstage before the song ends. So then it's over, with a big flourish from Olivia, and she's turning and walking right toward me, and I'm just standing there like an idiot. *Smiling* like an idiot, too.

"Enjoy the show?" she sneers.

"You were great," I say, just before she can breeze past me in her little cloud of flippy-skirted triumph.

"Psshh. Right."

"No, hang on."

She glares at me and for a second I consider snapping something bitchy at her.

But I'm tired of having an enemy. Now that I have someone I really need to avoid in the hallways, school is feeling way too small and spiky.

"Really. You were the best audition all day. By far."

The faintest hint of confusion crosses Olivia's face, and then when she smirks again, it's almost friendly.

"Well, that's not really saying much, is it?"

I smirk back. And when she turns and keeps walking, I feel like . . . I don't know.

Like maybe girls aren't so hard to get along with, after all.

> I don't know if I can make it this wknd.
>
> Ok
>
> I'm sorry
>
> I know. It's ok.

The screen glows at me, too bright in the dark room. Too insensitive to how hard this is.

> Soon.

It's so much and not nearly enough. But I can be strong. I have to be—this isn't a hookup at a party. This is a real relationship.

> I'll be here.

There's a long pause. Then: You're incredible.

"No, I'm not!" I whisper to the screen. "I'm dying! Come back now!"

But what I type is: Aw, shucks.

Then we send about a hundred smiley faces and hearts and even some flowers back and forth. It starts getting silly after that— weird hand symbols, cats, row after row of just pine trees—and I'm laughing in the dark, by myself. I don't tell him about how I made an appointment to talk to Mrs. Walsh tomorrow, and Mom is going with me. About how school is kind of great and completely awful depending on whether I'm in the theater or the hallways or the art room, which feels so empty without him.

Alex would listen if I wanted to talk. But I think I'm saving my energy for whatever I'll have to tell Mrs. Walsh. And for now, it's enough that I don't feel alone.

Maybe he feels the same way, because he doesn't explain how he's able to not be at school for so long, if he's doing homework out there or what. After some more silly exchanges, he says goodnight. We don't even bring up Homecoming again.

I get it now, why Alex was so quiet when he came to Midcity. Sometimes you have bigger things on your mind. It doesn't mean you don't care about the people around you, it just means you're thinking.

I click off my phone and pad out of my room to the bathroom. Ayla's brushing her teeth, but the door is open. I join her at the other sink and pick up the makeup remover.

"What're you laughing about?" she asks around her toothbrush.

I shrug. "Nothing. Just, you know. Alex."

She raises her eyebrows in the mirror at me, then leans down to spit. "Alex *Goode?*"

"Yeah. You know we're friends."

"I thought he was back in Iowa, though."

"Well, Ayla, there's this magical thing they've invented called *phones*, and people are able to communicate across vast stretches of space—"

She reaches over and punches my arm—not softly—and I stop talking to laugh.

"You're a dork," she says.

"Well, let's not get carried away. What about you? How's Henry?"

She gets the floss out of the cabinet. It always amazes me that my sister actually flosses her teeth. She seriously has to be the only almost-thirteen-year-old in the *world* who does.

"He's okay."

"Are you going to the Halloween dance with him?"

She sighs like I'm killing her with all my stupid questions, but I know better because I've been there—what would really kill her is not talking about it.

"Everybody goes in groups," she says.

"What about your birthday?"

"What about it?"

I lean forward, hitting my head lightly against the edge of the sink in frustration. "You have to give me a break, kid," I groan. Standing back up, I finish wiping off my eye makeup, throw away the cloth, and ignore her rolling her eyes at me in the mirror.

"Mom said I can only invite three people," she finally says.

"So? One of them could be Henry, right?"

"Yeah, but it's supposed to be a sleepover."

I lean my hip against the counter, crossing my arms over my tank top. "Or you could go *out*, maybe to the movies and out for pizza. That way, it could be a bigger group, and if you still want to have a sleepover, just a couple of girls could come home with you afterward. Right? And if everyone gets dropped off at the mall, you guys can hang out for a while without parents all over you."

She narrows her eyes at me. "That's maybe genius."

"Don't sound so surprised. Being alone with boys is *kind* of my specialty."

The words are out of my mouth before I remember that I'm not sure how I feel about that specialty of mine anymore . . . but then again.

It's not your fault Cory is a shithead.

Yeah. Maybe that.

"But you know," I say as Ayla rinses her mouth and grabs the towel behind me. I've never noticed that she dries her face the same way I do. What a weird thing to run in the family. "I always try to spend my birthdays with Maddie or Maddie and Ryan. I'm sure Henry is great, but boys come and go. And it's kind of nice being able to look back and remember how your friends were always there. Better memories."

Ayla shrugs. "But friends come and go sometimes, too."

"Yeah. But not the right ones."

She watches me for a minute without saying anything, then asks, "Why are you being so nice to me lately?"

"I'm always nice," I joke, but then I really stop to think about it. "Maybe it's because of the storm and everything."

"What, like, life is short, so stop driving your little sister crazy?"

"You're still crazy, though, so I guess it didn't work. . . ."

I jump out of the way before she can punch me in the arm again. She scowls and puts the towel back on the hook.

"I don't know why, Ay. Why've you been so cranky all the time?"

She sighs. "I don't know."

I push off from the counter and wrap my arms around her shoulders. She stiffens up and gives me a look in the mirror, but I hang on. "Hey, I didn't mean it. I know why you're cranky—I'm the mean one, remember? We're just sisters. And teenagers. All teenagers are supposed to be nutjobs. It's like a law or something."

To my surprise, she keeps standing there for a minute before she pushes away.

"Thanks for the idea," she says. "For my birthday."

"No problem."

"But maybe it'll just be a friends thing. Like you said." She shrugs again and then she squeezes past me and leaves the bathroom.

I brush my teeth, skip the flossing like a normal person, then go back to my room and crawl under the covers. In the dark, the headlights of passing cars move the stripes of my blinds across the ceiling, then the wall, then out of sight. I think about what Mom said about worrying about me every day. She must feel the same about Ayla. She won't want Ayla going on any kind of date this year, not even with a science nerd, not even in a group.

But I wish she wasn't so worried. Obviously I mostly wish she didn't *have* to be—just the thought of anyone grabbing Ayla the way Cory grabbed me, even the times I *liked* being grabbed, makes me want to stab someone. But I also want Ayla to see how much fun it is to go out with a boy like Henry. Or whoever. To feel good about that—to feel all that self-confidence and equality that Dave's always telling us we deserve. Mom thinks we deserve it, too, but I don't know. Maybe all her worrying just pushes us away even harder.

I wish there was something I could actually *do* that would help me, help Ayla. Help everybody. Even Cory, maybe. There's still a tiny part of me that feels like he might've been confused, that night at Gabe's house. Not that it makes it okay, I know that. But still. What if I could really explain it to him? What if he didn't actually mean to hurt me?

But if that was true, wouldn't he have apologized?

Either way I hate being left with this hopeless feeling, like there's no way to make anything better. Like he's a monster and that's it, I was lucky to get away from the monster, lucky that he's left me alone since that night.

That word again: *lucky*. Like the storm.

At least before the storm, though, we got a warning.

My thoughts are fast-forwarding too quickly and I roll onto my side, pulling the blanket over my head. I don't want to think about it anymore. Any of it.

I have friends. I have a house with a roof and running water and electricity. And I have two tickets to Homecoming. Just in case.

26

"MY EYESHADOW LOOKS stupid. Is it too late to start over?"

"Yes. Let me see—you look great!" I take Maddie's shoulders and turn her to face the mirror again. "Look at yourself."

We both stare, side by side in front of her long bathroom counter, at the hour of meticulous hairstyling and makeup application we've just finished. It's taken me so long to get my curls blown out that my arms hurt, but I have to say, we both look flawless. Maddie has a long braid over one shoulder and a thin headband with tiny fake diamonds. It looks like she has stars on her head.

"I guess we should put on actual clothes now," she says, smiling. We're both in oversized button-down shirts, our dresses lying on her bed in her room behind us.

"I'm sorry I'm your date," I say for the fifteenth time. "At least I got you a corsage."

"You did? But I didn't get you anything!"

"It's a wristlet. You don't have to wear it if you don't want to."

She sticks out her tongue at me. "You're a cornball, you know that?"

I walk toward my dress, calling over my shoulder, "I thought about a giant balloon bouquet, but I know you're too *cool* for that kind of thing."

"Shut yer piehole, Fuller."

We stare down at our dresses. "I can't believe we're ahead of schedule," I say.

"I think you not having a real date created a rift in the space-time continuum."

I look at Maddie. "I'm sorry, the *what*?"

She laughs. "I don't know. I think it's a saying?" She perches on the bed near her pillows, out of the way of the dresses.

I tug at the hem of my shirt. "Mads, my mom and I talked to Mrs. Walsh."

"What? Oh my God! Why didn't you tell me? I wanted to go!" Maddie sort of half lurches across the bed, but stops before she touches me. Suddenly she seems unsure.

"I don't know," I tell her, even though I do know—I just hate talking about this. "She said I could press charges, but it would basically be my word against Cory's. And Midcity doesn't have a policy for, you know. *Off-campus assault.*"

Maddie frowns.

"I know."

"So that's it? Just, like, get a lawyer or nothing?"

"Well, she wants to petition for better sex ed, and she thinks I could help." I sigh, circling the bed so I can sit on the other set of pillows. "Remember freshman year?"

"You mean the assembly where they told us if we had premarital sex we were going to get knocked up or die of an STI? That one?"

I snort. "Yeah. Well, Mrs. Walsh says the boys get a different one. I mean, I knew it was different—they talk about their penises or whatever—but they don't get the whole thing about not drinking, and the no-sex thing is shorter."

"Jesus."

"She's super pissed about it. I guess there are other girls at school, ones who've had similar things happen to them, and if we all get together . . ." I trail off, realizing that I shouldn't tell Maddie who the other girls are. I can't tell her the most surprising thing that happened at the meeting: Mrs. Walsh telling us that Olivia is a student coordinator for an anonymous support group at church, and I can contact her if I want to go.

It made me feel a lot better and a lot worse, knowing that someone like Olivia is working through something bad, too.

Maddie's silent for a while, and I'm sure she's thinking all the things I thought about when I was sitting in Mrs. Walsh's office next to my mom. How it all seems like a lot of work for something that could be totally pointless. How I have to do what I can, obviously—but I can't do much.

"It has to get better somehow, right?" Maddie says. I guess she's not feeling as hopeless as I do after all. "At least this is a plan."

"Yeah." I lean over and put my head on Maddie's shoulder, only worrying about my hair a little bit. "Thanks."

"And my mom's a lawyer, remember. If you want to talk to her," she says. I feel her body get kind of tense as she starts to say something else. "Rosie?"

"Yeah?"

"Why didn't you tell me what happened? You know, that night?

I know I was mad, and we'd all been drinking, but . . ."

I don't move. She's still, too, waiting.

"We already talked about this."

"Yeah, but not really. That day you came over to my house, you know? We talked about Cory. And me. But I didn't really ask if you were okay, and I've been wondering . . ." She spins the ring on her right hand, the ruby birthstone band she brings out on special occasions. "I was thinking maybe that was why you didn't tell me right away. Because you knew I'd make it all about me."

I sit up in surprise, and we look at each other.

"It *was* about you," I say.

Her eyebrows dip even lower, like what I've said has caused her physical pain. "No, see, that's the thing. It doesn't matter that Cory was dating me or whatever. Something bad happened to *you*."

"Mads, I—"

"Wait, just listen to me. I'm sorry that happened to you. And I'm sorry I didn't say that sooner."

"Oh."

"And I love you."

"I love you, too, Maddie. I'm sorry I . . ." I look down at the bed, the intricate flower pattern on Maddie's duvet cover swimming, twisting, blurring. "I'm sorry it happened to me, too."

A new kind of weight settles into the middle of my chest. Not the crushing heaviness of the secret, the truth of that night, but something different—the fact that *I'm* different. The fact that Cory made me different, and there's nothing I can do about it. I'm one of those girls now. One of those girls that something bad happened to.

I don't want to be one of those girls. I want the fact that he stopped, that I'm actually okay—I want that to be the end of it.

But it's not. I'm not that lucky.

"It's going to be okay," Maddie says softly.

I want to believe her. In some ways, it's already a lot more okay than it was. I have Maddie back; I never lost Ryan. Alex—I don't know. He's far away and it's still new, but this thing between us feels real. And there's my mom, going to Mrs. Walsh with me and doing a bunch of research on therapists, even if I don't want to talk about this anymore. . . . My mom has been great.

Maddie reaches over and takes my hands in hers. Her fingers are cool, soft. She squeezes.

I'd give anything to go back. To undo all of it, or to make it what I really wanted it to be—Cory mistaking me for Maddie or just not understanding. In the back of my mind I'm always replaying it, over and over, imagining him letting go of me while the lights were still off. Imagining what it would have felt like to push and have the weight of his body lift. What it would feel like to be strong enough. Stronger.

"Come on," Maddie says, shaking my hands a little. "We don't have to be sad about this all the time. Let's go out and enjoy your night of freedom."

I look up at her. I'm not crying, but my eyes are hot. Tired.

She leans over and rests her forehead on mine. "I'm with you, okay? School board, school dances, whatever. You're not alone."

I nod. It's true—I'm not alone.

Maddie's flowy, cream-colored dress practically glows. And even better, it's as bohemian as the clothes she was wearing when she got back from Spain—the new style that suddenly feels more like her than anything else. The neckline is gathered and it has little puffed cap sleeves, and around the waist a ribbon crisscrosses her rib cage flatteringly.

"You look like a Shakespearean lady," I say. "We don't exactly match, do we?" I'm in the bandage dress. It's tight but that's good—it holds me together.

She shakes her head, but not like she's disagreeing. "Your dress is *hot*. We should be going somewhere way more glamorous than a stupid school dance. We should be sneaking into a club or something."

"Where?" I laugh. "Omaha?"

"There are clubs! I've heard!" she cries, but then she laughs, too.

"Oh, look, Ryan's finally here."

I've been watching at the front window of Maddie's living room for Ryan's car, and as it pulls up I notice someone in the passenger seat.

"Mom, we're leaving!" Maddie shouts.

"No, you're not!" Mrs. Costello comes striding out from the kitchen, her shiny flats tapping briskly on the marble floor. "I need photos."

Maddie groans. "Please don't put this on Facebook."

Mrs. Costello ignores her, waving us toward the staircase and hurrying to open the door before Ryan even rings the bell. "Come in, come in!" she trills, and Maddie and I watch as Ryan and Gabe Richmond step into the entry, looking a little nervous in dark suits. "Oh, good, I thought you girls didn't have dates, but look at this!"

Ryan isn't quite making eye contact with any of us. I turn to see Maddie's face, wondering if this is some kind of weird surprise she arranged with Ryan, but she's obviously as confused as I am. Gabe stands near me and smiles, not saying a word as Mrs. Costello arranges us next to the banister and takes a flurry of pictures with her phone. He and Ryan are wearing matching corsages.

Oh.

Oh!

At last we're outside, Maddie and I skittering in our heels, hurrying to the car because it's freezing and we didn't want to wear coats. Behind us I can hear Ryan and Gabe whispering to each other.

"Ryan! Unlock the doors!" Maddie yelps, jumping in place next to the car.

When there's no answer—and no *chunk* of the locks being released—she and I turn to look back at the boys.

Ryan stands close to Gabe, his head down. Gabe is saying something we can't hear and seems to be trying to get Ryan to lift his gaze. He sees us watching and says something else. And then Ryan squares his shoulders.

And takes Gabe's hand.

Beside me, Maddie makes a little gasping sound. So she didn't already know—Ryan's been keeping this secret from everyone. I feel even happier.

The guys walk up to us, and Gabe is grinning from ear to ear, but Ryan still seems worried. His eyes flit from me to Maddie and back, uncertain.

"Are you ready to go?" Gabe asks. He's looking at us, but I'm pretty sure the question is for Ryan.

Out of the corner of my eye I see Maddie nodding, and I realize I'm waiting for her to say something. For her to say the *right* thing. Here we are, finally—Ryan is on a real date with a guy, it seems, and he's sharing it with us. Or trying to. Gabe has to be the boy I saw Ryan kissing at halftime, the football player who's about his height and now, I see, looks incredibly proud to be holding Ryan's hand. As he should be.

Maddie still isn't saying anything, so I finally jump in.

"You guys look really nice together," I say, and on impulse I step forward and kiss Ryan and then Gabe on the cheek.

"That's what *I* keep saying," Gabe says with a pointed look at Ryan. "This one thinks we're going to *shock* people."

I check Maddie, who, it should be noted, does look a tiny bit shocked. But she's smiling, too, and then kissing the boys' cheeks, and giving Ryan a hug. "I had no idea!" she breathes. "Why didn't you tell me?"

"Not everyone was ready," Gabe says, swinging Ryan's hand back and forth a few times. "And some of us have had to be *very patient.*"

Ryan's expression relaxes the tiniest amount as he rolls his eyes. "I still think coming out at the big dance is a total cliché."

"I don't think people will be as surprised as you'd expect," Gabe says. "Besides, it seems much more modern to have a Home*coming Out* party. Right?" He looks at Maddie and me, still grinning. "Get it?"

It takes me a second, but then I giggle. "Ryan, your boyfriend is a huge dork."

"And your best friends are *freezing*," Maddie adds.

"Oh my God, you guys are all the worst," Ryan says, finally pulling the car keys out of his pocket and unlocking his old SUV. Maddie immediately yanks open the back door and climbs in, and Gabe trots around the front to take the passenger seat.

Ryan doesn't move, though, so I step closer again and fiddle with the rosebud on his lapel.

"This is really great," I say softly.

"Yeah. So why am I so scared?"

I shrug, fiddling the delicate spray of baby's breath, the soft green leaf, the cold metal pin. "People are scary sometimes." I look up, into his eyes. "I'll have your back if you have mine."

"Great, now I'm on a clichéd reality show."

"Well, I got *real* dressed up. Might as well put on a show!"

Ryan groans and pushes me away with one hand as I cackle. "Oh my God. I'll do whatever you want, just *stop*."

I'm still laughing as we climb into the warm car. Gabe has the radio on, and Maddie is nervously touching the ends of her hair, and for a second I feel genuinely nervous. For me, for all of us. But then Gabe pats Ryan on the shoulder, and Maddie gives me an encouraging smile, and I figure, what the hell. We've all been through way worse than a crappy school dance.

27

"WELL, *THIS* IS disappointing."

Maddie swats Ryan's arm. "I told you guys, we gave most of the budget to the storm relief fund! It's really hard to decorate a whole gym with dollar-store stuff!"

Ryan gives her a look like she just grew a second head. "Not the décor, you weirdo. The lack of a, you know. *Reaction*."

We all pause to look around, and Gabe's expression is noticeably triumphant. It's true, no one has so much as given the guys a double take since they walked into school holding hands, stopped at the professional photographer for a portrait, and now stand at the gym doors waiting to hand over their tickets.

"We're a more empathetic generation," Maddie says, sounding wise.

"That's right," Gabe agrees. "Because of Harry Potter."

Ryan shakes his head and Gabe laughs.

"Really! It's science! Kids who grow up reading Harry Potter are more empathetic."

"He's right," Maddie says. "I read that study."

"Well, then, thank you, Harry Potter." Ryan catches my eye, and we stick our tongues out at each other at the same time.

As soon as we're inside, Ryan nabs a table, and the four of us stand around it, not sure what to do next.

Suddenly everyone's attention shifts back toward the doors.

Olivia is walking in, wearing a powder blue tuxedo. It's tiny—I wonder if she got it in the boys' department or something—and fits her perfectly. It also looks amazing with her long blond hair curling softly over her shoulders.

But what everyone's really staring at is the guy she's with.

"Come *on*," Ryan mutters.

"She is completely stealing the show here," Gabe agrees, but he's laughing as he says it. I never noticed how cheerful Gabe is—or maybe that's just when he's with Ryan.

"She did get the lead in the show," Ryan grumbles. "Drama queen."

Olivia's date has the highest pompadour I've ever seen in real life. He's super thin, like a rock star, and his extremely slim-fitting tux is bright purple.

"Who even *is* that?" Maddie says, sounding as impressed as I'm feeling.

I don't answer her, though, because just then I notice Cory near the refreshment table. Annabelle is tottering after him but looking over her shoulder at the same time. My stomach goes cold.

When I turn back to our table, I realize Olivia and the mystery hipster are headed our way. Olivia gives Maddie a hug, then nods at

Ryan and Gabe in a very approving way. When she catches my eye, I smile. It seems to surprise her, which is kind of satisfying.

"Hi," Maddie says to Olivia's date. "I like your hair."

"Thanks," he says.

"This is Tristan," Olivia says. Tristan nods at us in an incredibly cool way.

"I'm sorry, you guys; I have to go do committee stuff," Maddie says, making a face. "I'll be right back, though! Have some punch! Before some idiot spikes it!"

She hurries off and there I am, dateless. Not that anyone's paying any attention to me.

I concentrate on not looking over at Cory. I've been able to ignore him completely at school, so why does this feel different? I just wish he wasn't here. I wish I could be all-the-way happy—happy that Ryan is finally smiling, happy that some people, at least, got to bring the date they really wanted.

Under the table, I send another text to Alex. He hasn't been writing back tonight, but I've sent photos of my dress and a few messages just so he knows I'm thinking about him. And that I'm not mad that he couldn't come—but also still hoping he'll be back for Winter Formal.

"Gross, Annabelle really came with Callahan?"

It takes me a second to realize that Olivia's talking to me. "Yeah, I guess." We both look over at the dance floor, where Annabelle has found more cheerleaders to dance with. Cory's off to the side with Marcus and some other seniors from the team.

"I told her not to."

Olivia and I look at each other with something like an understanding.

Then the moment passes and she turns to Gabe. "Isn't this going to make life kind of hard for you?"

He shrugs. "A lot of the team already knows. It was a lot harder pretending I wanted to talk about boobs, honestly."

Ryan snorts. "Oh, come on. Everyone likes *boobs*."

Everyone laughs and then Ryan drags me onto the dance floor. After two fast songs, Gabe taps me out. Olivia and Tristan try to dance with me, but it's awkward, so I go to find Maddie at the food table.

She's not there, but someone walks up behind me.

"Nice dress," Cory says.

I'm shaking a little before I even turn, but I manage to take a step back and hold my head up like I'm not bothered.

"I don't want to talk to you," I say, but my voice is barely audible over the music.

"You wanna go somewhere?" he asks, closing the space I've made between us. Looming over me.

The paper plate I'm holding drops to the table as I flinch. It's not that tonight is worse than seeing Cory during the day at school—it's that *Cory* is worse. I could feel it all the way across the room. He must be feeling all-powerful, after winning last night's game and having yet another girl to pick up where Maddie and I left off.

I've been thinking about Cory so much, or trying to *not* think about him, and now that we're actually breathing the same air, standing too close, my head spins.

"Come on," he says, starting to reach for me.

"You seem to have a problem with people telling you no," I say. I don't even know where the words come from, but I'm kind of proud of them. My stomach feels a little firmer as his face twists in confusion.

"But you *don't* say no, Rosie."

See, I told you so, the voice in my head hisses.

"But I'm saying it now." Everything is wavering. My voice, my vision. And he's just smiling at me—why is he *smiling* at me?

"Why, because of Annabelle? That's no big deal, she's totally—"

"*No*, Cory, okay? Is that loud enough for you? *NO!*"

I'm pretty sure everyone in the gym turns to stare at us, but I'm too focused on Cory's shitty smirk to care.

"Jesus, Fuller, what's your problem? You used to be cool."

I can feel, more than see, Maddie's milky-white dress hurrying across the room toward us. The music is still blaring, bass pounding through my rib cage, batting my head around like a balloon.

I keep my eyes on Cory's. I can see what he sees. A girl who drinks, who wears short skirts. Who gets dressed up so that people will look at her, think she's pretty. A girl everyone *does* think is pretty. A girl who likes attention and dark rooms and boys and parties and dumb, flirty conversation.

It's my fault he sees me like that—I *am* like that.

But it's not my fault he doesn't see that I'm a person, too.

Maybe, in that split second, I think about all the people picking up after the storm and moving on, my sister helping in the small ways she can. Maybe I think about Ryan and Gabe, Olivia and her tuxedo, being themselves even if it's scary, or even if it's not that big a deal. Maybe I think about Maddie and how she's still coming, just outside my peripheral vision, ready to say the thing that will make Cory shrink or apologize or simply go away. Maybe I think about Alex and how sometimes what looks like bravery is just bad timing, but brave nonetheless.

But honestly I don't really think of anything at all. I just reach out, grab a cup of punch from the refreshment table, and throw it in Cory's face. There's a satisfying splash of red, followed by an even better sputtering noise from his stupid mouth.

And then I walk away.

And it's okay that I'm shaking, that I might fall down at any moment, because before I'm at the doors of the gym Maddie is there holding me up, helping me out into the hallway where it's quiet and cool and no one can see me burst into tears.

"It's a little creepy how your mascara still looks good."

I lean closer to the mirror in the girls' locker room. "They're pretty serious when they say waterproof," I say.

Maddie has a tiny brush that she's gently running through my hair. I don't know how long we've been hiding in here, but I'm starting to feel normal again, and the crying stopped long enough ago that I'm breathing evenly, which is nice.

"I still can't believe you did that," she says. On the counter, our phones both buzz with new messages. Ryan's been checking in on us every five seconds, but Maddie says he needs to wait. "It was badass."

I bite my lip. "It did feel pretty good."

She meets my eyes in the mirror again. "Listen, I was going to tell you this sooner, but . . ."

"No. I don't want any more surprises tonight. Even good ones."

"Yeah, I know. But I think you might like this one."

Putting down the brush, Maddie grabs her phone and taps through her texts. Then she holds the screen where I can see it.

"Why is Alex texting . . ." I stop when I see the message.

"He wanted to surprise you, and then he was running late. But he just got here a few minutes ago."

A hundred different feelings crash through me. Just when I thought I'd had all the feelings I could have tonight.

"Oh," I manage to say.

"I mean, normally I'd tell him to leave you alone, but he did say you invited him. Did you? Invite him?"

I nod. I guess I never told Maddie that, either.

"He can't get in without the ticket."

I laugh, but not because it's funny. "I left it at home." I lean all the way over, letting my hair fall, brushing the tops of my feet through my strappy sandals. "Maddie?" I say, my voice all weird from being upside down.

"Yeah?"

"Would you be mad if I left?"

"God, no. I'd leave, too, if I could."

"I love you, Maddie." I'm still dangling. It feels nice to be dizzy on purpose. It's sort of balancing out all the other dizziness in my head right now.

"I love you, too, but you're going to tip over." She finds my hand through my hair and helps me stand back up.

"You take good care of me."

"I don't know, Rosie. I think you did a pretty good job taking care of yourself tonight."

I let her lead me out of the bathroom and back to the front doors of school, where I give her a hug and wish her luck in the crowning ceremony I'm going to miss. I text Ryan a dozen *sorry*s.

Then I walk out into the cold, dark night, and at the end of the sidewalk that leads up to school I see a parked car with a guy leaning against it. He looks like a movie star.

"Sorry I didn't call," Alex starts to say, but I'm already kissing him. And he kisses me, his hands warm and careful on my back.

After a long time, or long enough, at least, I pull my face back far enough to say, "Sorry I don't have your ticket."

"I'm a bad dancer, anyway."

"That can't be true."

He shrugs one shoulder, lifting my arm up with it. "You can judge for yourself at the next one."

"The next—dance?"

He nods, his mouth pinched with a secret smile.

"So you're really back?"

"For the rest of the year. And then my mom wants to *revisit the issue*. What do you think—do you mind having me around for that long?"

Instead of answering, I kiss him again.

"Good," he says against my lips.

When we finally get in the car, Alex says he has a surprise. He starts driving and I dig around in the backseat, finding his new Midcity letter jacket and putting it on. He gives me a funny look.

"What? Am I not allowed to wear it?"

"No, I just—I never noticed how beautiful you are." He's quiet for a long minute, watching the road, then shakes his head. "I'm kidding. Obviously you're gorgeous."

"I'm other things, too."

He reaches over, takes my hand, and doesn't let go.

When he pulls onto the familiar dirt road, I smile. We have a spot.

"Um, Alex, it's freezing."

"It's not that cold. It's still October."

"No, it's literally freezing—look, your car knows. It says thirty-two, which according to my shitty level of high school science is *actual* freezing."

"Wow, you're whiny in the cold. Is this what I have to look forward to all winter?"

Despite everything, the inside of my body goes instantly warm. *All winter.*

He turns off the car and opens his door. A blast of *freezing* air rushes in, making me gasp.

"Seriously, why don't we just go to Village Inn or something?"

Alex laughs and climbs out, slamming the door. Then he's opening the trunk and disappearing from view.

I sit in the warm car, rubbing my hands together, until I hear the trunk slam. Then I watch as Alex makes his way over to the ladder on the side of his dad's shed-barn and turns back, waving to me in the glow of the headlights.

"There's *snow* on the ground," I mutter to no one. It's really just a frost. And I don't actually care; I'd follow him anywhere.

Alex is starting to climb the ladder with one hand, holding the big basket in the other.

I sort of walk-jump over to the shed, then bounce there while he finishes climbing and turns back to look at me.

"Sorry, will you be okay climbing in that outfit? It's worth it, I promise," he says.

I don't doubt it.

It's not easy negotiating heels and a tight dress on the cold, slippery ladder. But as soon as I clamber onto the roof, I forget everything else.

There's a big wool blanket spread out on the tiles, and Alex is unpacking things from the basket that look a lot like bread and cheese and maybe even cake. There's a Thermos full of something that smells like hot chocolate when he uncaps it. There are three of those candles that run on batteries.

"It's nice up here," he says, holding the Thermos closer so I can smell that it's definitely cocoa. "You'll see."

I do my awkward crawl over to him and sit back, speechless.

"We don't have to stay long," Alex promises. "I just brought a few snacks and—oh!" He reaches back in the basket and shows me a small speaker plugged into his phone. "Music."

Clear, shimmering notes float into the air a minute later, and it's beautiful and romantic, but it also makes me laugh.

"What?" Alex says. "Do you not like this? I can change it—"

"No," I say, grabbing his hand. "It's just—this is the Flaming Lips, right?"

He nods. "I know it's kind of old, but I really like this album."

"Yeah, me too. It's just funny because my parents got married to this song. I mean, when my mom married Dave. It's kind of a family song at our house."

"Oh," he says. He stares at me for a minute, his eyes dark but his face clearly visible under the low clouds. "So would it be weird if I kissed you right now?"

"No," I say. "It would be weird if you *didn't*."

We kiss for a long time, so long that the song ends, and another one plays, and another.

I try to hang on to every second, appreciate every note and every kiss and every minute that led to this one. It's impossible, of course, but I have to try. Finally Alex pulls back and says, "The cheese is going to get cold."

"The cheese?"

"I mean, the hot chocolate. Did I say cheese?"

I nod. "It's probably all a *little* bit cold. Considering that it's freezing out here." I give him one last, quick kiss, and then I let him hand me the hot chocolate. It's still warm.

We look out over the fields to the city lights in the distance, and we don't shiver at all. Not even when it starts to snow, tiny specks of white filling the world around us, hanging in the air like they're in no hurry to fall. Like a million tiny, perfect stars.

Acknowledgments

A REALLY GIGANTIC, everlasting thank-you is owed to my editor, Donna Bray, for patiently guiding this book from a random assemblage of words to an actual story; I could not (and let's face it, probably *would* not) have done it without your wise counsel and inexplicable faith in me. Also instrumental to my sanity and productivity: Holly Root, Alison Cherry, Kayla Olson, Erica Jensen, Abigail McAden Rubin, and Rebecca Mazur. Endless gratitude as well to everyone at HarperCollins Children's Books/Balzer + Bray, particularly the gracious Viana Siniscalchi and genius Erin Fitzsimmons. And to Andy, Calvin, and Virginia: I'm so grateful to be on your team. Thank you.

You May Also Like

"Horrifying. Satisfying.
Remarkable in so many ways.
Tease is a brave debut."
—**ELLEN HOPKINS**,
New York Times bestselling author

TEASE

A novel by
AMANDA MACIEL

BALZER + BRAY
An Imprint of HarperCollins*Publishers*

www.epicreads.com